Unfair!

Jenna wanted to cry, "Stop!" But the word simply wouldn't come.

Mark gave her a long, speculative appraisal from beneath his lashes. His tender smile had melted her insides. "You realize, of course, if you go now, you'll never find out."

"Find out what?" Her voice sounded detached and foreign.

His mouth widened into a grin. "Whether it's boxers or briefs."

She stared at him in mute misery. The dark, heavy truth descended on her in full force. She might as well acknowledge the terrible inevitability of this moment, that something was breaking like a cord in her mind.

Jenna nodded slowly. "You're right, damn you. I have to know."

She tossed her remaining shoe over one shoulder. By the time it hit the floor she had lifted her arms around Mark's neck and pulled him to her. She kissed him, thoroughly. And he responded.

If this was a mistake, she'd find a way to make it right somehow. And if there were regrets, she'd never lay claim to them. A premonition of danger flared at the edges of her mind, but her body was already on a wild journey, and the feeling didn't last long enough to become a nuisance.

Dear Reader,

It's wonderful to feel safe in the life you've built for yourself. We should all be so lucky as to have stress-free, secure, peaceful lives that never cause us a moment of concern.

But sometimes that kind of complacent existence can get…well, boring. You get stuck in a rut. You never feel challenged. You stop taking chances. And the people you love? They think they know you inside and out.

Which is why sometimes your life needs a swift kick in the pants. Or, as in the case of my heroine, you need to shake things up a bit. That's what Jenna Rawlins decides to do one night when she meets Mark Bishop. Something new. Something unexpected and out of character. And that adventurous decision results in big changes in both their lives.

Resolving their problems was a great way for me to shake up my own little world, too. I've never written a story about two people who are drawn to one another so quickly, with such life-altering consequences. I hope I've met the challenge, and that you'll find Jenna and Mark's story interesting and fun.

May all your challenges in life be exciting, rewarding and, as always, may they make for wonderful stories!

Sincerely,

Ann Evans

Books by Ann Evans

HARLEQUIN SUPERROMANCE

After That Night
Ann Evans

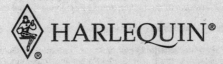

HARLEQUIN®

TORONTO • NEW YORK • LONDON
AMSTERDAM • PARIS • SYDNEY • HAMBURG
STOCKHOLM • ATHENS • TOKYO • MILAN • MADRID
PRAGUE • WARSAW • BUDAPEST • AUCKLAND

ISBN 0-373-71136-0

AFTER THAT NIGHT

Copyright © 2003 by Ann Bair.

This edition published by arrangement with Harlequin Books S.A.

® and TM are trademarks of the publisher. Trademarks indicated with ® are registered in the United States Patent and Trademark Office, the Canadian Trade Marks Office and in other countries.

Visit us at www.eHarlequin.com

Printed in U.S.A.

For my good friends Lanny Reddick and Sherri Angell,
who never say "No" when I want to play "What if…?"

I couldn't do it without you.
Well…I could, but it wouldn't be nearly as much fun.

CHAPTER ONE

JENNA RAWLINS really disliked Atlanta's Regent Street Grill. The restaurant, situated in the upscale suburb of Buckhead, was too sleek, too cold and too uncomfortable. The waiters thought they were doing you a favor by taking your order. And the *prices!*

Jenna swallowed as her eyes drifted down a dessert menu as thick as a Russian novel. Where did they get the nerve to charge so much?

Of course, she had to admit that Vic was right about one thing. This place *was* the latest trendy eatery in the city for that important business lunch. Already two of the magazine's advertising clients had stopped by their table to say hello and buss everyone on the cheek. But honestly, with the small portions they served, what good did it do you to make contacts in the restaurant if you were too weak from hunger to remember their names?

She must have been scowling, because Victoria Estabrook, seated beside her, snatched the menu out of her hand and closed it with a snap.

"Stop that!" Vic commanded. "I don't want to hear about how the company can't afford this right now. This is a celebration, and we're all having dessert."

They were celebrating the anniversary of *Fairy Tale Weddings,* the specialty magazine she, Victoria and their friend Lauren Hoffman had founded three years ago. As a CPA and the person who kept the books for the magazine, Jenna knew perfectly well whether the company budget could stand the cost of an expensive lunch for its three partners. It could. Just not too many of them. Vic, however, had been in a contrary mood all through lunch, so it was probably pointless to argue.

"I didn't say a word," Jenna said.

"You didn't have to. We can see it on your face. It's always given you away." Victoria looked at Lauren, seated across the table. "Am I right?"

Lauren offered an agreeable shrug and sent Jenna an apologetic glance. "She's got you there, kiddo. How do you think we could always tell when things weren't going well with Jack?"

Jenna didn't want to talk about her ex-husband. More than five minutes, and she'd have a headache for certain. "Be nice, you two," she warned. "I'm still trying to get over last night's argument with Dad."

Victoria tossed down her soiled napkin. "I'll tell you how to get over it. Tell him that if he wants to continue to have you and his grandsons in his life, there are some opinions he needs to keep to himself. And anything involving Jack-ass Rawlins, no matter how true, is one of them."

Lauren and Jenna exchanged knowing smiles. This was the kind of advice they could expect from Vic, who'd been born assertive and who resented anyone trying to tell her how to live. But Jenna wasn't like that. She might be a fully grown woman of twenty-eight, but she couldn't imagine talking to her father that way in a million years. He'd probably have a coronary right on the spot.

Still, it would have been nice to find a better way to handle the "men" in her life. Taking care of two rambunctious young sons, living back home with Dad since her divorce, having two protective older brothers offering more advice than Dear Abby…

The truth was, it could make you nuts. She knew they only wanted the best for her. She knew they all loved her. But… Was she the world's worse mother/sister/daughter to sometimes wish she could just pack her bags, hop in the car and never look back? Probably.

Instead of commenting, she watched as Victoria motioned for their waiter, Dexter, who'd taken their lunch orders once a week for the past six months. He waltzed around several tables to get back to them.

"Tell us what's good today, Dexter," Victoria demanded.

"The mousse is very refreshing," he suggested brightly. "And easy on the diet if you're watching your calories this week."

"Six dollars for pudding," Jenna couldn't resist muttering. "Ridiculous."

Victoria shot her an evil look before smiling back up at Dexter. "We'll all have the Chocolate Sin cake," she told him. And probably because she felt pricked a little by that "watching your calories" remark, she added, "Make sure they put extra whipped cream on top of mine, darling."

"Of course," he said smoothly. He knew who to count on for a big tip.

Once Dexter left, Lauren leaned across the table. "What's bothering you, Vic?"

"What makes you think anything's bothering me?"

"Because besides dessert, you had a fried appetizer, a buttered roll, a salad *without* the dressing on the side and a dinner-size portion of the lamb. You only overeat when you're worried or angry about something. So what is it?"

Victoria tossed back the last of her chardonnay, then poured herself another glass from the bottle they'd ordered. "It's Cara," she said morosely. "She wants to quit school and traipse off to Europe with that moron she's dating. She's not listening to me at all. I swear, if I could convince her to come home, I'd lock her in the attic and toss the key off the top of Stone Mountain."

Jenna laughed. "And I thought I was the only one being tortured by overprotective older siblings. Poor Cara."

"You know I'm not like that. But after Mom and Dad died, I worked hard to get her future settled. I won't let her toss away law school just because this guy gives her multiple orgasms."

Lauren's brows arched. "Multiple? Wow. Sounds like someone I'd like to meet."

"Well, he's not. He's crude and ill-mannered and unemployed. Last week he almost talked her into having a nipple pierced."

"Ouch!" Lauren said with a grimace.

"I'm not a prude, but honestly, he's…" Victoria made a low, annoyed sound and raked her fingers through her long hair. "Forget him. I refuse to let him spoil our celebration. Now where were we?"

Again Jenna exchanged a glance with Lauren. She was concerned for Vic, but they both knew her well. Vic wouldn't elaborate further if she didn't want to. There would be another time, another place to tackle the problem of free-spirited baby sister Cara who just wouldn't listen to reason.

Lauren said calmly, "You were telling us about the one who bit the dust."

Victoria turned her attention back to the file folder she'd set on the table in front of her. She opened it, and Jenna saw that it contained the guts of an article the magazine had run the year before—a fluff piece listing the Ten Most Eligible Bachelors in the South. Lauren had taken the pictures. Victoria had written and edited the text.

Jenna vaguely remembered that it had been well received. No reader really expected it to help them catch one of these paragons of manhood. But there wasn't an unmarried woman in the world who wasn't at least curious to know what kind of high-end matrimonial material was out there.

That was the heart of *Fairy Tale Weddings'* appeal— dreams and fantasies. Besides the latest trends in catering and wedding attire, it specialized in the fantastic. Honeymoon locations that no one else had found and spoiled yet. Weddings that could be performed in mountaintop yurts or underwater on a sunken ship. And though the publication was a pretty small fish in the publishing pond, *FTW,* as they referred to it, had seemed to find its niche at last.

"So which one is getting married?" Jenna asked, leaning over to get a better look.

Truthfully, she wasn't all that curious. She might be an equal partner in the magazine, but most of the time she was strictly back office: paying the bills, budgeting and because she was so savvy with a computer, helping with the layout of each bimonthly issue. Occasionally she helped out in other areas, but the content of *FTW* was generally left up to Vic.

And since her divorce last year, Jenna found that the idea of men and dating and all that matrimonial hype had about as much appeal as yesterday's cold soup.

Victoria sorted through the stack of glossies with their attached profiles, then edged the photos apart. Lauren had done a great job with them. Ten gorgeous-looking men surrounded by boats, planes and polo ponies marched in a line toward Jenna's side of the table.

"Number six," Victoria said, rescuing one picture from the row. "Mark Bishop."

Lauren moved her chair so she could see better. "I remember him. Ivy League college. Newspaper business. A very intense way of sizing you up. I'm surprised he's the first to get married."

"Why?" Jenna asked.

The picture of Mark Bishop revealed a good-looking, dark-haired man in a custom-made suit. Unlike most of the other subjects, he wasn't surrounded by the playthings of the rich. He sat perched on the edge of a boardroom table, arms crossed, unsmiling. His eyes were locked with the camera in a way that made him seem dangerous, in

spite of the tasteful civility of his clothing and surroundings.

Lauren pursed her lips as though searching her memory. "He wasn't very cooperative about having his picture
taken. He didn't seem to care one way or the other
whether women found him attractive. Wasn't that your
take, Vic?"

"I don't think he believed our readers would find him
interesting."

"Too shy?" Jenna asked. The picture didn't seem to
indicate a guy who was at all reticent.

Lauren took a sip of wine. "Too arrogant, if you ask
me."

Victoria seemed to mull over that comment. "No, not
arrogant," she said at last. "Just very self-assured. He
only agreed to the interview as a favor to Debra Lee."

"Debra Lee Goodson?" Jenna asked in surprise.

"How many Debra Lees do you know?" Vic asked
with a smile. "When I first had the idea for the article, I
called every woman I could think of who might know
someone, and she suggested her boss. She didn't want to
ask him at first, but eventually she caved in."

"That's because she adores you," Lauren pointed out.
"If you asked her to take a swim in toxic waste, she'd
dig out her snorkel and fins."

That was certainly true. Back in high school, Debra Lee
Goodson had idolized Vic, who had taken the gawky teenager on as her pet project and been the one to introduce
her to her future husband.

Still, it didn't sound as though Mark Bishop had wanted
to do the original interview at all. Debra Lee, persuasive
and extremely loyal, had probably been impossible to turn
down.

Jenna flipped up the picture to scan the attached bio
and Mark Bishop's answers to the list of questions that
had been posed to every one of the Ten Most Eligible.
Thirty-two. A Leo. Educated at Princeton. No siblings.

Aloud she read, "'My life's passion is…*my work*'?" Jenna smiled at her friends. "Gosh, every woman's dream. A workaholic."

Lauren frowned. "Yes, and if I remember correctly, Debra Lee shared with him a few of our more embarrassing tales of adolescence. The nitwit."

"He found them amusing," Victoria said. She seemed determined to raise Mark Bishop's profile. For *my* benefit? Jenna wondered.

Lauren shook her head. "Ha! He blew us off professionally. I got the distinct impression he thought we were goofy, naive teenagers who grew up to be goofy, naive adults."

Jenna looked at Vic. "And you think he'll make an interesting follow-up piece?"

A tiny frown marred Victoria's brow. "He's the first one to get engaged. I think it will be interesting to follow each of these guys as they come off the list. What made them choose the woman they're going to marry? What made—" she checked the back of the profile, where she'd added a notation or two "—Shelby Elaine Winston the one for Mark Bishop? Why her?"

Lauren snorted. "Why should we care? So the rest of us can copy good old Shelby and hope that one day we'll snag a Mr. Right for ourselves?" She shook her head in disgust, sending loose auburn curls over one shoulder. "God, sometimes I think we need to give up on *that* fantasy."

"What makes you think some of us haven't?" Jenna surprised herself by saying. Damn Jack Rawlins! He really had soured her on any notion of happily-ever-after, hadn't he?

Victoria looked genuinely disconcerted. "What's wrong with you two? We're all firm believers in fairy-tale endings, remember?"

"Not lately," Lauren said, playing with her wineglass. Something in her tone made Jenna wonder just how much trouble there was in Lauren's current relationship. Earlier she'd mentioned that Brad had begun to pressure her to make more of a commitment. She'd responded by taking an assignment for a travel magazine that would have her flying to New Zealand next week. Get some breathing distance between them, she'd said.

Vic cocked her head at Lauren. "Trouble in paradise?"

Lauren didn't pretend not to understand. From the moment they'd met in grade school there'd been few secrets between the three friends. "Brad's driving me crazy," she admitted.

"In what way?" Jenna asked.

"In a dozen different ways. Everything he does lately gets on my nerves. Did you ever notice how many times he ends a sentence with '…and so on and so on and so forth'? He'll be telling a story, and it's as though he's suddenly lost interest. Then I'm just supposed to *guess* how the rest of it goes. And if I say anything, he looks at me like I'm an imbecile." Lauren narrowed her eyes at Jenna. "Why are you smiling?"

"I was just wishing I'd had that problem with Jack. He *always* finished his stories. And then he'd repeat them again and again. I could recite them in my sleep. He never shut up." She caught sight of Lauren's scowl. "Sorry. You were saying?"

Lauren played with her spoon, still frowning. "He attacks his spaghetti," she said in a soft voice.

Vic sat forward. "I beg your pardon?"

Lauren looked at her friends impatiently, then made quick slicing motions with her silverware. "He *attacks* it. Like it's a plate of snakes. It doesn't matter that he's got a pasta spoon right beside his plate. He just starts whacking at it with a knife and fork until every piece is no more than an inch long. It's disgusting to watch."

"Sounds serious," Vic said, barely suppressing a grin.

"Wait till Chef Boyardee hears about this," Jenna added.

Lauren gave them both a stern look. "I know what you're thinking. But little irritations like that can really kill a relationship, you know?"

Jenna nodded sympathetically. "Mom used to say you could sit on a mountain, but you couldn't sit on a tack."

Although, she had the sudden, wry memory that little transgressions hadn't been the death of her own marriage. Forget how Jack had repeated stories or treated his spaghetti or neglected to cap the toothpaste. That long-term affair with his secretary had pretty much distracted her from small annoyances.

She pushed thoughts of Jack to the back of her mind and tried to concentrate on Lauren's dilemma. Both Jenna and Vic had heard this same sort of complaint from their friend before.

Lauren claimed to love her independence so much that the idea of settling down with one man horrified her. Her career as a freelance photographer had really taken off in the past few years, and she now made a comfortable living regularly contributing to several different publications. While photo assignments for *FTW* were still a top priority, she loved flying out of the country on a moment's notice, marching through steamy jungles and climbing steep mountains in search of just the right shot. Where would a husband and kids and a picket fence fit into that kind of life? she'd once asked her two best friends.

It was Jenna's private theory, however, that a loss of independence wasn't Lauren's real fear at all. Jenna would have bet money that Lauren was more afraid of duplicating her parents' disastrous marriage.

Her mother was on her fourth husband. And Lauren's father, husband number one, was still referred to in their old neighborhood as Womanizing Walter. He'd been the first guy in Bear Hollow to greet any new neighbor with an armload of lawn-care products for the men—and eventually, a key to the nearest motel for young and willing wives. The scandalous details of the Hoffmans' divorce had set the neighborhood on its ear for months.

"Has Brad asked you to marry him?" Jenna inquired.

Lauren stiffened and rolled her eyes. "No. But I think he's going to soon. Hell, I think he's in love with me."

Vic placed her hand over Lauren's. "Lauren, you know what you're doing, don't you? Every time a guy gets too close you start running."

Jenna sat back in her chair, a little unnerved. "What's wrong with us?" she asked. "Vic's right. I can remember a time when we would have been dancing on this table at the thought of someone being in love with us. We're only twenty-eight. This can't be *it* for romance."

Vic, who had recently broken off with her boyfriend of six months, shook her head vehemently. "Of course it isn't. Let's just acknowledge that we're all going through a bad patch right now. But that doesn't mean we've given up on finding true love. Or it finding us. Haven't we built a business on the idea of romance and grand passion?"

They fell silent for a few moments, each of them caught in her own thoughts. Dexter approached the table with the dessert tray and placed a dish of sinful-looking chocolate cake in front of Jenna. She smiled her thanks. She had to admit, expensive and as calorie-laden as it was, it looked wonderful.

Vic pushed her fork into the moist slice of cake before her. "I'm not going to spoil a perfectly divine dessert with talk about how pathetic our love lives are." She tapped a finger against the nearest photograph on the table. "I still think the women who read *FTW* want to believe there's a Ten Most Eligible out there for them. Wouldn't you like a few hints that might allow you to snag one of these guys?"

"I suppose that would depend on how much of myself I'd have to give up in order to get him," Jenna said.

Catching sight of the picture of Mark Bishop, Dexter's eyes lit up. "Oh, honey, I wouldn't let *him* get away. Do whatever it takes. Get a complete makeover if you have to. He's a hottie.''

They all laughed and the mood at the table lightened. After Dexter sashayed off, Jenna said, ''Well, whatever secrets the happy couple want to share, I'm sure you'll put a great spin on it, Vic.''

A short silence fell as the three women took their first bites of dessert, sighs of appreciation escaping their lips. As she slipped her fork into the cake for a second mouthful, Victoria looked at Jenna and said, ''Actually *I'm* not going to do the article. *You* are.''

Jenna frowned. ''Me? What are you talking about?''

''I want you to do the piece.''

Jenna shook her head. She reached over and pushed Victoria's wineglass to the opposite side of the table. ''No more wine for you.''

''I'm serious.''

The cake in Jenna's mouth suddenly became flavorless. She gave Victoria an incredulous look, though she noticed that Lauren didn't seem completely surprised. ''Why aren't *you* going?'' And then, because she realized that Vic was serious, she added, ''I can't go in your place.''

''Why not? You have perfectly acceptable skills. You did that article last Christmas about gift suggestions.''

''You know very well that was a last-minute filler, and it amounted to no more than three paragraphs. That doesn't make me a journalist.''

''It still required a way with words. Which you have.''

Jenna set down her fork, her dessert forgotten. ''Yeah, and I'm thinking of a few choice ones right now.''

She looked across the table at Lauren for support. The redhead was mysteriously quiet. No help from that quarter evidently.

''Absolutely not,'' Jenna said firmly. ''No.''

Victoria lifted her head, all haughty tyranny. ''Technically, I'm your boss. I order you to do it for the sake of the magazine.''

Lauren and Jenna burst out laughing, and even Victoria cracked a smile.

"I might let you order my dessert," Jenna said, "but I'm an equal partner of *FTW*, and you can't send me off to—" she flipped back to Mark Bishop's bio to see where he lived "—to Orlando just because you don't want to do it."

"You don't have to go to Orlando," Victoria said.

"Good."

"He and Shelby will be in New York."

"What?"

"They've agreed to squeeze in a joint interview while they're in New York this week. He's there on business, and she's picking out her trousseau. It'll be easy. They'll be in a lovey-dovey mood. Flush with the glamour and glitz of New York, the city of love..."

"I thought Paris was the city of love," Lauren cut in.

Victoria shot her a sour look. "Thanks for your support."

Jenna crossed her arms, annoyance tinged with the tiniest bit of fear beginning to take hold of her. Searching for the right argument, she looked down, straight into the steely, hooded eyes of Mark Bishop. The guy was in the newspaper business, for heaven's sake. He'd certainly recognize that she was completely out of her element. He'd chew her up and spit out the pieces.

She cleared her throat. Loudly. "I can't just drop everything and go to New York. I have two children who—"

"Don't play the little-homemaker card with me," Victoria said in exasperation. "You have a father and two older brothers who dote on those boys, and they'd be quite willing to baby-sit if you asked them. God knows, you do everything for *them*."

"Send Lauren."

Lauren gave her a small smile of commiseration. "I'm already going. To take the pictures."

"She can't do the article," Victoria said. "She might be a genius with her camera, but you know her thought processes can be hopelessly disorganized. Doesn't allow for good writing."

Making a face at Victoria, Lauren replied, "Keep it up, and you'll be looking for a photographer, *as well as* a journalist."

Vic reached across the table and squeezed Lauren's arm. "You know I love you, darling. Desperation always makes me cruel."

"What about one of the freelancers?" Jenna suggested.

"Aren't you always telling me we need to watch costs where we can? Why should we pay a freelancer when there's a perfectly good writer in-house?" Victoria developed an interest in scraping crumbs from her plate. "Besides, there's no time. You and Lauren have to show up at his penthouse suite tomorrow afternoon."

"Tomorrow!"

Seeing Jenna's consternation, Lauren decided to speak up. "Come on, Jen. We can do it. Then we can go shopping. Or take in a show. We can have a 'wild woman weekend' just like in the old days."

"The last time I acted like a wild woman, I ended up married to the most inappropriate man in the world."

"Well, you certainly don't have to worry about that this time," Victoria said. "Shelby Elaine isn't going to turn number six loose without a fight."

Jenna tried again. "I can't go anywhere tomorrow. I have an appointment."

"With whom?" Vic asked suspiciously.

"With a real-estate agent. I wasn't kidding before. I've got to find a place of my own. The boys need it. I need it. Independence Day is long past due."

How irksome it was to see the open skepticism on both her friends' faces! Vic, of course, was the first to weigh in with her opinion. "I don't know why you think you can fool us with all this nonsense about buying a house.

You're not going to move out of your father's place—at least not until you get married again. You claim to be eager to get back out on your own, but there's still a part of you that wants to stay there."

"Why would I want to stay there? It's too small for all of us. Dad can drive a person nuts. It's too far from—"

"Because it's safe." Vic cut across the conversation.

Jenna stared down at her abandoned dessert. She wanted to refute Vic's words, but she had no grounds.

She longed for independence, longed to make a home for herself and the boys, but at the same time she was scared to death. Afraid to fail. Afraid to find out she couldn't manage on her own. It was horrible to be this age, have come this far, and still suspect that deep within, the same old insecure Jenna was sabotaging every move.

She could feel Vic and Lauren's eyes on her and felt a surge of rebellion. "Why *can't* you go, Vic?" she asked, determined to keep the conversation on the problem at hand. "And I want the truth."

Victoria looked down for a moment, running her fingers through her blond hair in a familiar gesture that told her friends the teasing time was over. When she lifted her eyes, Jenna saw the uneasiness there, tinged with an uncharacteristic fear.

"I'm flying out to California tomorrow morning," Victoria said, the lightness gone from her voice. "I'm not going to let Cara flit off to Europe to ride around on the back of a motorcycle without trying to make her see reason. That guy is no good for her, and maybe face-to-face I can convince her of that."

During Victoria's last year in college, her parents had been killed in a car accident. Cara, six years her junior, had been seriously injured. Vic had dropped out of school and come home to take care of her sister. She'd nursed her back to health, settled their parents' estate and overseen the sale of the family business. The sisters loved each other dearly. But that didn't mean Cara would let Vic tell her how to run her love life.

Jenna knew firsthand how such interference could sometimes produce a result just the opposite of the one desired. She leaned closer to her friend. "Vic…are you sure this is the best way to handle the problem? Don't you remember when everyone in my family tried to persuade me not to marry Jack? We couldn't get to the justice of the peace fast enough."

"It won't be like that," Victoria replied. She pressed her lips together tightly, as though her anxiety had leaked out before she could catch it. "My mind's made up, the tickets are bought, so don't try to talk me out of it."

They all subsided into thoughtful silence. The rest of their desserts remained uneaten. Jenna stared down at the picture of Mark Bishop, seeing nothing but the potential for disaster. She would do anything to help the magazine and her friend. But this? How could she hope to succeed?

Eventually the silence became charged and uncomfortable. Jenna picked up the picture again, releasing a huge sigh. "Lord, he looks so intimidating."

"Debra Lee says he's a prince to work for. And he's fallen in love since that picture was taken," Victoria said. "He'll be a pussycat."

Jenna opened her mouth to refute that, but Lauren touched Victoria's sleeve and said, "Give her some time to think about it, Vic. You know Jenna. She likes to weigh everything very carefully. I'm not surprised she's hesitant, the way you've sprung this on her."

Victoria looked back at Jenna. "All right. I'll give you until tonight to make up your mind."

"And then what happens?" Jenna asked.

"And then I start begging."

Lauren laughed, but Jenna frowned. She wouldn't go. She just couldn't. No more thought on the matter would make a difference.

And she wasn't going to let this foolishness keep her

from enjoying a dessert the company was paying good money for. She picked up her fork again and deliberately placed a sizable bite of Chocolate Sin into her mouth.

The icing was thick, cloying. She tried to savor its richness, but all she could see were Mark Bishop's dark eyes staring up at her from his picture beside her plate.

"Don't look like that," Vic commanded. "You're not being sent to the executioner's block."

Maybe not, Jenna thought. But the cake sure tasted like part of a condemned man's last meal.

CHAPTER TWO

BY THE TIME Jenna got home that afternoon, her mind was more made up than ever. There was no way she could face a powerful, sophisticated businessman like Mark Bishop and ask him a bunch of silly questions about love and romance and how he'd found the girl of his dreams.

But at the same time she couldn't help sympathizing with Vic and her dilemma with her sister. The easiest solution, Jenna decided, was to farm out the article to one of *FTW*'s many freelancers. Even on such short notice, one of them would be glad to take the job. She could start calling them right after she got the boys settled down for the night. If she had to, she'd pay for the piece out of her own pocket. End of problem.

That decision made, Jenna turned her attention to dinner. She would have preferred to take a warm bath and put her feet up with a good book, but no such luck.

Her older brothers were coming over. Christopher had been in a major funk this week because his girlfriend, Amanda, was out of town visiting her family. Trent, now a full partner in the family construction business, wanted to celebrate the completion of their most recent job, a large office complex on Magnolia Street. Jenna's sons, Petey and J.D., always enjoyed having their uncles in the house, and her father was eager to try out his new grill. The evening promised to be noisy, lively and exhausting.

She fixed a salad and baked potatoes to go with the steaks her father grilled. While Christopher and Trent roughhoused with her sons in the living room, Jenna slipped peach cobbler into the oven and swallowed two aspirins to quell the headache building behind her eyes.

The meal was a success. The fellows were always appreciative of her cooking and had the good sense to remark on it. Afterward, as Jenna placed the cobbler and ice cream on the table, there were groans that they were too full, but she noticed that this didn't stop them.

Her father launched into a speech about barbecuing techniques. Christopher said that Amanda had called him and missed him already. Trent was helping the boys scoop ice cream while they playfully fought over who got the biggest helping. The closeness, the good-natured ribbing, the relaxed laughter—it was into this familiar family patter that Jenna brought her own contribution to the conversation: Vic's attempt to coerce her to go to New York.

Talk at the table ceased as if someone had just discovered a bomb planted in the centerpiece. Five pairs of eyes turned in her direction.

After a lengthy silence, Trent was the first to speak. "Wow," he said as he returned to scooping ice cream. "Victoria must be really desperate."

Jenna was momentarily speechless. Maybe it was her headache. Maybe it was the heat from the kitchen that had caused an unpleasant line of perspiration to form along the small of her back. Or maybe it was just the offhand, incredulous way Trent had said it, as though Vic's suggestion was unthinkable. Whatever it was, her brother's comment rankled. Why was it so impossible to believe his kid sister might be able to handle the interview?

Jenna decided she had to know.

"Why *wouldn't* she ask me?" she said. "I'm an equal partner at the magazine. We share a variety of jobs. I can still carry on an adult conversation. Unless, of course, I'm trying to talk to you."

"Yeah, but…" If he'd missed the sting in her words, Trent certainly couldn't have misinterpreted her frown of displeasure. He subsided with a grumpy scowl of his own and focused on his bowl of ice cream.

Her father made the situation worse. "New York?" he exclaimed, as though he found the words offensive. "You can't go there."

Jenna turned her frown on her father. "Why not?"

"We need you here at home."

"That's a lousy reason and you know it. It's two days. I'll be back before you and the boys finish the leftover cobbler."

Her father's chin set in the same stubborn lines that used to irritate her mother so much. "I don't like it. It's much too dangerous. You're a small-town girl, and the big city's not the place for you, Jenny-girl."

Jenna could feel the spoon in her hand cutting into her palm she gripped it so tightly. "For heaven's sake, it's New York, not Bangkok. I commute into Atlanta five days a week. I think I can handle it."

William McNab apparently failed to notice the irritation in his daughter's voice. "Big-city Atlanta is not the same as big-city New York. Things are different here in the South."

She batted her eyelashes dramatically. In a heavy Southern accent, she said, "Land-sakes, Papa. I think I can handle being among those darned Yankee carpetbaggers. But if I can't, why, I'll just skedaddle back here to the plantation."

Trent chuckled around a mouthful of cobbler. "Make up your mind, Jen. Are you Lois Lane or Scarlett O'Hara?"

"Knock it off, Trent," Christopher warned softly, obviously sensing trouble ahead.

Trent looked momentarily confused. Her father sighed, then tossed his oldest son a humor-her look. "Explain the difference to her, Chris."

Christopher was an Atlanta police detective and could probably regale them with a dozen grim tales from the mean streets of New York. But Jenna, feeling more annoyed by the minute, wasn't willing to listen. She raised a hand to stop him, then addressed her father.

"You know, Dad, I'm a grown woman now. I've been married and divorced, and I'm the mother of two children. What I am *not* anymore is Jenny-girl. I am not a child, and I am perfectly capable of conducting this interview and hailing cabs and riding the subway and— J.D., stop that!"

Six-year-old J.D. had been trying to start a duel with his brother using a spoon that still dripped ice cream. He jerked his head up guiltily. Jenna gave him "the look," then went around to his side of the table to wipe at the spot he'd made on the tablecloth. She kept her head down, focused on the task at hand because her throat was suddenly clogged with frustrated, angry words unfit for the boys' young ears.

Used to defusing potentially dangerous situations, Christopher spoke up. "Take it easy, sis. Dad didn't mean anything by it. He just worries about you. We all do."

She glanced up, looking at her brothers and her father in turn. They didn't appear a bit apologetic, only surprised by her attitude. She was a little surprised by it herself. Just how long had this resentment about the way they saw her been boiling up inside?

Next to her, seven-year-old Petey finished scraping out his bowl. He smiled at her. "I think you'll be great, Mom. You can do anything."

Probably just a ploy to get a second helping of dessert, Jenna thought. But she couldn't help feeling a swell of ridiculous pleasure. At least *someone* at the table thought she was an adult capable of more than baking a passable peach cobbler.

She leaned over, captured her son's tousled blond head with one arm and planted a kiss on his forehead. "Thank you, sweetheart," she said as he reddened and squirmed out of her grasp. "You believe in your mom, don't you, honey?"

"Uh-huh," Petey replied. "You can tell him all about us. How you ran the pumpkin patch for school last year and how you got Randy's dad to pay for Little League uniforms and the special Easter baskets you made for Gramma Resnick's nursing-home people..."

"And how you're a good cook," J.D. offered.

The smile froze on Jenna's face. Neither one of the boys had a clue what conducting an interview was all about. It was also horribly clear just where they thought her talents lay.

In being a mom. Not a real person at all. Just the family facilitator who made sure they got to school every morning with full stomachs and clean clothes. The one who carted them to soccer practice. The one who read them stories at night and cried silly tears over the pictures they drew. *Just being a mom.*

At the other end of the table, her father and Christopher remained judiciously silent, but Trent, never one to catch subtle changes in the air around him, couldn't help grinning at her. "There you go, Jen," he said with a twinkle in his eye. "Offer the guy some peach cobbler. He'll spill his guts about romance faster than one of Christopher's collars trying to beat a rap."

This time all three men laughed. Even the boys joined in, not fully understanding the conversation, but tickled by the goofy face their uncle made.

Jenna ignored the laughter, refusing to make the discussion any more unpleasant with the boys present. She retreated to the kitchen to wash the dinner dishes while Trent helped Petey with his homework and her father flipped on his favorite television program. Perhaps sensing her irritation, Christopher made a half-hearted attempt to clear the table and help with the dishes, but she shooed him into the living room to join the others.

She usually ran the dishwasher, but tonight she filled

the sink with hot, soapy water and slowly lowered the dishes into it. She wasn't that eager to join the rest of the family. Maybe tonight she'd distance herself entirely from them. Even the boys.

It didn't matter that some of the things they'd said were the same arguments she'd used at lunch with Vic. They should have been supportive. They shouldn't have made fun of the idea. At the very least, they should have *pretended* to think she could do it. For heaven's sake, she was a college graduate. A working mother. She wasn't stupid.

She supposed it was her own fault if her family discounted her, tried to run her life. Growing up, she'd allowed her brothers to do most of her thinking for her. It was habit with them now. And since her mother's death a few years ago, her father had become more protective of her, as well.

The circumstances of her failed marriage hadn't helped. Jack Rawlins had been the sweetest-talking, handsomest man she'd ever met. He had dreams of running away from the ho-hum world of corporate accounting, living in wild, indolent grace on some tropical island. The unreliable heat of physical desire had sparked and flared between them, and over the objections of her entire family, they had eloped.

For a while, even after the boys came, they'd both worked toward that fairy-tale goal. Jack had bought a boat to fix up. He wanted to sail around the world, and Jenna could see herself on the deck, warmed by the sun, her hair tangled with salt spray as she kept a journal detailing their escapades. They would share a life bigger and grander than anything hot, humid Atlanta had to offer.

But by the fifth year of their marriage, Jenna had begun to modify that dream a little. The boys needed roots. They would be in school soon. The house they'd bought required repairs that were more crucial than the rotting, rusting boat sitting in drydock in the backyard. Could you really support yourself on a small island in the Pacific? Live on coconuts and fish? Maybe it was time to consider occasional vacations, instead of a permanent relocation.

Foolishly, she'd thought Jack had come to that conclusion, too. Passion became a missing ingredient in their comfortable, suburban lifestyle, but Jenna was certain that Jack still loved her. That whatever hopes they'd had to compromise, it would be all right. Sooner or later, didn't everyone have to accept reality?

And then she woke up one day to discover that Jack hadn't settled at all. That he'd emptied their bank account, run up their credit cards and booked a flight to Tahiti.

For two.

Evidently his secretary had similar dreams of an adventurous life.

The divorce had been painful, but mercifully quick. The boys had been spared the details of their father's desertion. Jenna had sold the house, moved back in with her father and begun to rebuild her credit. Her family had closed ranks around her, and she'd been so devastated she'd gone right back to letting them take care of her.

Her one moment of spiteful retaliation? Jack's boat, left behind because it simply wasn't grand enough, had mysteriously burned to a crisp. She wasn't a saint, after all.

Yet she couldn't honestly say she missed Jack all that much. He'd been so emotionally distant for so long. The boys were finally getting used to the fact that he never called or wrote. Not even a card to them on their birthdays or at Christmas. Those were the only times Jenna thought she could really hate the man.

Perspiration beaded her forehead from the dishwasher's steamy heat. She swiped it away with one arm. The moonless night had turned the window over the sink into a mirror. She caught her reflection in it, and her submerged hands stilled.

Who is that woman?

It had been years since she'd really evaluated her looks.

Now she gave herself the most thorough once-over she could remember. And what she saw made her throat go dry with panic.

Because her mousy-brown hair lacked body, she'd always worn it short, a perky style she'd considered becoming to her long neck. But when had carefree become careless? And her eyes. It wasn't just the unflattering overhead lighting in the kitchen. There were shadows under them that made her look downright unhealthy. In their dark depths there was no gleam, no energy. Only an unnervingly bleak, fenced-in look.

It was the sight of her mouth that troubled her the most. It had always been her best feature, and truthfully, she was a little vain about it. A lovely bow shape, it curved upward at the corners, the lower lip lush and mobile. In their romantic early days, Jack had told her that it just begged for a man's kiss.

Of course, he'd probably told his secretary that, too.

But it didn't matter. What she saw now was nothing she wanted to lay claim to. Her lips seemed thin and down-curving, as though she were the type who constantly manufactured grievances. And tight, as though her teeth were clenched on despair. When had that happened? And how could she have missed it?

She hardly noticed when the dishwater turned too cool to do much good. She kept looking at that stranger in the glass. She knew the divorce had left her pride in tatters, had left her feeling rudderless and *finished,* but she thought she'd finally come through all that. She was picking up the pieces, moving on with life, moving *into* life again.

You sure about that, Jen? If that was so, then who was this stranger who stared back at her? And how long before the years took an even greater toll? Once the boys no longer needed her... Once life was filled with more disappointment than fulfillment...

I'm not going to let that happen, she swore to the

woman in the glass. *I refuse. It's not too late to change things.*

She set the rest of the pots to soak and dried her hands. The family was engrossed in some sitcom blaring on the television and hardly noticed as she made her way upstairs to her bedroom.

She dialed Vic's number before she could change her mind and was relieved when her friend picked up on the second ring.

"What are you doing?" Jenna asked.

"Packing, of course." There were muffled sounds from the other end of the phone as Vic readjusted the receiver. "What will take hollandaise sauce out of a white cotton blouse?"

"Try some club soda mixed with baking powder."

"I knew you'd know. So what's the answer?"

Jenna didn't hesitate. "I'll go."

Vic whooped with delight. "Terrific! I told Lauren that once you got home and really thought about it, you'd come up with a dozen reasons why you should go."

Jenna couldn't resist smiling. "Actually I couldn't come up with a dozen. Only six."

"And they are?"

"Dad, Christopher, Trent, Petey and J.D."

"That's only five reasons. What's number six?"

Jenna drew a deep breath, then let it out slowly. "Me."

CHAPTER THREE

"STOP LOOKING at me like that," Jenna told Lauren for the third time.

"I can't help it," her friend replied with a silly grin. "I'm still in shock."

They were alone in the small elevator of New York's Belasco Hotel, headed up to the penthouse suite. The hotel was a pleasant surprise. Jenna had expected someone of Mark Bishop's wealth and position to be drawn to a place more pretentious, more dazzling. Instead, the Belasco boasted Old World charm and discreet elegance—no doubt at horribly expensive rates—but enchanting nonetheless.

Lauren, whose exposure to these kinds of places was much broader than Jenna's, didn't seem a bit impressed by their surroundings. Instead, her appreciative gaze roamed over Jenna again. "When did you find the time to do all this?"

This was the transformation Jenna had attempted to make in her appearance before their plane had taken off that day at noon. She'd decided that if she couldn't actually lay claim to *being* a serious journalist, she ought to at least *look* like one. Confident. Sophisticated. Savvy. Judging from Lauren's reaction, her efforts had been worthwhile.

"It's amazing what you can accomplish once you decide to eliminate sleep from your life," Jenna told her friend. "I raided the cosmetic counter at my all-night drugstore. I did my nails and gave myself a facial. Then

I called Max early this morning and promised him a month's salary as a tip if he'd do something with my hair."

"The change is incredible," Lauren said.

Self-consciously, Jenna touched the wispy ends of her new haircut. "You don't think the blond highlights are too radical?"

Lauren shook her head as though she still couldn't believe what she was seeing. "I think they look fantastic."

"It's not helping that you're this shocked. How bad did I look before?"

"Sorry. You just look so…"

"Professional?"

"I was going to say sexy."

Jenna frowned. "Oh, dear. That's not the image I was going for."

"Maybe not. But it can't hurt." She gave Jenna another long, sweeping glance. "And red is really your color."

Jenna looked down at the suit she wore with its short jacket and stand-up collar. She hadn't had time to shop for clothes, and this had been the closest thing in her wardrobe to a "power suit." She'd faced down an IRS auditor in this suit during her brother Trent's tax investigation the year before.

She noted that Lauren, on the other hand, looked casual and breezy in a khaki shirt and pants with about a dozen deep pockets. Her hair was swinging freely in a ponytail, and the camera bag that went with her everywhere was slung over one shoulder.

"I just hope I don't make a fool of myself," Jenna muttered.

The elevator doors opened, and they started down a short hallway where the carpet underfoot was as thick as a blanket of snow. They stopped in front of the penthouse door. As Lauren rapped on it, Jenna said softly, "Just promise me one thing. If you hear my knees knocking, you'll start talking to cover the noise."

Vic had provided her with a list of questions, along with a copy of Mark Bishop's original interview. Jenna hugged it close to her chest. Some of the questions were harmless, just for fun. Some informational. Others, maybe half a dozen, made Jenna blush just to read them. She couldn't imagine asking them. Or Mark Bishop being willing to respond.

What would Vic do if she came back without a single sizzling nugget about the man? Probably pronounce her a complete failure and never send her on this kind of assignment again. Which, come to think of it, wouldn't be such a bad thing.

For the hundredth time she ran through the interviewing tips her friend had coached her with over the phone. *Listen, listen, listen. Don't interrupt him in the middle of an answer. Look interested in what he says, never as if you disapprove. Make eye contact, lots of it. Don't let him see that you're nervous....*

Oh, Lord, what had she been thinking? She couldn't do this! Why did she think this suit would help? She wasn't a journalist. She was an accountant, and power red or not, he was going to see through her in two seconds flat. She should bow out now, while she still had the chance. She should—

And then suddenly the door to the suite opened, and there was their old friend Debra Lee. She looked a little older, much more sophisticated than Jenna remembered, but her smile was the same. Warm and welcoming. She greeted them with hugs and ushered them inside.

Jenna barely had time to register that the suite was probably big enough to hold most of her father's house before Debra Lee led them through sliding glass doors and onto a wide terrace that ran the length of the suite.

The summer air was surprisingly cool and refreshing. From the balcony, the tops of the tallest trees from the nearest park were barely visible, waving like ruffled fans in the slight breeze. Beyond them lay Manhattan, its impressive skyline caught in the late-afternoon sunlight.

Lauren, always looking for that next wonderful shot, immediately crossed to the railing. She pulled her camera up, made a few adjustments and began clicking away happily. Never fond of heights, Jenna was content to hang back closer to the sliding glass doors.

"Make yourselves comfortable," Debra Lee said, indicating a pitcher of iced tea and glasses on a patio table. "Mark and Miss Winston had an appointment this afternoon, and I'm afraid they're not back yet."

One of Jenna's pet peeves was being kept waiting, especially since she knew *FTW*'s office had reconfirmed their appointment just this morning. She'd read once that people who were chronically late were subconsciously flexing their muscles, trying to show who had the upper hand in the meeting. She could just imagine someone like Mark Bishop wanting to send that kind of message. *You're not important enough for me to care about being on time.*

But on the plus side, a delayed interview would certainly allow her an easy out. "We can reschedule if necessary," Jenna said, knowing Vic would be the one to show up next time.

Lauren stopped taking pictures and turned toward them. "No, we can't," she said to Debra Lee with a pointed look in Jenna's direction. "We'll wait."

"Good," Debra Lee replied. Then she suddenly looked sheepish. "I suppose I should have told Vic, but Mark never actually agreed—"

There was a sound behind them, the door to the suite opening and closing with a bang, then a strong male voice calling out, "Deb! Where are you? Get in here!"

Debra Lee gave them a quick smile. "Wait here, please," she said, then spun around and stepped back into the living room.

Still absorbed in taking pictures, Lauren had wandered

farther along the terrace. She was almost completely hidden now by an enormous ficus in an oriental tub. Jenna was standing so close to the exterior wall beside the sliding glass doors that she couldn't be easily seen, either.

It occurred to her that she should probably move out into the center of the terrace, make sure her presence was noted by whomever had just entered the suite. Instead, she instinctively moved closer to the wall.

The man spoke again, harshly, and though she couldn't see him any better than he could see her, Jenna felt sure it must be Mark Bishop. "I just spent two excruciating hours listening to that idiot Benchley. He claims there was a major change in top management at Castleman Press last week. Find Scott. Tell him I want to know why it wasn't in his report. A shakeup like that should have been a red flag that a blind man couldn't have missed."

His voice was exactly what Jenna expected—deep, commanding and leaving little room for argument. Nervous tension danced up her spine.

"Right away," she heard Debra Lee say. And then, "Miss Winston isn't with you?"

"I didn't have the heart to make her stay and listen to Benchley, so she went on to Ken's office to sign some papers. She'll be here soon. God, I'm whipped. And I need a drink. Benchley's voice is still making my ears vibrate."

There was silence for a long minute amid a few small sounds of settling. The rustle of cloth against cloth. The clink of ice being dropped into a glass.

"Your five-o'clock appointment is here," Debra Lee said at last.

"I don't have a five-o'clock."

"My friends from the magazine. You remember, we discussed this yesterday."

"I remember I told you to cancel it." There was a quizzical note in Bishop's voice now. Jenna was sure he must be frowning at his secretary.

"That was before you kept me working on the Brazleton deal all night. I believe you owe me a favor, Mark."

"Deb, come on. I did this once. How many times do I have to be tortured by these people?"

The remark put Jenna immediately on the defensive.

"I suppose that depends on how many times you expect me to leave my husband and family at a moment's notice just so you'll have someone at your beck and call twenty-four hours a day." Debra Lee didn't sound a bit intimidated. She'd worked for Mark Bishop a long time, and maybe their relationship had developed beyond the usual employer/employee dynamic.

"You know, there are women at the paper who would kill to work shoulder to shoulder with me. I could have you working in classifieds by tomorrow morning."

Jenna could hear fondness in his voice and knew he was joking. Debra Lee laughed lightly. "I'll get the transfer forms. Simple work. Normal hours. No having to second-guess or cater to unreasonable whims. Sounds like heaven to me."

"Why don't *you* do the interview?" Mark Bishop suggested. "You know me well enough to answer any asinine question they might have. Tell them all my secrets. Tell them anything you want. I don't care. I haven't slept in…God, I can't remember how long."

"Then let's get started now, and when Miss Winston gets here, most of it will be done. It'll be over before you know it."

"That's what my mother used to say when she took me to the dentist. I didn't believe her, either."

"Come on, Mark. These are my friends. I—"

"Owe them," the man finished her sentence impatiently, and Jenna could imagine him lifting his hand to halt her continued efforts to sway him. "I got it, I got it."

"It's true. I could never have gotten through high school without their friendship. Besides, you need to be more visible, more approachable."

"I don't want to be more approachable."

"Then think of it as good PR for the company."

"Fine. Let's just get this over with."

Again there was a rustle of movement from inside the suite. Jenna froze. She was about to come face-to-face with Mark Bishop, and when she did, it would become abundantly clear she'd been standing close enough to the doorway to hear every nasty word. But it was too late now. She remained where she was, feeling resentful and embarrassed and pinned to the spot.

Mark Bishop walked out onto the terrace, Debra Lee only a couple of steps behind him. Because Jenna was so close to the wall, he didn't see her, and Debra Lee obstructed her view of him. All she got was the impression of broad shoulders and dark hair.

From the far end of the balcony, Lauren turned and approached quickly, hand held out, a smile on her face. "Hello," she said as they shook hands. "Nice to see you again."

"It's a pleasure to see you, too," the man said mildly, and if Jenna hadn't heard his complaints with her own ears, she'd never have guessed this was the same man.

"Lauren Hoffman." She tilted her head past him to catch Jenna's eye. "And this is Jenna Rawlins, one of the partners of *Fairy Tale Weddings*. She's taking Victoria's place for the interview."

Bishop pivoted immediately. He was frowning; he clearly hadn't been expecting anyone behind him. Blood surged giddily through Jenna's veins and she could imagine color rushing to her cheeks. She stepped forward swiftly, her hand held out in greeting.

"Pleased to meet you, Mr. Bishop," she said in her most authoritative voice. "We'll try not to take up too much of your time. It's very kind of you to agree to be…tortured once again."

He blinked quickly—just once—but it was enough to give her a moment of confidence. If there was no way to gracefully admit she'd been eavesdropping on his conversation with Debra Lee, she might as well let him know she hadn't misunderstood a single, unkind word.

Her poise, however, didn't last. Mark Bishop took her hand in his, holding it a shade longer than necessary. An awkward silence stretched between them like a thin, tight wire.

His head had tilted slightly, as though she was something he'd never seen before, and his mouth, so serious only seconds before, curled up slowly in one corner. It was his eyes that fascinated her, though. They were a dark gray-blue, the color of a stormy sea, yet flecked with light.

"Deb's told me all about you," he said pleasantly.

She couldn't tell what he meant by that, whether he was making fun of her or just making small talk. Either way, she wasn't going to let him see how much he unnerved her. "And Deb has told us all about you, too."

He looked as if he might address that, but Debra Lee interrupted smoothly with "Shelby should be here any minute. Shall we get started without her?"

Without waiting for them to answer, he nodded and turned, stepping back into the suite's living area. She and Lauren followed in his wake, and Jenna couldn't help noticing how tall he was and the easy, confident way he moved. From shopping with her father and brothers, Jenna knew men's clothing, but nothing they had ever chosen off the rack could match the fine-tailoring of Bishop's charcoal double-breasted suit.

He offered them the couch, while he took the easy chair across from them and Debra Lee disappeared into another room. Jenna assumed it was to locate Scott, the poor guy who'd missed the management changes at Castleman Press. She wondered if he would lose his job over it.

Unbuttoning his jacket, crossing one ankle over the opposite knee, Mark Bishop spent a few minutes listening to Lauren as she discussed the pictures she intended to take. He didn't seem to mind the idea that she wanted mostly candid shots. In fact, Jenna was left with the impression that he didn't care one way or the other.

Jenna continued to stare down at his file in her lap. The questions in front of her were only a black-and-white blur. She could feel her heart racing. Random questions popped out at her as she tried to settle on which one to ask first. Should she start slowly and build to the more intimate ones? Or jump in with something daring, as Vic was likely to do?

· *Oh, hell,* Jenna thought, *what does it matter? You're not on* 60 Minutes, *trying to unravel a political scandal. Just pick something.*

But when her eyes finally focused and she did, she saw that the question dealt with positions in bed, one of Vic's naughty inquiries, and Jenna knew it would take more than a red power suit to prepare her for that one. She swore she could feel the tips of her ears turning pink and wished she'd told Max to give her a haircut that covered them.

"Any time now, Miss Rawlins," Mark Bishop said into a silence that had become foolishly long.

She jerked her head up to discover that he was staring at her. Dark, curious and assessing, it was the sort of look that could make you forget about breathing for a heartbeat or two. *There,* Jenna thought. *Those eyes are what made Shelby Elaine Winston fall in love.*

Her heart began to beat faster; she could feel it in her temples. She blurted out, "Do you wear boxers or briefs, Mr. Bishop?"

He let out a little huff of surprised laughter, and Jenna was aware that even Lauren had turned her head to stare at her.

Somehow she kept from lowering her glance in mortification.

His lips had curved into a smile. "I must say, you get right to the point."

How had the situation gone so wrong, so fast? The part of her brain still capable of rational thought took over again, thank goodness. She cleared her throat and offered him a smile full of regret. "I apologize for being so personal," she said. "Let's start with something less… intimate, shall we?" A quick look down at her notes. "How did you and Miss Winston meet?"

He nodded, obviously willing to forget that first question. "We met a couple of years ago at a charity auction. We spent a very pleasant evening together trying to outbid one another."

"And you've been dating ever since?"

"No. I didn't see Shelby again until three months ago when one of my newspapers was doing an investigative piece on Senator Winston's involvement with the Texanol scandal. She stormed into my office and accused me of trying to start a smear campaign against her father."

It was Jenna's turn to frown, though she hid it by pretending to flip through her list of questions. It seemed odd to her that Mark Bishop could have met the woman of his dreams two years ago and then been perfectly happy not to see her again until just recently. Evidently it hadn't been love at first sight.

She looked up when Bishop spoke again. "Senator Winston is the senior senator from Texas." He paused, as though she needed time for that to sink in. "And by the way, he was found to be completely uninvolved in that debacle at Texanol."

She knew that, and it irritated her that he would think she didn't. Did he imagine they were idiots? That they never read the paper? There he sat, cool and elegant in his expensive suit, in his expensive hotel penthouse, like a king greeting his subjects. Was she supposed to find his insults acceptable because they'd been presented with subtlety and finesse? He'd been friendly and charming so far, but what did she really know about the man? He certainly hadn't wanted to do this interview, she remembered.

Annoyed, she gave him a bright, completely false smile. "Actually, Mr. Bishop, we do stay abreast of current events at *Fairy Tale Weddings*. In fact, I'm almost sure I read a story about Senator Winston one day in the grocery store checkout line. It was right next to a story about a two-headed baby born in Nebraska."

Nothing in his posture or features indicated he found her sarcasm offensive. He just continued to stare at her, waiting. Lauren got up suddenly, lifted her camera and began taking another round of pictures.

Debra Lee appeared in the living room at that moment, cell phone in hand. "I've got Scott on the line," she told her boss. "Do you want to take it?"

"Yes," Mark Bishop replied. He gave both Jenna and Lauren apologetic smiles. "Will you excuse me for one moment, ladies?"

He stood and wandered back out to the terrace for privacy. Debra Lee scooped up their empty iced-tea glasses and retreated to the kitchen.

Lauren was digging in her camera case for more film. She said under her breath, "What are you doing? Don't piss him off, Jen."

"He thinks we're idiots!" Jenna hissed.

"Who cares?"

"I do."

Before they could say any more, Bishop was back. The breeze on the terrace had fingered his dark hair into soft, imperfect waves. Jenna liked the look better on him and was sorry when he pushed back a lock from his forehead with an impatient hand.

He didn't sit down again. A beautiful mahogany desk took up the entire corner of the room, and he perched on it, one leg cocked over the edge. The refined, athletic grace of that movement sent an unexpected dart of sexual heat to Jenna's stomach.

"Now, where were we?" he asked. "Oh, yes. I believe you were taking exception to something I said?"

The question was mild, nonthreatening, but Jenna couldn't help feeling as though he was watching her a little more closely now. She could feel a blush creeping higher and higher up her neck.

Suddenly she didn't want to ask any of Vic's silly romantic questions. She wanted to see Mark Bishop as a real person. Wanted him to see *her* as a real person. Someone to be reckoned with and taken seriously. He'd piqued her interest with his earlier mention of a buyout of Castleman Press. Curiosity overcame her. "Are you going to buy Castleman Press?" she asked.

He seemed unperturbed by such a bald question. "That depends on the financial climate next quarter."

As the investment counselor for the magazine, Jenna knew a little bit about Castleman. She read the *Wall Street Journal* religiously, followed every trend in the stockmarket and was always looking for companies *FTW* could add to their tiny investment portfolio. "Castleman's stock plummeted sixteen points last week. It's ripe for a takeover."

She sensed a restless movement from Lauren's side of the couch, but she couldn't take her eyes off Mark Bishop. He was watching her in that silent, assessing way again. Only this time Jenna was also aware of a *pull* between them, something electric and subtle, something unmistakably sexual. It didn't seem possible, yet Jenna was sure she wasn't imagining it; it hadn't been *that* long since a man had looked at her this way. Too bad it was coming from someone who was already engaged to be married.

The corners of his mouth lifted into another smile. "Is that opinion coming from your supermarket tabloid?"

She started to smile back, then sobered when Debra Lee leaned close to him. Mark Bishop turned away to speak to her. His comments were brief and businesslike. Jenna felt a stab of pain on her thigh and swung her head around to find that Lauren had pinched her.

"Forget about Castleman," Lauren whispered tightly. "You're the only one who cares about that. Find out whether it's boxers or briefs."

"But…" Jenna began, then closed her mouth because Mark Bishop had finished his business with Debra Lee and turned his attention back to Jenna.

"My apologies. You were saying?"

Jenna consulted her list and moved on to the next question on it. "So you and Shelby were at odds at first. What, eventually, attracted you to Miss Winston?"

"She's quite beautiful, of course. She has a good head on her shoulders and comes from an excellent family. Honest, socially conscious. I found her loyalty to her father very admirable." He stopped, tilting his head inquiringly at her. "Something amuses you, Miss Rawlins?"

How much could she safely say? And how could she put it? *Wow, Bishop. Are you sure we're talking about your fiancée here and not Lassie?* No, he'd definitely take offense at that. Jenna's tongue slid out to wet her lips. "Pardon me, Mr. Bishop, but the readers of *FTW* would find your answers rather…" She hesitated.

"Unromantic?" he finished for her. "Yes, I expect they would be disappointed. But I'm not eighteen anymore. For me, marriage isn't about poetry and flowers and silly love songs. It's a partnership, and I see nothing wrong with two people wanting to make the best arrangement they can."

She could see he was dead serious, and she hardly knew what to say in the face of his calm practicality. His eyes were like polished steel now, untroubled and frank. Maybe she'd imagined that earlier awareness between them, after all. Her overriding thought was that she hoped Shelby Elaine knew just what kind of bargain she'd made.

"So you see your upcoming marriage as a satisfactory business alliance," Jenna stated. She tried to keep Vic's advice uppermost in her mind. *Never look as if you disapprove.*

"I can see I've offended you somehow," Bishop said, killing her hope that she'd managed to keep her thoughts off her features. "I'm sorry. I'm afraid I've always found the idea of grand passion rather—" he stopped, searched for the right word and evidently found it "—unreliable."

"No, I understand," she replied, although she wasn't sure she did. "Shall we continue?" Beginning to feel a little edgy and out of sorts, she chose the most foolishly inane questions she could find. "What's your favorite flower?"

"Artificial. Silk, I suppose. It's more costly, but ultimately lasts longer."

Sorry, Shelby Elaine. Looks like there will be no roses smelling up the house on your birthday. "Your favorite movie?"

"I rarely have time to go to movies."

"Favorite color?"

"Gray."

Should have seen that one coming. "Favorite animal?"

"I'd have to give that some thought. I'm not really an animal person. No pets."

Probably too messy for his tastes. All that mushy unconditional-love stuff.

"I'm a Leo," Mark Bishop offered. "But then, I think that was established in the last interview."

She narrowed her eyes, certain now that he was making fun of her. His expression seemed guileless, and yet she imagined he knew exactly what she was thinking.

Changing tacks, she said, "Have you set a date yet?"

"Shelby would like to get married next spring."

"Where?"

"On her father's ranch in Texas."

"And your honeymoon?"

Bishop shrugged. "That hasn't been decided yet. I've told Shelby to pick out any spot that pleases her."

Are all the decisions Shelby's? Except for showing up, are you participating in this wedding at all? She clenched her teeth, trying to keep every bit of skepticism she had about these nuptials way, way down inside her. "Do you plan to have children?"

He took a moment to answer that one. Finally he said, "Shelby and I were both only children. We may want a child eventually, but I don't think either of us is ready to give up our freedom just yet."

She asked a dozen more questions. None of them seemed to upset or interest him. He danced around the more personal ones, and by the time the interview wound down, Jenna was pretty certain she'd discover later that she'd bitten her tongue completely in two. She wondered how she was going to make anyone find her article the least bit interesting.

Mark Bishop didn't have a romantic bone in his body. Poor Shelby Elaine was going to find it tough going. Jenna felt sorry for the woman, and oddly dispirited herself, like a child who opens the most promising package under the Christmas tree only to find nothing she wants inside. Even the question of boxers or briefs seemed pointless now. She searched her list of questions, trying to come up with *something* to take back to Vic.

She settled on, "What advice could you give our readers if they wanted to catch a man like you, Mr. Bishop?" *Not that anyone ought to try.*

"I'd tell them not to bother."

Her head snapped up. "I beg your pardon?"

His gaze was impersonal now, roaming over her in a way she didn't like at all. In a bland, dispassionate voice he said, "No man should want any woman who makes it her life's mission to catch a husband."

Thrown off stride by that answer, Jenna was momentarily speechless. And then speech wasn't necessary at all because the door to the penthouse opened and closed—

again with a bang—and a gorgeous blonde stalked from the foyer into the living room.

The woman completely ignored Lauren and Jenna, and even Debra Lee, who'd come out of the kitchen area. She had the delicate, sculpted profile of an antique cameo, but there was nothing delicate about the way she approached Mark Bishop. She was breathing heavily, as though she'd just run a marathon.

A frown starting to form in his brow, Bishop straightened. "Shel? What's the matter?"

The words were barely out of his mouth before Shelby Elaine Winston lifted her hand and slapped him hard across the face. He didn't move or react in any way, but his cheek turned bright red immediately.

"You despicable son of a bitch! Did you really think I would sign this?" Shelby raised her other hand and waved a sheaf of legal-size documents in Mark Bishop's face.

"Be reasonable," he said calmly. "A prenup is hardly out of line in a merger like this. Legally, it only makes sense to—"

She threw the documents on the desk beside him, where they scattered wildly. "I was wrong. I thought I could change you, but I should never have doubted my instincts. You really don't know how to love or trust anyone, do you, Mark? I feel sorry for you, but I'm glad I got the wake-up call before it's too late."

"Shelby, if you'll just think about it rationally—"

"I've done nothing but think about it the whole way over here from Ken's office. Is that how you see our future? Is that what you think marriage between us will come to?"

Mark Bishop never looked in Jenna or Lauren's direction. He kept his gaze focused on the angry woman in front of him. "I would hope not. But I don't have a crystal ball. I don't know what the future holds, and neither do you."

"Oh, but I do," Shelby Elaine said in a tight voice.

Lifting her hand, she twisted her engagement ring off her finger, then tossed it on the desk to join the papers. It bounced once, then rolled to a stop. "I see my future very clearly, Mark. And you're not in it."

CHAPTER FOUR

"WELL," LAUREN SAID as they waited for the elevator to take them back down to the lobby. "That was interesting."

Jenna was still trying to catch her breath. "Interesting! You mean dreadful."

After Shelby Winston had stormed out of the penthouse, Mark Bishop had turned to them calmly, apologized and said that the interview appeared to be over. Then he'd left the room. They'd gathered their things so quickly that anyone watching might have found their departure comical. Except that Jenna couldn't find a single amusing thing about the whole sorry incident.

She stared up at the elevator numbers over the door, wishing it would hurry. She wanted to get back down to the sidewalk outside the hotel, where the last of the summer sun would warm her, make her feel less chilled.

Lauren glanced at her. "Oh, come on, Jen. Didn't you learn anything from Jack about the rotten things men are capable of? Obviously Mr. Wonderful wanted to make sure Shelby Elaine couldn't touch a single penny of his hard-earned money. If you ask me, she got out just in time."

Jenna frowned. Something about that didn't make sense. The elevator arrived, and all the way down she thought about it. Over the phone last night, Vic had prepped her pretty thoroughly about Mark Bishop, and Jenna, who had a mild interest in politics, had always kept current with what was happening in the wealthy and political Winston family.

Sure, a prenuptial agreement for a rich guy like Bishop might be a given, but he wasn't exactly marrying Daisy Mae from Dogpatch. Her father was a senior state senator. The family history went back to Texas land grants deeded to her ancestors before the Alamo. Shelby herself was on the fast track as a campaign manager for Senator McDill from Nebraska. Why would money be the deal breaker?

Jenna said as much to Lauren as they strode through the lobby.

Lauren shrugged as she stepped through the revolving front door and didn't reply until they were both on the sidewalk. "Maybe it was just the principle of the thing. Who cares? Except now we don't have a story for the next issue." She craned her neck to see if she could spot a taxi. "Vic's gonna go ballistic when we come back empty-handed. I wonder if Bishop would be willing to be part of a new list—the South's Ten Most Unromantic Males."

Jenna shook her head. "I don't see how you can be cavalier about what we just witnessed. It was so…unpleasant."

Lauren stopped watching the traffic and turned to give her friend an incredulous look. "God, Jenna, don't tell me you think there was any hope for that relationship! I mean, really, he'd buy her silk flowers? And why? Because you get better value. Yep, the blowup had to be a money thing. Men are always so generous before the wedding, aren't they?" She spotted what appeared to be an available cab and waved her arm, but the driver whizzed right past them.

Jenna blew out a long, frustrated breath. It still didn't make any sense. Mark Bishop struck her as a lot of things, some of them annoying, some of them downright infuriating, but not stingy. "It sounded as though he was willing to go to any expense for the wedding and honeymoon.''

''Why are you worrying about him? He looks like the kind of guy who knows how to land on his feet. And as good-looking as he is, he won't have a difficult time finding someone to fill Shelby Winston's shoes.''

''I just find it puzzling, that's all.''

A cab squealed up to the curb at last. ''Let's get out of here,'' Lauren said, clearly finished with the topic of Mark Bishop and his ex-fiancée. ''I want to shop.''

Jenna backed away from the taxi. ''I'm really not in the mood. It's only a couple of blocks to the hotel. I think I'll walk.''

''Spending money will put us both in a better mood.''

''You go on. It will give me time to think, let my nerves settle.''

''We're in *New York*,'' Lauren said. ''You told me yourself that we blew all the frequent-flyer points the magazine has to come here. You can't let this opportunity go to waste. Surely there's something you want to see or do.''

''Maybe this evening.''

''Jen—'' Lauren stared at her in complete exasperation now ''—do you even *remember* how to have fun anymore?''

The question stung, but she wasn't going to get into an argument. ''I'll see you later,'' she said with a wave of her hand. Before Lauren could say another word, Jenna slipped into the thick, urgent river of people making their way home.

Back at their hotel, the phone was ringing as she unlocked the door. She kicked off her high heels and snatched up the receiver as she sank onto one of the beds. It was her father, calling from Atlanta.

''Nothing's wrong,'' he reassured her quickly. ''I just wanted to see if you made it there safely—since you didn't call me.''

Jenna stopped rubbing one sore calf muscle and switched to massaging her temple. After a day like today, she wasn't prepared to handle a guilt trip for not checking in. "Everything went fine, Dad," she said between gritted teeth. "I didn't need to have a note pinned to my jacket, after all."

Her father laughed, unfazed by her sarcasm. "You know I can't help worrying."

"I know." She supposed there were a lot of things William McNab couldn't help doing out of habit, but that didn't mean she had to like them. She'd canceled her initial appointment with the real-estate agent, but now she made a mental note to call the woman again once she got back home. Time to start an earnest search for just the right place. "Are the boys there?"

"Chris took them out to the batting cages. He's going to work on Petey's swing. Fat lot of good it will do, just between me and you."

Her oldest son was probably the worst Little League player in the history of the game. Her brothers and father had worked with him quite a bit over the summer, but he still "stunk to high heaven," as his coach so charmingly put it.

"How did your interview go?" her father asked.

"Fine," she replied. He didn't need to know what a bizarre and miserable failure the whole experience had been. "We'll be home tomorrow afternoon."

For some reason not clear to Jenna, her father was a huge fan of the weather channel, and in no time he was lecturing her about a storm watch in effect for the whole eastern seaboard starting around midnight. The flight home was bound to be bumpy. She should remember to take her antinausea medicine. Barely listening, Jenna began paging through the hotel's guest-information book that sat on the nightstand.

"Are you listening to me, Jen?"

"Every word, Dad," she said absently. She squinted

down at the laminated page in front of her—the list of contents of the room's honor bar. *Good grief, I can see charging a fortune for macadamia nuts, but can two ounces of vodka really be worth twenty-six dollars?* She rubbed her temple again as her father warned her about a cold front blowing down from Canada. Maybe twenty-six dollars *was* a bargain, if you were desperate enough.

"Go to bed early tonight," her father advised. "You'll manage better tomorrow if you get a good night's rest."

Irritated that even her bedtime didn't seem to be her call anymore, Jenna took perverse enjoyment in saying, "This is my only night in New York. I was thinking of painting the town red."

There was a long pause. Then her father said in a low, serious tone, "Do you think that's wise?"

"Maybe not," she said. Then, remembering her last conversation with Lauren, she added, "But I'd like to think I haven't forgotten how to have fun."

"You haven't forgotten, honey. You just grew up. You're a good girl. And whatever else Jack may have been, marriage to him taught you some valuable lessons about responsibility and the dangers of reckless disregard and—"

Advice about the weather and keeping late hours she could tolerate. Discussions about her failed marriage were something else entirely. "I have to go, Dad," she interrupted him. "Kiss the boys for me. I love you."

Feeling frustrated and edgy, she crossed to the bar and started to remove every tiny bottle in the fridge. She hadn't concocted mixed drinks in years, but she was pretty sure she could manage it. But then she put everything back. Not because she'd changed her mind, but because if she really wanted to improve her mood, she stood a much better chance if she was to go out, be around other people. Feel the ambiance of New York City, a little excitement, a touch of the unknown.

Though her feet were killing her—she hardly ever wore

heels these days—she slipped her shoes back on, applied fresh lipstick and ran her fingers through her hair to give it a less-structured look. On the walk back to the hotel she'd passed at least a dozen bars and restaurants. One of them was bound to offer what she needed.

She didn't know when Lauren would be back, but one thing was certain. She wasn't going to spend the evening checking the weather channel, eating stale nuts and washing them down with thimble-size bottles of liquor. It had been one hell of a day, and she deserved to let her hair down.

After scribbling a short note to Lauren, she dropped the small container of macadamia nuts into her jacket pocket and headed back out the door.

Forty-five minutes later found Jenna sitting at a small table in Willowby's Tavern. The floor-to-ceiling windows offered a great view of the avenue and a golden, fading sunset that had turned the windows of every office building into a pretty caramel color. She was on her third drink, some festive rum mixture that was more appropriate for a tiki bar in the South Pacific than a dim, crowded watering hole in Manhattan. She'd drunk more today than she had in six months. But at least she no longer felt as though someone was sawing on her nerve endings with a dull knife.

The bar was noisy and full of New Yorkers having a few drinks with friends after a long day at work. Jenna ignored them, concentrating, instead, on the *FTW* file in her lap, which she'd pulled out of her purse.

Undoubtably Vic would find her interview with Mark Bishop lacking in substance, and they still needed something to fill pages. Maybe one of these other guys on the Ten Most Eligible list would be a better candidate. Of course, none of them were engaged to be married, so they'd have to come up with some other hook.

She flipped through the pictures, reading bios and trying to imagine having better luck with one of these rich, powerful, attractive men. Not surprisingly, when she came upon it, she couldn't help focusing on the picture of Mark Bishop in his sleek mahogany boardroom.

She tried to see what Lauren and Shelby Elaine had accused Mark Bishop of being—a man who didn't know how to love or trust, and a cheapskate to boot.

Nothing she saw in the picture hinted at that. He was arrogant. Audacious. A snob, probably. Without a doubt he was the most unromantic man on the planet. But the photograph made him look isolated and lonely, too. Incapable of feeling? She just didn't see it. And when she'd interviewed him, she'd hadn't *sensed* it, either.

Growing up around men, Jenna felt she had a special insight into the male psyche. With the notable exception of her ex-husband, Jack, she was pretty good at figuring out what made them tick. Who they really were. What they really wanted out of life.

Mark Bishop could antagonize. Seduce. Confuse. But she'd seen flashes of humor and kindness in him. Most of all, he had a kind of genius for making a person believe they were the sole, fascinating center of his attention. Something in the eyes. A certain lift of the mouth that made you want to... She shook her head and had to smile at her foolishness.

He was just so different from the men in her tiny, civilized universe, that was all. Or maybe it was the liquor she'd consumed on an empty stomach. It might be time to break out the macadamia nuts.

She became aware of a presence at her shoulder. She looked up to find an attractive blond man gazing down at her. His eyebrows lifted in encouragement and his mouth sketched a smile, revealing that the drink in his hand wasn't his first.

He indicated the empty chair across the table from her. "Is this seat taken?"

"Well, I…" Jenna stopped. She recognized that predatory look. This man had more than conversation in mind.

It might be fun to practice her flirting skills, which were pretty rusty, but she didn't want to have to eventually fend off a drunken advance. Especially since her own mind wasn't all that sharp right now, either.

You're a good girl.

Yes. And a boring one.

Do you even remember how to have fun?

No, but I'm willing to relearn.

But starting now? Starting with…him?

Lauren and her father had helped her to realize the depth of the rut she'd been living in for so long. The truth was, her level of boredom with her life was rising above her level of fear. But that realization couldn't keep a cold, clammy mist of insecurity from settling over her.

The guy was waiting for her answer, his hand on the back of her chair as he leaned close. She returned his smile, trying to recall male/female banter that had been in mothballs for too many years. "Actually—"

Surprise jolted into her at the warm touch of a hand on her shoulder. At first she thought it was the blond man, but quickly saw that it wasn't. Surprise turned to shock as Mark Bishop edged past her would-be companion and slid into the chair opposite her.

"Sorry to keep you waiting," he said to Jenna. "Did you order my usual?"

He sent the other man a friendly glance of regret. Without a word the man drifted away and back into the crush at the bar.

Jenna blinked at Mark as he settled in. She'd just been looking at his picture, and now he was here. She felt as though she'd conjured him up.

He arched a dark brow at her. "What's the matter?"

"What are you doing here?"

His gaze slid away from hers momentarily, back to the blond man at the bar, who had already linked up with another woman. "From the looks of it, saving you from making a big mistake."

His answer annoyed her. Jenna took a big swallow of her drink to get her wits back. The cute little umbrella got in the way and almost took out her eye. She tossed the wretched thing on the table as the alcohol swirled in her system. "I don't need saving. I was looking for a little conversation, and now you've spoiled everything."

"Really?" he said. He frowned absently out the window as though something on the street displeased him. "I seem to be very adept at spoiling things today."

His tone sounded raw. There was such regret carved in his profile that she found her annoyance lessening somewhat.

"How did you find me?"

"I wasn't actually looking for you. I took a walk to clear my head." He nodded at her red suit. "That color's hard to miss, and when I saw you in the window, I thought I'd come in. Where's your partner? Why are you drinking alone?"

"Lauren's out enjoying New York. And I didn't think I was going to be drinking alone for very long."

He gave her a strange look, and she knew she'd surprised him. Good. The last thing she wanted right now was for one more person to think they knew everything there was to know about dull Jenna McNab Rawlins.

Mark jerked his head in the direction of the bar. "Do you want me to call him back?"

"No."

"Do you mind if I stay awhile?"

She should have told him to go. He confused her. Her *reaction* to him confused her. If she ever had a hope of stepping back into the real world and facing the prospect of dating again, Mark Bishop was the last man she should consider practicing her feminine charms on.

Instead, ignoring the sudden racing of her heart, Jenna found herself shrugging nonchalantly. "It's a public place."

He laughed lightly as he motioned at a passing waiter.

"That's a pretty tepid reception. Where's all that warm hospitality Southerners are supposed to be so famous for?"

"We're not in the South."

His humor faded. "No," he said with a rueful shake of his head. "We definitely are not. Today, I feel like I've landed on a completely different planet."

Jenna would never have thought a voice could sound so tense and utterly devoid of hope. She observed him for a long, quiet moment while the waiter took his order. Maybe he really wasn't the rat Lauren and Shelby Winston claimed him to be.

She watched him play with the napkin the waiter had left. He had beautiful hands. When the silence between them stretched too thin, she cleared her throat. "I'm sorry about what happened between you and Miss Winston. Can you salvage your relationship, do you think?"

His manner was brusque, but not ungracious. "No. It's over between us."

"You don't strike me as the kind of man to give up easily."

He looked at her. His features were full of fatigue. "Some things just aren't salvageable."

"I'm sure…" She stopped, unable to think of anything inspiring to say. He was right. Some things couldn't be fixed. But she felt the need to say *something*. She thought of all the lectures she'd endured from her family.

"If you're made of the right material, a hard fall is bound to result in a high bounce," she said at last.

His mouth lifted. "Sage advice from your last fortune cookie?"

Her senses swam for a moment, but she knew it wasn't just the alcohol. She would need to watch out for that smile of his. It was lethal. She shook her head. "No. Unsolicited wisdom from my father after my divorce. And I wasn't any more receptive to it than you are. Sorry. Force of habit, I guess. In my house, someone's always getting positive reinforcement. I'm either giving it to my boys or getting it from my father and brothers.''

"Sounds like an interesting family."

"Sometimes 'interesting' is just a polite word for 'peculiar.'''

"Tell me about them," he said, clearly ready to move the conversation elsewhere.

She settled her chin on her hand. The discomfort of talking about his breakup with Shelby had passed. God, he was beautiful to look at. Who looked this way outside of Hollywood film actors?

She drew a deep breath. "I have two wonderful sons. Six and seven. I live with my father in Atlanta. I have two older brothers." She frowned. "I can't remember how old they are, but they still think of me as their kid sister." Somehow she'd drained her drink, and now she lifted the glass in the air. "If you want anything deeper than that, you'll have to buy me another Rum Blaster, because without benefit of liquor, I don't find my life remotely worth discussing."

He pinned her with a shrewd glance. "How many of those have you had?"

"This makes three. But they're girlie drinks, so you really can't baste the tooze." She blinked in confusion. "I mean, taste the booze. Gosh, I guess it's true what they say—the tongue's the first thing that dissolves in alcohol. Or was that dignity?"

"Have you had any dinner?"

"No." A colorful row of pineapple, oranges and cherries lay forlornly on a long toothpick in her glass. She pulled them off with her teeth and munched happily for a moment. "Unless you count this fruit."

"My turn to give advice. Drinking on an empty stomach isn't a good idea."

"I'll write that down," she said in mock seriousness, patting herself as though looking for a pencil. Her hand stumbled across the bulge in her jacket pocket. "Oh wait,

I *do* have dinner!'' She pulled out the small jar of macadamia nuts, tilting it toward him. ''Want some?''

''I was thinking of something a little more substantial.''

''They're awfully expensive, you know? The fact that I'm willing to share them with you means that you must be very, very special.''

Silence. Then he sent her another one of those slow, confusing, blinding smiles. ''That's nice to know,'' he said softly.

He was looking at her intently, filling her with an acute and perfect pleasure. How wonderful, she thought, to have a man look at you the way Mark Bishop was. She knew with a helpless, hopeless shudder that she no longer cared what Shelby or Lauren or anyone thought about him.

''Jenna—'' her name on his lips was the most seductive sound she'd ever heard ''—would you have dinner with me? A *real* dinner?''

''I suppose,'' she said. ''I don't want to throw up.''

''I'll take that as a yes,'' he said with a short laugh. He rose, deposited a few bills on the table and held out one hand. ''Come on, I know just the place.''

She seesawed up to her feet, a little surprised at how unsteady she felt. Was it the rum or her damned heels or the effect of standing this close to Mark Bishop? With one hand on her elbow, he led her out of the bar and onto the sidewalk.

They walked in silence, side by side. Jenna clutched her file folder to her chest as if it was the most valuable possession she owned.

Sunset was over, but night had yet to claim the streets completely. The air was soft, full of the promise of rain and a dozen different city scents. They passed bookshops and travel agencies and restaurants too numerous to count. Honky-tonk music drifted out to them from a cowboy bar, beckoning the sinful.

Jenna drew in a deep lungful of air. ''I love this time of day, don't you? All the anxiety and tension you've struggled with all day suddenly seem rounded out and smoothed over.''

''Yes,'' he said. ''It does seem to put all the complexities of the day into perspective.''

She hadn't meant to remind him of any earlier unpleasantness. To change the subject, she touched the top of her *FTW* file. ''You know, I'm really not a journalist.''

''You're not?'' he replied with no attempt at all to sound sincere.

She pressed the file against her face, grimacing. ''I knew I wasn't fooling anyone. Least of all you. Tell me I didn't disgrace myself.''

''You didn't. Regardless of the way it ended, I enjoyed it. I don't think I've ever been interviewed in such an inventive manner.''

She turned her head to look at him, trying to read his features, trying to interpret the play of light and shadow on his face. The slight breeze had tossed his dark hair into a sexy, windblown tangle. She managed to swallow and find her voice.

''I'm an accountant,'' she admitted. ''A partner in the magazine, but a number cruncher at heart.'' Briefly she explained why she'd been given the task of interviewing him, leaving out how desperately she'd tried to avoid the assignment in the first place. ''Vic is going to scissor me up when I tell her there's no article.''

''That's hardly your fault.''

''True. Actually, I think it's yours. We didn't really get to finish the interview, you know.''

''I do business with several of the men that were on that list.'' He touched the corner of her file. ''One of them is about to announce his engagement to a very hot Hollywood actress. Maybe I could persuade him to give your magazine an exclusive.''

She halted abruptly. Turning, she looked at him in amazement. ''Why would you do that for me? I mean, for us?''

"Because you're right that we didn't get to complete it. And because you deserve it," he answered simply.

They traded a long, silent look. She had no idea what to say. A few people detoured around them. She must have swayed a little, because he stepped closer and took her arm.

When he pulled her into the stream of foot traffic and took her hand in his, she didn't try to pull away. They continued to walk, hand in hand like lovers. The odd thing was how right and natural it felt.

Jenna's senses were completely muddled now, afloat in rum-soaked, guilty delight. It wasn't until they went through the revolving doors of the Belasco Hotel that she came suddenly back to earth.

"This is your hotel," she said.

"Yes."

Automatically she moved toward the direction of the hotel dining room. Mark steered her toward the elevators, instead. "Actually, I was thinking of my suite."

She came to a dead stop and frowned up at him. "I can't go up to your suite!"

"Why not? You were up there earlier."

"That was different."

"I'm not trying to seduce you. I'm trying to feed you."

"Oh." She dropped her chin to her chest, thinking hard, then lifted her face to eye him with renewed suspicion. "No ulterior motives?"

"Not right now," he said with a smile. He didn't look a bit perturbed or offended. "Maybe later, after you've sobered up."

"I'm not drunk. Pleasantly buzzed, maybe. But not drunk. So what's wrong with going to a restaurant?"

"Nothing. Except…"

He glanced away, as though debating something, then turned back to her. "Look," he said with a long sigh. "Believe it or not, upstairs is a dining room full of balloons, a huge spread of food, a waiter to serve everything and a chef who, by now, is no doubt pouting. Having dinner with me in my penthouse will probably save my life.''

Maybe she was more buzzed than she thought. None of his words made much sense. She settled on trying to sort through something easy. ''Why do you have balloons in your dining room?''

''Because before this afternoon's fiasco, Shelby had asked the hotel to plan a private dinner for the two of us. She evidently forgot to cancel it. Once I saw all the preparation going on, I just walked out. I sure as hell wasn't in the mood to celebrate anything. Then I found you. Now I'm thinking it would be a shame to see it go to waste.''

The idea of spending more time in Mark Bishop's company held a lot of appeal. But she wasn't sure she wanted to do it surrounded by a bunch of party decorations meant to celebrate the engagement of this man to another woman. ''A celebration?''

''Actually—'' he grinned, and for the first time looked a little embarrassed ''—today is my birthday.''

Taken aback, she stated sternly, ''It is not.''

His grin became almost wicked. ''You're right—you are a lousy journalist. Check your file,'' he said, tapping the folder that was clutched back to her breast again. Somehow during the course of this conversation she'd lost his hand. ''My birth date should be in there. Thirty-three today.''

Quickly she flipped open the file and found the date on the back of his picture. She gasped. ''Oh, my gosh, it is! Happy birthday.''

He lifted her chin with one finger. She thought she saw amusement in the gray depths of his eyes—not at her, but at the situation, possibly even at himself. ''Now will you come up? Save me from self-pity? Not to mention a chef with a bad attitude and a meat cleaver.''

How could she refuse such a charming appeal? Caution

flew away like a bird let out of its cage. "When you put it that way…"

The penthouse dining room was just as he'd said. The table was surrounded in a sea of burgundy and blue balloons, gleaming with cutlery and china that was finer than anything Jenna had ever seen, much less eaten from. The waiter snapped to attention the moment they walked in, and a few moments after Mark entered the kitchen, Jenna heard him calming the temperamental chef.

Trays of artfully arranged hors d'oeuvres covered the coffee table in the living room. From the look on her face, Mark must have realized how little she wanted to be part of Shelby's elaborate plans for a celebration. He wisely suggested they skip the formal dinner and have a champagne picnic on the terrace. Jenna went outside, settled into one of the comfortable chairs at the patio table and kicked off her shoes.

A few minutes later Mark appeared with two huge plates in hand, followed by the waiter. In no time, a champagne bucket, place mats, glasses and cutlery were added to the table. The waiter disappeared behind the glass doors without a word.

The moonlight was sweetly romantic, but not very illuminating. While Mark popped the cork of the champagne, Jenna tried to make out what he'd brought her. Oysters still on their shell. Caviar-stuffed celery that she wrinkled her nose at. The rest was a mystery. Pretty to look at, but a little too fancy for her tastes.

Mark pointed to the various delicacies. "Citrus salmon. Red-curry braised duck. Crabmeat on avocado. Squab liver pâté." He frowned, catching sight of her still-empty plate. "What's the matter?"

"I make it a habit never to eat anything my cat would fight me for."

He laughed and speared a marinated shrimp on his fork. "Let's start with something simple and work our way up."

They ate, sharing and comparing, and eventually Jenna's nerves settled. Mark had a quality of quiet self-containment that made him easy to be with. They talked about everything and nothing, even the challenges she faced with her overprotective family. He didn't try to force his opinions on her—a refreshing change from her relatives.

The Rum Blasters had worn off. She'd had only one glass of champagne, and she was pleased to see that he didn't try to press more on her. It occurred to her that she'd told this man far too much about herself.

They both settled into a companionable silence and gazed up at the night sky. The moon was a pale, watery disk. Jenna had slid down in her cushioned seat and her bare feet were propped on an empty chair. She sighed heavily and closed her eyes, savoring the moment, feeling relaxed.

"Do you want to move closer to the railing?" Mark asked from beside her.

She turned her head back and forth against the back of the chair. "Afraid of heights," she said.

"That explains why you were plastered against the penthouse wall when I met you this afternoon."

"I wasn't plastered against the wall. I just don't see any reason to get close to the edge of anything. Nothing dramatic in my past. I just don't like being up high and looking down."

"What else should I know about you?"

She met his gaze. "I'm an open book."

"With a couple of pages missing." He reached to spear a Spanish olive with his fork, then extended it toward her. "Last one. Want it?"

Without taking the fork from him, without thinking, she leaned forward and closed her mouth around the olive. She saw that Mark's eyes suddenly glittered with desire. The heat in his look made her toes curl. She hadn't meant her action to send a sexual message, but it was too late to worry about that now. She took another breath and tried to calm the panic that stitched up her spine.

Inspiration struck. "Oh, I got you a birthday present." She swung her arm in his direction, and he laughed when he saw the jar of macadamia nuts in her hand. "I didn't have time to wrap it."

"I'll treasure these always," he said playfully. "I know you share them only with special people."

"That's right," she agreed, filled with a pleasant silliness. "Don't forget it. They're a unique gift from a unique person." *Someone who remembers how to have fun.*

"A very special person," Mark agreed softly.

She found herself locked in his all-consuming gaze. He didn't seem to be breathing. She knew she wasn't.

The need to kiss him rose in her like a powerful thirst, and he must have seen it, because in the next moment he leaned forward, lowered his head and placed his mouth against hers, very gently. At some point during their picnic he'd eaten an orange, and his lips were flavored with it now. He stroked his tongue along the seam of her mouth, soft and curious, slow and suggestive. He didn't touch any other part of her, but blood rushed through her as though she could feel him everywhere.

She couldn't have said how long the kiss lasted. Short enough to make her want more. Long enough to make her realize she was perilously close to tripping over the edge and sliding down a very steep slope.

Mark sat back. He stared at her, and she knew he didn't regret a single moment. Come to think of it, neither did she.

"Jenna…"

Traces of heat lightning zigzagged across the Manhattan sky. A sudden breeze made Jenna shiver.

"What time is it?" she asked.

"Almost midnight."

Her father's storm warning. Right on time. He'd be worried about her flight tomorrow. He always worried.

His good little Jenny-girl. What would he think to see her now? Ready to make love to a man she hadn't even known twenty-four hours ago.

Oh, Lord, what am I doing? This wasn't like her. She was the kind of person marriage had been invented for, and Mark…well, Mark wasn't. He was probably used to having women throw themselves at him. She'd been begging to be kissed, and he'd been more than happy to oblige. But it would be foolish to take this lovely interlude any further. It was midnight. *Pumpkin time.*

"I have to go," she said.

She pulled her feet out of the chair and stood, snatching up her shoes and jacket.

"You don't have to," Mark said, coming to his feet, as well.

"I do. I'm sorry. I didn't mean to give you the wrong idea. I didn't mean…" She realized she was starting to babble and stopped, void of explanations that would make any sense even to herself.

She pulled the sliding glass doors wide and passed quickly through the suite, Mark close on her heels. She plunged her arm into one of her jacket sleeves, missed and tried again just as Mark came up behind her in the foyer.

Mark settled one of the sleeves up over her shoulder. "Didn't mean to what, Jenna? Let me kiss you?"

"Yes. No! What I mean to say is, I liked it. Too much."

"So did I. So stay here. Let's find out what else we have in common."

Dammit! Why wouldn't her jacket cooperate? She fished around in it awkwardly, finally finding the second sleeve and shrugging into it. She turned to face Mark. "I can't. I'm not a one-night-stand kind of girl."

His brow furrowed as he stiffened a little. "Do you think that's the way I would treat you?"

"No. Well, yes, probably." She took a deep breath. "I

just think that where that kiss was heading is someplace that's a lot easier for you than it is for me. My life is very structured. Very simple. Very *sane*. Some people even find me boring. Ask Lauren, she'll tell you."

She finished yanking her jacket into place, then realized she was still barefoot. She pulled one shoe on, but the other refused to slip into place. She took a couple of ungraceful hops. "Damn! I hate these shoes."

"I don't care what Lauren thinks. Or anyone else. I don't find you boring at all. I think you're one of the most intriguing women I've met in a long time."

Her attention swung away from her shoe and back to his face. "For a man who claims not to believe in romance, you're very good at it."

She was losing her balance. Mark reached out to steady her, his hands on both her shoulders. "Will you stand still? Let's talk about this."

She wobbled on one foot for a moment, then steadied. She should have known he wouldn't make this easy for her. Her mind was a jumble of guilt and confusion and embarrassment, and Mark wasn't willing to play fair. Forget nice and friendly. His hands were quiet on her shoulders, but his thumbs were massaging the base of her throat, and that touch was so warm. Supple. Alive.

She shook her head. "Stop that. It's not going to work."

Now his hands did move. Up her neck in a gentle, whispery caress. Cupping the base of her skull so that her head was drawn upward and back, and his fingers stroked pulse points that had been sleeping for years.

Unfair! Jenna wanted to cry. *Stop!* But the words simply wouldn't come.

He gave her a long, speculative appraisal from beneath his lashes. His tender smile had a melting effect on her insides. "You realize, of course, if you go now, you'll never find out."

"Find out what?" she asked. Her voice sounded detached and foreign.

His mouth widened into a grin. "Whether it's boxers or briefs."

She stared at him in mute misery. The dark, heavy truth descended on her in full force and without mercy. She might as well acknowledge the terrible inevitability of this moment, that something was breaking, breaking like a cord, in her mind....

Jenna nodded slowly. "You're right, damn you. I have to know."

She tossed the remaining shoe over one shoulder. By the time it hit the floor, she'd put her arms around Mark's neck and pulled him to her. She kissed him, thoroughly. And he responded.

If this was a mistake, she'd find a way to make it right somehow. And if there were regrets, she'd never lay claim to them. A premonition of danger flared at the edges of her mind, but her body was already on a wild journey now, and the feeling didn't last long enough to become a nuisance.

CHAPTER FIVE

THINGS HAD HAPPENED pretty much as Jenna expected when she and Lauren returned to Atlanta. They called Vic in California, giving her the bad news that the interview with Mark Bishop was a bust. Their friend had been so thoroughly immersed in talking sense into her little sister that she hadn't been able to give it much attention.

But now, a week later, Vic was back. Disappointed and annoyed. Ready to hear the full story. Eager to find out if there was anything that could be salvaged. Lauren and Jenna, seated in Vic's plush office chairs, had just given her all the details.

Well, not *all* the details, Jenna admitted. Some things just weren't meant to be shared with anyone. Even your best friends and business partners.

Victoria Estabrook's disheartened sigh cut into Jenna's musings. In the merciless sunlight pouring through the glass windows of the office, Vic's expression was crestfallen. "So you just dropped the interview and *left?*" she repeated as though she couldn't have heard correctly. "Without even *trying* to find out what was in that prenup to make Shelby Elaine go nuts?"

"We couldn't ask," Jenna said. "It wasn't appropriate to intrude. And certainly it was none of our business."

"Of course it's none of our business," Vic agreed with an incredulous snort. "But it's newsworthy. Readers have a right to know."

Jenna frowned. "Our readers want to know where to buy wedding gowns that are designer knockoffs and what kind of mother-in-law gift costs ten bucks but looks like a hundred. I seriously doubt they care about Mark Bishop's prenup agreement.''

Lauren, who had been polishing one of her camera lenses, stopped long enough to grab Vic's attention. ''Maybe you could find out more from Debra Lee.''

Vic nodded thoughtfully and rifled through her Rolodex. ''She might be willing to talk.''

''I think we should consider it a dead issue,'' Jenna got out with some desperation. After everything that had happened, she was eager to see the incident—including her part in it—put well behind them.

''Maybe by now they've patched things up,'' Lauren suggested.

''That's not going to happen,'' Jenna said. When Lauren gave her a mildly surprised look, she realized she'd sounded too vehement. More reasonably she added, ''I mean, Shelby looked very distraught and determined to put an end to the engagement.''

''She could rethink it,'' Lauren said.

Seated behind her desk, Vic rested her chin on her hands. ''Well, right now we still seem to be short one article. Any suggestions?''

Lauren lobbed a few ideas, but nothing that seemed to solve the dilemma. Jenna mostly sat back in her chair and listened. She'd brought the latest company expense reports to this meeting to go over, and she fingered the edge of the file lovingly. Numbers were so wonderfully cut-and-dried. So finite. As a partner in *FTW,* why couldn't she have stayed firmly behind the scenes, instead of getting pulled into these kinds of discussions? They always seemed to underscore how completely unimaginative she was when it came to brainstorming.

Although…

She remembered the conversation she'd had with Mark that night on the sidewalk. He'd promised to help the magazine get an interview with one of the other eligible bachelors. Considering how their night together had ended and subsequent events, it seemed very unlikely now that he would help her. But he might be willing to talk to Vic.

She cleared her throat, and both her friends glanced her way. "Supposedly number eight on the list is about to pop the question to some Hollywood actress," she said. "We could contact him. See if he'd give us the story."

"How do you know this?" Vic asked, and already Jenna could see the wheels turning in her head.

"Mark Bishop told me," Jenna said without thinking.

Lauren frowned at her. "When did he tell you that?"

Jenna realized her mistake instantly. "I'm sure I heard him mention it," Jenna said with a shrug. "Or maybe it was Debra Lee." *Think, Jenna. Don't just sit there!* "What time is your flight to New Zealand, Lauren? I'd be so excited about this assignment. Aren't you?"

She ducked her head, certain that the furious blush creeping up her neck would give her away. Lauren was too sharp not to wonder just when that information had passed between the two of them without her hearing it.

Luckily, just then Vic's secretary interrupted to say Lauren had a phone call from one of the magazines she regularly contributed to. Lauren wanted to take it in her office, which was only a couple of doors down, leaving Jenna and Vic alone.

Jenna was about to leave the office when it occurred to her that, since Vic's return, she hadn't mentioned the problem with her sister, Cara, at all. She turned back to her friend. "Is everything all right? How did it go with Cara?"

Vic surfaced from the distraction of a desktop filled with phone messages she had to return. Her small smile was hopeful. "Cara agreed to slow things down a little. She's promised me she won't run off to Europe with him."

"Then why don't you sound happier?"

"You know the really horrible part, Jen? Once I got to

know this guy and see what Cara saw in him, I couldn't honestly disagree with her. There was a time when I would have run off with him, too. Isn't it awful how stodgy we've become?''

''We're not stodgy. We've just learned that spur-of-the-moment decisions and impromptu actions usually have a price. One we're not so eager to pay anymore.''

''I suppose.'' Vic leaned back in her chair. ''But if you could have seen how happy Cara is. This guy makes her feel like she's flying…''

''Which is just fine until you try to land. Once you crash and burn a couple of times, you're not so willing to—''

''Jenna!'' Vic sat forward in her chair. ''You can't become this jaded over the idea of falling in love. I forbid it. Jack was an unfortunate choice, but he's out of the picture now. Someday a new guy will come along, and you'll have to make yourself take a chance again. You must.''

Oh, if only you knew the chance I took recently, Jenna thought. But she couldn't share with anyone what had happened that one night in New York. It was still too painful even to think about. And Vic would try to fix things, even though some things were unfixable.

She gave her friend a bright smile of agreement. ''You're right, of course. But I really don't have to worry. If a new guy comes along, you and Lauren will be pushing me at him no matter how hard I dig in my heels.''

''We certainly will.''

Jenna turned toward the door. ''Until that day comes, I have expense reports to go through. Carve out some time this afternoon to go over yours.''

''If I must,'' Vic said with a grimace. She hated accounting tasks.

''You must.''

Jenna was almost out the door when Vic stopped her. ''Jen, thanks for filling in for me with this interview thing.

I know if you could have made it happen, you would have.''

"I did try," Jenna said. "I'm disappointed for us. And I feel as though I let the magazine down even though it wasn't my fault."

"If we can snag agreement from one of the other bachelors, number eight maybe, you could make it up by agreeing to interview him."

"Okay."

Vic's playful grin turned into a look of surprise. "What? I expected an argument."

Jenna shook her head. "I did most of the interview before Shelby Elaine came in with her big announcement and spoiled everything. It wasn't nearly as terrifying as I expected. You see? I'm not completely unwilling to take chances. Mind you, I still prefer a calculator and spreadsheets." With a smile she tapped the expense-report file in her hand. "Call me when you're ready to discuss how we can justify full-body massages to the IRS."

She returned to her office, feeling oddly deflated and edgy. Refusing to give in to it, she dug into the latest accounts-payable report. *FTW* was paying too much to outsource its mass mailings. There had to be a way to get the costs down, and finding it would keep her brain fully focused on practical matters. Too bad it wasn't tax season, when dealing with the mountain of government forms left absolutely no time for daydreaming.

But ten minutes later she found her mind wandering back, as it had so often these past few days, to the same question. How could that one night in Manhattan with Mark Bishop have happened?

Had she been so desperate to prove she was willing to take chances, mobilized by family and friends who saw her as someone she no longer wanted to be? Had a little alcohol, a few hours of satisfying conversation and being around the most sexually potent man she'd ever met given everything such a rosy glow that she hadn't been able to resist him?

And truthfully, not a bone in her body had regretted where all that had led. They had moved to the bedroom with identical haste and few words. The longing she felt to touch Mark, just touch him, was something she couldn't explain and only dimly comprehended. Was it just foolish, romantic gibberish to say that making love with Mark Bishop had taken her to places she'd never imagined? Well, it had.

But the soft, dreamy hour before dawn had brought sanity. Feeling headachy and heavy, she had remained tucked in Mark's arms and tried to envision what could come next for them. Half-a-dozen complications and possibilities teased her mind, but in the end, she dismissed them all. No point in hoping for more. She was nothing but what she'd told Mark she did not want to be. The epitome of dating clichés—a one-night stand.

That realization had caused her to slip quietly out of his sleeping embrace. She'd left him a note—keeping it short and breezy had seemed the way to go—and then she'd made her escape.

"Got a minute?" A voice from the office doorway made her jump.

She looked up to find Lauren standing there. As always, one of her expensive cameras was clutched in her hands. "Sure. What's up?"

Lauren entered, shutting the door behind her with a soft click and then leaning against it. "All right," she said quietly. "Confess."

"To what?" Jenna asked. She knew where this conversation was headed, but she wasn't going to cave in without a fight. She grinned and snapped her fingers. "Okay, I admit it. I lied this morning. I did eat the last jelly-filled doughnut."

Lauren moved closer to Jenna's desk. "Don't play

dumb with me. You saw Mark Bishop after that interview, didn't you?''

"What makes you think that?"

"Because I was with you the entire time we were in his suite, and he never mentioned another guy on the list getting engaged."

"I said I could be wrong about where I heard it."

Lauren's eyes narrowed. "I don't believe you."

"That doesn't make it any less true."

"Right now your neck is as red as a beet."

Damn! Why did she have to have such fair skin? Was the best defense a good offense? She was about to find out. "That's because I'm not used to being called a liar by someone I consider one of my best friends. My feelings are very hurt."

Lauren didn't look a bit apologetic. She ignored the possibility of Jenna's hurt feelings completely. "When you staggered into our hotel room at five in the morning, you said you'd walked all over the city. But I knew that couldn't be true."

"Why not?"

"In those heels you were wearing? Not a chance. They were killing you even before we got to New York. Besides, being that adventuresome isn't like you."

"Wow," Jenna said with an annoyed look. "You ought to work for Scotland Yard."

"And when I asked, you told me you'd met a very nice man who bought you dinner and showed you some of the sights."

"What's wrong with that?"

"Was Mark Bishop that 'very nice man'?"

She didn't have to think twice about that answer. "No, as it turns out, he's not a 'very nice man' at all."

Lauren came up to the desk, laid her camera aside and planted her hands on the cherry surface. Lowering her head and her voice, she said, "Stop playing word games.

Tell me the truth or I'll sic Vic on you. You know she'll be much more ruthless than I am.''

That was certainly true. Jenna sighed heavily. What was the point in denying it any longer? It wasn't as if she was likely to ever see Mark Bishop again. ''All right,'' she said with a grimace. ''Yes. I ran into Mark Bishop. We had dinner together.''

''Where?''

''In his suite.''

''Just the two of you?''

''That's generally what together means.''

''And that took until five in the morning?''

''Time…got away from us.''

''Oh, my God,'' Lauren said, standing upright suddenly and staring at Jenna. ''You slept with him!''

Jenna was ready with a denial, then changed her mind. ''Oh, hell, yes. I slept with him. Are you satisfied?''

''You slept with him!'' Lauren repeated, as though she couldn't believe it.

''I don't think technically what we did could be considered sleeping,'' Jenna said dryly.

Lauren shook her head. ''I can't believe it.''

''Neither can I. But it happened.''

''Are you going to see him again?''

Jenna's heart lurched. She bit her lip and scowled. ''No. Absolutely not.''

''Why?'' Lauren asked, then gave her a knowing glance. ''He's lousy in bed, isn't he? I knew it. The best-looking ones always are.''

Jenna suddenly felt as if her lungs were encased in a small, tight box. She struggled to draw a breath. ''I'm not going to discuss it, Lauren. And neither are you. It was a mistake. One I won't repeat. I'm asking you, as one of my closest friends, to drop this conversation and never talk about it again. Not with me, not with Vic, not with anyone.''

Unlike Vic, Lauren never pushed further than she

thought she could reasonably go. In spite of all her teasing accusations, something kind and nonjudgmental came into her eyes. "He really got to you, didn't he?" she said, then shook her head. "Oh, kiddo, I'm so sorry."

Jenna gave her friend a small smile. "Me, too. But just promise me—not a word."

Lauren held up her camera. "I swear on my best camera. Not a peep. Not even to Vic."

Lauren left her alone after that. Jenna sat at her desk for a long time, thinking. Nothing had turned out the way she'd hoped.

When she'd returned to Atlanta, she'd found two messages on her answering machine. One from the office. Mark Bishop had been calling for her and had finally been given her home phone number. Since she'd just done the interview with him, they didn't think she would mind. The second message had been from Mark. Asking her to call him.

To say that she'd been pleased was an understatement. Going to bed with Mark Bishop so soon after his breakup with Shelby Winston had made her feel slightly uneasy, but he'd seemed so sincere at the bar when he'd told her there was no way to salvage that relationship.

She'd wanted to see him again. Orlando, his home base, was only eight hours by car from Atlanta. His apparent eagerness to talk to her had seemed like a good sign. She'd been about to pick up the phone and return his call when it had rung under her hand.

Mark.

Jenna had known almost immediately that the conversation wouldn't go well. His voice had sounded too cautious, his words too rehearsed. He'd asked why she'd left him that morning—not with scorching anger in his tone, but something far worse. Vague, sterile disinterest. She'd started to explain, then stopped. She'd found his tense silence oppressive and known that nothing she said would make it better.

And then, *he* had made it worse. Unforgivable.

Dear God, how could she have misjudged him so badly? she'd thought.

He'd implied that the details of the previous night's interlude would somehow make it to the pages of gossip tabloid. For a long, horrible moment she'd been frozen in shock. He'd gone on, asking her to remember that his company employed a lot of people, people who depended on him for their living. Scandal that touched him also affected them, and he didn't really believe she wanted that, did she?

She'd responded by hanging up on him.

He'd called back. She'd cut off his apology and told him what he could do with it, told him he didn't need to worry and that she had every intention of forgetting she'd ever met him, much less slept with him. Then she'd banged the receiver down in his ear.

He'd made a few more attempts to call over the next two days. She'd made a science of ignoring them. On the third day, he'd stopped calling.

Now a week had gone by, and it appeared he'd truly given up.

Jenna stared down at the numbers on her accounting report, seeing nothing but blurry columns of black ink.

Lauren had been wrong about Mark. Sex hadn't been a problem at all. In fact, it had been fantastic. "Great in bed. Not lousy," Jenna muttered quietly to the four walls of her office. "Just lousy in life."

ORLANDO WAS NOT New York City, not by a long shot. But if you could get past the summer heat and the tie-ups on the interstate and the fact that tourists never seemed to bring their brains with them on vacation, it had a certain picture-postcard splendor. A clean, bright lushness that made a person glad to live there.

Most days.

Not today.

Mark Bishop stood at the window of his twenty-sixth-floor office in downtown Orlando and wondered where the day had gone. It had been a week since he'd left Manhattan, and he'd done nothing but go from one pointless meeting to the next, field a bunch of complaints from Human Resources about new employee policies and fight with his accountants over their never-ending suspicions about the books in the Atlanta office.

Now he just wanted to go home. Relax. Watch a game on television.

Check the answering machine. See if maybe, just maybe, Jenna Rawlins had finally responded to any of the voice messages he'd left on her phone.

Grimly recalling their last conversation, that seemed unlikely. He knew that whatever magic they'd shared that night, it was definitely long gone. He'd blown it.

Years ago Mark had learned how to separate desire from need, and the truth was, all women looked the same to him now, indistinguishable versions of eligibility. There had been more lovers in his life than he cared to think about, but not one of them had left him so hungry for more. Not even Shelby.

Poor Shel. For a while he'd thought her the perfect woman—beautiful, smart, accomplished. Hypocrisy was not one of his vices, and when things had finally heated up between them, he'd made no bones about what he wanted in a wife.

With her own agenda in mind, Shelby hadn't objected. She'd been completely focused on her career goals. She'd wanted a husband as a helpmate, someone who could open doors for her own political ambitions. As for children, they were a nuisance better enjoyed at a distance.

When Mark had finally popped the question, there had been no giddy laughter, no breathless excitement, no tears of joy. Just the safe, satisfying belief that marriage between them nicely fit both their agendas.

But as their engagement moved forward, Mark began

to suspect that Shelby wanted more, and worse, that she thought she could actually change him to accomplish it. The prenuptial agreement had cleared up any misconceptions she'd had on that score, and however painful the end turned out to be, it had been better to see it happen *before* they actually went through with the ceremony.

In a few days he'd contact Shelby in Texas. He'd start the conversation with the very real need to find out how she wanted to handle dissolving some of the joint business ventures they'd agreed upon. But he'd make sure she was all right. He'd never had a relationship with a woman end in ugliness, and he didn't intend for this one to, either.

Maybe he was losing his touch. Those few golden hours with Jenna Rawlins hadn't ended any better. For the thousandth time he asked himself why he hadn't been able to manage a better outcome.

When he'd walked into the Belasco's penthouse suite that afternoon and come face-to-face with her, his reaction had been purely visceral.

God, he could still remember every tiny detail of that interview. Watching the pale satin of her cheeks turn pink with every question or answer. Enjoying the long curve of her neck as she'd pored over her notes. The sight of her pulse pounding at the base of her throat had fascinated him. He'd wanted to place his fingertips against it, just to see what effect his touch would have. But it was her lips that captivated and intrigued him, hinting, in an entirely artless way, at any number of possibilities. Even now, just thinking about her sent an odd twist of pleasure through him.

Bright. Funny. Sexy. And he knew she felt it, too, that sizzling awareness. By the time Shelby had walked into the penthouse, he'd caught himself indulging in erotic fantasies that an engaged man would have to be extremely foolish to pursue.

Of course later, after everything with Shelby had gone to dust…

He'd spent an hour alternately indulging in self-pity and giving himself hell for creating such a mess with Shelby, for turning her world upside down. He was glad that she'd be the one on record for calling off the engagement. If there was any face-saving to be had from the fiasco, it was only fair it be hers. But he'd turned thirty-three that day, too, and the thick, heavy hopelessness that seemed to be his life lately had settled on his heart, making him feel more like ninety-three.

To say he was sorry he'd come upon Jenna Rawlins alone in that bar would stick in his throat like the lie it was. That evening spent with her had been like stolen treasure.

No sly, feminine tactics. No harsh judgments. She was so...alive. So completely herself. Jenna made him laugh and think and question. But most of all, she made him feel as though his whole world *wasn't* unraveling.

And no doubt about it, by the time midnight had rolled around, the thrill of desire, the expectation of things to come, was as crisp as pain within him, and blatantly reflected back from her own eyes.

The sex had been some of the best he'd ever known. They'd made love more than once that night in the dark luxury of the penthouse bedroom. The summer storm had raged outside the windows, but every tremble of thunder, every strobe of lightning felt as though it was happening between them in that bed.

By four in the morning, they'd lain exhausted, satisfied, their energy spent. He'd pulled her close, wanting that feeling of completeness never to end, savoring the idea that, for now, they were beyond the touch of time or change. He'd fallen asleep stroking the soft curve of her cheek, wondering how he could persuade her to lengthen her stay in New York. A dozen different arguments had played in his head, but he'd never gotten to use them.

When morning had come and he'd awoken squinting into the sunlight, she was gone. For the first time in his life, a woman he'd made love to had left his bed before he'd wanted her to go....

A clatter of noise pulled Mark out of his reverie and made him turn from the window. Debra Lee was fussing at his desk, clearing away the remnants of the unsatisfying day—empty coffee cups, balled-up pieces of paper, stacks of computer reports that had proved to be outdated and useless. He was surprised that she hadn't gone home already.

"Deb," he said sternly, "what are you still doing here? Don't we have a cleaning crew who can do some of that?"

"You'll feel better if you leave tonight with a clean office and clean desk."

Debra Lee was the best administrative assistant he'd ever had, but he still hated it when she puttered. "Leave it," he said. "Go home."

She ignored that. Instead, she lifted the jar of macadamia nuts off his desk and favored him with a frown. "Are you eating these?"

"No." He still wasn't sure why he'd stuffed them in the bottom of his garment bag. *I'll treasure them always,* he'd joked to Jenna. But now all they did was remind him of how wrong everything had gone.

"Shall I trash them?"

"No," he said more harshly than he intended. "Don't you know how expensive they are?"

She gave him a sour look that said the obvious—if it was nuts he wanted, he could afford to buy a truckload.

Feeling annoyed, he jammed his hands into his pockets and stared back out the window. What was the matter with her? She knew him as well as she knew her own husband. Couldn't she tell he wanted to be left alone?

The office windows were floor-to-ceiling, and he looked down. The street traffic below offered little interest.

Women! he thought. Could a guy ever completely understand them? If Jenna Rawlins didn't want to see him again, why should he chase after her? His ego was healthy enough to handle the occasional rejection. When he got home tonight, if there was no message from her on his phone, that would be the end of it. He didn't need to be hit on the head. Lots of fish in the sea, and he knew how to offer some pretty attractive bait.

He didn't know how long he'd been standing there, lost in thought, when he heard a harshly indrawn breath and became aware of the subtle sound of weeping.

He turned to find Deb hunched over his desk. One hand covered her face. In all the years he'd known her, he'd never seen her cry, not once. He was flabbergasted, completely at a loss. And ashamed that his first thought before he crossed the distance between them was *Oh, hell, what's this?*

"Deb?" he said quickly. "I'm sorry if I snapped at you. Throw the damned nuts away if you want."

She shook her head, holding one hand out to ward off his approach. "It's not that. I'm sorry. It's been a long day. I'm fine. Really."

She wasn't fine. He could see it in her eyes—a bleak, cold misery that said something was definitely wrong. He hated getting involved in people's lives, really hated it. But this was Deb. Tough. Efficient. His right arm. He couldn't just wave her off and pretend he hadn't noticed.

He took her elbow and steered her toward the leather couch that sat against one wall. She looked as if she might refuse to cooperate, but he said in his most authoritative voice, "Sit." And when she did, "Don't move."

From a decanter on the mini-bar he splashed a couple of fingers of whiskey into a glass. He placed it in her hand, then took the chair across from her. She looked completely undone.

When she didn't make a move, he leaned forward and touched her hand. "Drink it."

She complied. Her hand shook visibly, rattling the ice in her glass.

"Tell me what's wrong. Is it Scott? If that son of a bitch has done something inappropriate, I'll get Human Resources on his sorry ass first thing in the morning."

"It's not Scott."

If it wasn't the office Lothario, what was it? *Oh, damn!* "It's not me, is it, Deb? Am I pushing you too hard? Do you want me to get a temp—"

"It's not you," she said with a watery smile. "When it is, don't I always tell you?"

"Always," he agreed. He was relieved to see her rally this way. Women and tears made his gut ache. "So, what is it?"

"It's Alan."

Oh, damn. Not a husband-and-wife thing.

"What about Alan?" he asked cautiously.

Alan and Debra Lee's marriage had always had one of the few happy ones he knew of. If she'd caught the jerk cheating… *Why the hell didn't I go home earlier, when I had the chance?*

She swiped her hand across her wet cheek. He offered her the box of tissues that sat on the side table. She gave him a tiny smile filled with regret and embarrassment. She was a pretty woman, not beautiful, but with a certain regal way of carrying her few extra pounds that could make a man feel privileged to have her all the same. Right now her face was blotchy.

"I shouldn't be discussing this with you," she said, her lips pressed into a pale line. "I know how you hate to get involved in people's personal lives."

"I don't hate it," he lied. "I'm just not very good at it."

"That's true," she said in a matter-of-fact way that irritated the heck out of him.

"So what's Alan done?"

"I don't know."

"What do you mean, you don't know? If you don't know, then why are you crying?"

"I've been married for twelve years, Mark. There isn't a thing I don't know about Alan Goodson. I can tell you things about his childhood that even his mother doesn't know."

He grimaced. "You're not going to, are you?"

Debra Lee looked at him as if he were a half-witted child. "My point is, I know my husband inside and out. And yet suddenly he's keeping secrets. He's not talking to me. He's angry sometimes for no reason. He wasn't at work yesterday. On my lunch break I was at the mall and saw him sitting in the food court. He lied to me about it."

It seemed pretty clear to Mark what the problem was. God, members of his gender could be such asses sometimes. He reached to place his hand over hers. "Jeez, Deb," he said gently. "You know what that sounds like, don't you?"

"He's not cheating on me."

"How can you be so sure? Sometimes men—"

She sat up straighter, emphatic disagreement etched in every bone and muscle. "I told you. I know Alan. But there *is* something wrong, and he won't tell me. I've been trying to find some way to ask you, but I didn't have the courage."

"Ask me what?"

"To talk to him. Find out what's wrong."

It was Mark's turn to sit up straight. In fact, he almost came out of his chair. "What? *No.* Hell, no. No way am I getting involved in this."

"He trusts you. He likes you."

"Doesn't he have any buddies?"

"His closest friends are my brothers, and he might be afraid they'd tell me. Or maybe he'd be ashamed for them to know. It could be anything. Problems at work. Maybe he's developed a gambling thing. Or he's sick or...or dying."

Screwing around, more like it. But it was clear she wasn't willing to entertain such a notion.

Mark sighed heavily. He really didn't know what to say.

She stood up. Patting a tissue to her eyes, she sniffed and brushed imaginary lint from her skirt. "I'm sorry. You're right. I shouldn't impose on you this way. You've had a tough time of it yourself lately, haven't you."

He'd risen as well, and now she looked up at him. Her smile was weak, but determined. "What I'm asking is way beyond what an employee should ask of an employer. I'm not using reverse psychology here. It's true. It's too much to ask. Sorry. Please forget about it."

He watched her head for the door, relieved she'd changed her mind. He felt like a heel, but he wasn't comfortable traipsing around in other people's lives. He never had been. Tomorrow they'd go on as if this unpleasant conversation had never taken place. In a few days he might ask her if she'd ever learned Alan's secret. But only if she looked as if she wasn't on the verge of tears. Only if it felt safe.

"Deb," he called to her. *Keep your chin up, kid,* he'd say. *You're tough. You can do it.* Nothing wrong with offering a little encouragement.

Her hand on the office door, she turned. Waiting.

"What time does Alan get off work tomorrow?"

CHAPTER SIX

FIVE WEEKS LATER, feeling resentful and fuzzy-minded, Jenna stared down at the article headlines she'd been working on for the next issue of *FTW*.

When a Lassie Comes Home—Planning Your Scottish Wedding. Haunted Honeymoons—Where the Dead Were Wed.

No. Definitely not right.

Mollie Baxter, in charge of the magazine's layout, was home with strep throat. Production of each issue being a team effort, Vic had asked everyone in the project meeting this morning to try to come up with some catchy headlines for the articles they planned to run. Jenna had told Vic she wasn't any good at that sort of thing. Besides, she felt sick and might be coming down with something herself.

No luck. Vic was always ruthless where the magazine was concerned.

Sighing, Jenna pulled the next article in front of her— a humorous piece on ten wedding gifts that could be made out of cardboard.

Nothing came to her. She was dead from the neck up, it seemed.

The next article was about a new wedding trend— brides and grooms getting matching tattoos. She didn't even know where to start with that one.

Her stomach rolled unpleasantly, and for one horrible moment, Jenna thought she might throw up. If it wasn't Mollie and her darned strep infection—*Deadly Plague Kills Entire Office*—then it was probably the horrible new barbecue restaurant her father had dragged them to last night. Now there was a headline waiting to be written: *Board of Health Shuts Down Greasy Spoon after Diners Poisoned.*

Only one more article was left to be dealt with, which was a good thing. For then Jenna was going to head home, swallow a couple of aspirin and some antacid and hide under the covers until the boys got home.

Feeling more nauseated by the minute, she pulled the article in front of her and read through it quickly. It was a short piece on five new ways to prevent pregnancy. She dashed off her idea on her notepad: *Jack and Jill Without the Pill—What to Do When the Drugstore's Closed.*

She rubbed her stomach as it fluttered again, and for a moment, she actually felt dizzy. "Stop it!" she commanded. "Can't you see I'm trying to work?"

What was up with her body this morning? *Atlanta Saint Impregnated by Aliens.* Jenna laughed at her foolishness. If any aliens had done a mind-meld and gotten her preg—

She threw up in her garbage can. Loudly. Painfully. And somewhere in the middle of all that retching, the possibility hit Jenna like a blow to the back of her head.

Not aliens, but worse. Much worse. *Oh, my God. It's not possible. We used protection.*

As soon as she could keep her head up, Jenna shuffled through her purse, searching for her date book. She always kept close tabs on her monthly cycle. She wasn't late, was she? Maybe a couple of days. But surely…

The calendar revealed the worst. More than a couple of days. More like a week and a half. But that could be explained. She'd been under a lot of stress lately. Arguing with her father and brothers over her determination to buy a house. J.D. had fought with some kid in his class, and she'd been called into a teacher-parent conference. With a family like hers, it was a miracle she wasn't *more* irregular.

Jenna put her head in her hands. *I am not pregnant. Not by him. Not by anyone.*

With shaking fingers, she dialed her gynecologist's office and begged for an appointment that day. Then, unable to stand the suspense, she jumped up from her desk, raced down the street to the drugstore and bought two home pregnancy tests. Even before she sat in the doctor's office, she knew what *that* headline would read.

Atlanta Idiot Impregnated by Arrogant SOB.

ALL THE WAY HOME, driving in stunned disbelief, Jenna wondered how she was going to break the news to her family.

Six weeks pregnant. Six weeks to the day she'd slept with Mark Bishop in New York City. Lauren had been dead wrong about her. She *did* remember how to have fun. And look where that fun had landed her!

It wasn't just that she was pregnant. And single. It was that she was pregnant by the most inappropriate, arrogant, confusing man on earth. Aliens *would* have been better. At least they didn't pretend to be something they weren't.

She just couldn't believe it. Pregnant by a man who had obviously thought she was capable of the most obscene behavior. What would he say when she called to give him the news?

As she pulled into her driveway, Jenna made a sudden decision. She wouldn't tell him. There was no question in her mind that she would keep the baby, but that didn't mean he had to be involved. In the interview he'd made it perfectly clear he wasn't looking to become a daddy anytime soon. So let him keep to his cold, power-hungry world, and she'd keep to hers.

She loved children. She was a good mother. She wouldn't ask him for a thing. Eventually Mark Bishop's contribution to her current situation would become less and less an issue. By the time the baby came in late spring, she wouldn't even remember what Mark looked like.

She was strong.

Capable.

She could raise this baby by herself.

PETE RAWLINS was just hitting the ball out of the park when loud voices pulled him from his dreams. Turning over in bed, he blinked into the moon shadows, trying to focus on his brother's bed. J.D. talked a lot in his sleep—chasing some alien menace, yelling for invaders to halt and be identified, marching prisoners off to space-jails. No matter *who* was trying to get some sleep.

But J.D. was sound asleep, his arms still hugging the space cannon he always took to bed with him. *Goofball,* Pete thought. Everybody knew you didn't have to worry about two-headed, one-eyed space aliens. Not when there were plenty of Spiderman's enemies creeping around.

He heard the noises again and recognized Uncle Trent's voice. Pete glanced at his clock. Almost eleven, according to Mickey's hands. That meant the family conference was running late.

Sometimes, like tonight, Mom would invite his uncles for dinner, and then everybody had a family meeting later. He and J.D. got sent to bed early. Pete didn't mind that much. Who wanted to listen to a bunch of adults talk about something bad called income taxes? Or whether the house needed a new roof? It was boring stuff. Even playing alien invasion with J.D. was better than that.

But those meetings never got so loud they woke him up. Even with Uncle Trent there, who could outholler anyone at Pete's Little League games. Maybe he'd better see what was going on.

On bare feet, Pete crept across the bedroom, trying to remember where all the squeaky stairs were. He'd almost made it out the door when J.D.'s voice nearly made him jump out of his skin.

"Where ya goin'?" his brother whispered from his bed.

"Downstairs," Pete hissed back. "Go back to sleep."

J.D. was suddenly wide awake, sitting up. "Are Cyberlons in the house?" He jerked his cannon blaster to his chest. J.D. was the mortal enemy of Cyberlons.

"Shut up! It's just Mom and the uncles and Grampa."

"Oh," J.D. said with noticeable disappointment.

"I think they're having a fight. I'm just gonna take a look."

J.D. slid out of bed, weapon in hand. "I'm coming with you."

It was useless to tell J.D. to go back to sleep. He knew as well as Pete that the family never really fought. They talked loud sometimes, but their mother told them that was because they all had strong "pinyons," whatever they were. But yelling could be bad. Something serious. And worth checking out.

They settled across from each other on a step midway up the stairs. It was their Christmas and Easter waiting spot. Close enough to hear what was going on downstairs, but still out of sight.

"...still don't know how you could have let this happen, Jenny-girl." That was Grampa Will, sounding sad. In his mind Pete could almost see his gray hair flopping as he shook his head.

"Well, I'm certainly not going to explain *how* it happened, Dad. It happened. There's nothing I can do about it now except move on."

His mother sounded upset. Then a chair scraped as his uncle Trent spoke. "The hell we can't do something about it. Tell me his name. I'll pound the guy into the dirt with my bare hands."

"Yeah, that'll help," Pete's mother said calmly. "Stop being dramatic. You'll wake the boys."

Pete and J.D. exchanged looks. They'd better not get caught listening.

"The baby needs a father," Grampa said.

"Not this one," their mother answered.

"Jen, don't be stubborn," Uncle Chris said. "Give me his name, and I'll run it through the department computers. With a little luck, I can know everything there is to know about him in twenty-four hours. Criminal records, finances, personal history."

"And what will that get me, Detective?"

"You'll know what kind of guy he is. Whether he'll take responsibility for his actions. If there's anything in his past you need to worry about."

"I already know what kind of guy he is," she replied. "He's not going to want any involvement with this child. I've already accepted that I'm going to have to raise this baby alone."

Pete jerked in astonishment. *Huh?* Mom was gonna have a baby?

J.D. had heard it, too. He leaned across the step to whisper to Pete, "What baby?"

Pete made a face at him. "Mom's pregnant, you dope."

J.D. blinked like a baby owl. "But I thought Daddy was gone."

"I still say we break his legs," Uncle Trent was saying. "No one messes with my sister like this and gets away with it."

"Trent, stop behaving like a Neanderthal," Grampa Will said.

Pete heard his mom sigh. "Look, I appreciate everyone's concern. But I'm really tired of discussing this. I know you want answers, but I'm just not willing to give them right now. I'm still trying to absorb the fact that I'm going to have another child."

There was a long silence, and when his mother spoke again, Pete thought her voice sounded shaky, like when she told them about getting a divorce. "I'm sorry if you're disappointed in me, Dad. But it's done, and now I have to find a way to deal with it. I can do this alone, but I'd much rather know that my family's behind me. That I'll have your love no matter what. And that this baby will have your love, too.''

"Oh, Jenny-girl," Grampa Will said. "Why didn't you just find a nice, sensible young man who'd be a good husband and father to the boys? Why do you always want something more than what you have?''

Again no one said anything for a long time. Then it suddenly seemed like all the men in the family were talking at once.

"You know we'll be there for you," his grandfather said in a low voice.

"Whatever you want, sis," Uncle Chris agreed.

"I still think we should break his legs," Uncle Trent complained, and then added, "But all right. It's your call, Jenna.''

"I don't know how I'm going to tell Petey and J.D.," their mother said.

At the mention of their names, both boys crept silently up the stairs and back to their room. They jumped back in bed, just in case their mother meant to wake them up and tell them right now. After some time had passed and she still hadn't come to their door, Pete's heart stopped thumping so hard in his chest. He tucked his hands under his head and stared up at the ceiling.

A baby in the house. What was that going to do to everything? Was Mom happy about it? She didn't sound like it. Not really. Did she wish Daddy was here to help her?

Out of the corner of his eye, Pete saw J.D. flop over on his side to face him. "I still don't get it," he said in a whisper.

Pete didn't look at him. If he ignored his brother, maybe he'd go back to dreaming about alien battles or something.

No such luck.

"Petey," J.D. hissed at him. "Pete! What's it mean? Tell me, or I'll blast you to Saturn with my cannon."

Feeling slightly sick, Pete propped himself on one elbow to face his brother. "It means Mom's going to have a baby."

"But I thought we were getting a dog."

"Well, we're not. We're getting a little brother." His mouth curled in disgust. "Or sister."

"If Daddy's not with Mom, how can she be gonna have a baby?"

Under his breath Pete swore like his grampa Will had when he'd stuck a fishing lure through his thumb. He wanted to jump out of bed and take that cannon blaster and throw it out the window. He glared at his brother. "J.D. ought to stand for 'Just Dumb,' instead of James David."

Mad now, J.D. plopped down on his back. "You don't know, either," he accused.

That was sort of true. Pete knew making a baby involved kissing and then sleeping next to another person. And he knew that person didn't have to be the one you were married to. He wasn't sure what happened after that, but he wasn't willing to admit that to his brother.

"I know one thing," he whispered back to J.D. "Mom's gonna need all the help she can get."

CHAPTER SEVEN

TWO DAYS LATER Pete was still waiting for his mom to tell him she was going to have a baby.

Although J.D. seemed ready to ignore or forget everything they'd overheard that night, Pete had been unable to think of anything else. He didn't understand why she hadn't told them yet. Grampa Will and his uncles didn't count. *He* was the man of the family now that his dad wasn't around, and he had to do something to make things easier on his mother.

Especially after last night.

He'd come into the bathroom and found her sitting on the side of the bathtub, crying. She'd pretended she wasn't and begun rushing around, acting like getting their bathwater just right was the most important thing she'd ever done. But Pete could tell by her red eyes and cheeks that she was upset, and he couldn't think of anything they'd done recently to cause it. So it had to be the baby.

He didn't know what to say or do. It scared him a little to see her this sad, so he hadn't argued when she insisted that they wash their hair and clean their ears. And later, when J.D. started whining about which pajamas he wanted to wear, he shut his brother up with a whispered threat that he'd never see his space cannon again if he didn't stop being such a baby. Threats like that always worked with J.D.

Then this morning, by accident, Pete had the answer to the whole baby problem.

Mom was in her closet, picking out something to wear

to the office. Pete had come into her bedroom to ask if he could have last night's cold pizza for breakfast, instead of cereal. He sat on the edge of her bed, running his hands over the bedspread, waiting for just the right moment.

There was a file folder on the bed, and when Pete peeked inside, he saw the pictures of the men Mom had talked about interviewing for work. He pulled them out, setting them out on the bedspread.

His reading was good, but he couldn't make out a lot of the words. The pictures were cool, though. Most of the guys were surrounded by lots of cool things like horses and planes and boats.

"Are you gonna talk to all these guys, Mom?" he asked. "I thought you were done."

His mother stuck her head out of the closet. "No, unfortunately. In a weak moment I let your aunt Vic talk me into trying again with another one of them." She watched him lift the pictures for a second, then added, "Don't mess those up, Petey. I have to take that file back to work."

The first page in the file was all writing, and he held it up. "What's this word?"

She sat down beside him. She'd recently taken her morning shower and smelled like flowers. It was a smell he liked, and if he hadn't been too old, he would have snuggled against her and filled his nose with it.

"Eligible," she said, then pointed out the words one at a time. "The South's Ten Most Eligible Bachelors. That was the name of the article."

"What does…el-elible…mean?"

"Eligible," she repeated slowly. "In this case it means available. To get married." She sighed and fluttered her eyelashes at him so that he knew what she was going to say wasn't really serious. "If only we poor, foolish women were smart enough to catch one of them."

"You could catch one of these guys, Mom," he said, wanting to make her feel good. "You're smart."

He got a sudden idea. The men in the pictures were obviously all rich, and they looked like movie stars. The kind girls got all goofy over. They might make good daddys. He scrunched his face up, trying to see his mother from their eyes. She wasn't like a movie star, but she was still pretty.

"Not so smart, Petey," his mother said with a sad little smile and a shake of her head. "At least, not lately." She rose suddenly. "Now scoot. I'm running late, and I need to get dressed. And no, you can't have leftover pizza for breakfast."

Pete made a shocked, disappointed sound. "I didn't even ask yet!"

"You didn't have to. I know everything that goes on in that devious little mind of yours."

But later, after she'd left for work, and he and J.D. were waiting for Grampa to take them to school, he realized she didn't have the folder with her. When he went back upstairs and peeked into her bedroom, he saw that it was still on the bed.

His mom was right—she *did* almost always know what he was thinking. But for the first time ever, he thought that maybe she didn't know *everything*.

That afternoon Pete could hardly wait for Mrs. Weatherby, the baby-sitter who watched them after school, to drop them off at home. He'd already told J.D. his plan. Now all they had to do was wait for the right time.

Grampa Will liked to mess around in the garage in the afternoon. Once he started on his latest woodworking project, he wouldn't stop for anything. Pete and J.D. could get to work on fixing Mom's problem.

They finished their after-school snack—still no leftover pizza—and he and J.D. charged up the stairs, pretending they wanted to play in their room. A few moments later, they slipped into their mother's bedroom. In another hour, their mom would be home from work, so they couldn't waste time. Pete went quickly to the bed.

"We're not supposed to play in Mom's room," J.D. whispered, hanging back. "We'll get in trouble."

"So? We've been in trouble before." Pete was feeling excited now. All day he'd been practicing in his mind, and it was finally here. "And we're not gonna play. This is business."

"I don't like it. If Grampa catches us—"

"Grampa's not gonna catch us. He's gone to the garage, and he thinks we're playing."

"Suppose he comes upstairs to check on us? Or goes to the bathroom?"

Pete had retrieved the file and put the pictures out on the bedspread. Over his shoulder he gave his brother one of his mother's stern looks. "That's why you're gonna keep an eye on the door while I make the call. Stop being such a goof. Do you want to help Mom get a husband or not?"

J.D. clamped his jaw tight, like an old turtle. "I don't see how getting Mom a husband is gonna help."

"Look at these guys, J.D.," Pete said. He pointed to the pictures, knowing that his little brother just needed to see what kind of man their mom could end up with. "They look like movie stars, and they've got money and cars and…and everything. They can make Mom happy and help her with the new baby. Mom needs someone like that."

"Why don't we just get her a baby-sitter? Like Mrs. Weatherby."

"Because what Mom needs right now is a man."

"How do you know?"

"Remember what Grampa said about the baby needing a father? Well, one of these guys has to be someone Mom would like. We just have to let them know she's not married."

J.D. swung his head back and forth, looking over the photographs that Pete had spread out in two neat rows. "What if they don't like her?"

That question made Pete scowl. "Why wouldn't they? She's pretty, and she's a good cook, and she smells nice. We don't have to tell any of them she gets mad if you don't pick up your stuff."

"We shouldn't tell them she doesn't like wrestling."

Pete nodded quickly. "So which one do we call?"

J.D. finally pointed to the one Pete had known would be his little brother's choice. A blond guy with a space rocket behind him on a launchpad. Probably an astronaut. "Him," he said. "He has good teeth. Mom likes that."

Pete slid the picture away, pointing, instead, to a smiling man in a cowboy hat. Next to Spiderman, Pete liked cowboys best. "What about this one?" he asked, trying not to sound like it mattered that much. "He's probably a rancher. We could ride horses and have campfires."

J.D. looked at his brother suspiciously. "I thought we were trying to find a husband for Mom. She doesn't care about horses. You do."

"That's true, but doesn't she always say that if we're happy, she's happy? And think about it, J.D. A space guy is gonna be on a rocket most of the time. Not with Mom and the baby. So how does that help?"

"I guess it doesn't," J.D. agreed with a sigh. "All right. Call him."

Hiding his excitement, Pete snatched up the bedroom phone and the cowboy's picture. He wasn't bad with telephone numbers. His mom had made both him and J.D. practice phone calls in case they ever got lost. He dialed the number on the back of the cowboy's photograph and sounded out his name. It wasn't too hard. *John Simm-ons. John Simmons.*

The phone rang a couple of times. Then it was answered by a woman who sounded a lot like the lady who answered Mom's telephone at work. Pete was disappointed. He wanted it to be a ranch, maybe with horses neighing in the distance. Not what sounded like a plain old, boring office.

"May I speak to John Simmons, please?" he asked in his most grown-up voice.

"I'm sorry. Mr. Simmons is not available."

Pete had listened to adult conversations a lot. He knew what came next. "Do you know when he comes back?"

"I'm afraid Mr. Simmons won't be back in the office for several weeks. He's on a business trip to Australia. If this is an emergency…"

"Yes. I mean…no!"

Pete punched the off button.

The phone call had not been what he'd hoped. J.D. was waiting for an explanation, and when Pete gave it to him, his brother lifted the pictures, pulling out the astronaut again.

"Now try him," J.D. said.

Pete wasn't willing to give up on the rancher so quickly. "Why can't we just wait a few weeks? We can call him again when he comes home."

"I thought we were trying to fix it for Mom *now*. We can't wait. Call him."

"Oh, all right," Pete said. An astronaut wasn't horrible. And J.D. was right. He had good teeth.

Terry Boyd.

He called the number, and again a woman answered. This time, at least, it didn't sound like he had called an office. In fact, he could hear music playing loud in the background and lots of laughing and splashing, like a pool party was going on.

"I'd like to speak to Terry Boyd, please."

"Who's calling?" the woman asked.

"Peter Rawlins."

The woman must've placed a hand over the receiver because the background sounds Pete heard were muffled.

"What's this call in reference to?" she asked eventually.

"Are you his mother?"

The woman laughed. "God, no! Are you kidding?"

"No, ma'am," Pete said respectfully. The last thing he wanted to do was make anyone mad. "I'm sorry. Are you his daughter?"

"No, although some people think he's robbing the cradle." The woman laughed, then stopped and lowered her voice. "Listen, kid—I can tell you're a kid—is there something specific you want? Because Terry isn't getting his butt out of the hot tub just to play games with you. Not when he's playing games with me, if you know what I mean."

Pete didn't know what she meant, but it didn't seem important. "I was calling to ask him about my mother."

"What about your mother?" she said in a suddenly sharper tone.

"I wanted to know if he would like to marry her."

The phone line went dead in his hand.

Stunned, Pete stood and stared at the telephone for several long seconds. Then he explained to J.D. what had happened, although he wasn't quite sure he understood what had made the lady mad enough to hang up. It wasn't like he'd been rude.

"You did it all wrong," J.D. complained, using the tip of his space cannon to scratch the side of his head. "Call him back and say you're sorry."

Pete was annoyed. "I'm not calling him back. He's got a girlfriend."

"So?"

"So he can't have a girlfriend and be married to Mom, too."

"Mrs. Weatherby's husband had a girlfriend."

"Which is why Mr. Weatherby doesn't live at home anymore, stupid. You can't have both." A little upset because his plan to help his mom didn't seem to be going very well, Pete shuffled through the remaining photographs. Eight left. "Let's pick someone else."

They settled on a dark-haired man surrounded by boats

in the water. He had a really good suntan. Going to the beach all the time would be fun, they decided.

His name was harder. Pete had to sound it out several times before he could say it without stumbling.

Rick-y Cas-ten-ello. Ricky Castenello.

As he punched in the man's telephone number, J.D. tugged on his sleeve. "Don't tell him right away that Mom needs a husband. Say something cool. So he'll like us."

This time the phone was picked up quickly, barely before it had rung once.

"Yeah?" a man said impatiently.

Pete squirmed a little, not expecting the man to sound so...so gruff. "Is this Ricky Cast—"

"Yeah," the man said again. "Who's asking?"

Pete searched for something clever to say and came up empty. His hand was sweating, making the receiver slippery in his grasp. He spied the headline he'd asked his mother about this morning. Desperate now, he stuttered, "Are y-you one of the South's m-most ill...el... Are you one of the South's most ill-egal bachelors?"

"Who the hell is this?" the man snapped. "I told you people, I'm not talking to the press. You want to talk about fraudulent claims, you talk to my attorneys. Got it?"

The phone slammed down in Pete's ear.

"What did he say?" J.D. asked when Pete just looked at him.

Bewildered, Pete shrugged. "I don't know. He yelled. Something about a frog he lent someone. I don't think he'd make a very good husband for Mom."

"Now what?" J.D. asked.

Pete wasn't sure. This wasn't going the way he'd thought. They should have had it settled by now. But none of the really cool-looking guys were doing what they were supposed to. J.D. had on his I-told-you-this-wouldn't-work face. To keep from looking stupid, Pete acted like it was no big deal and lifted the closest picture.

It was a dark-haired guy in a suit with nothing around him that looked even close to cool. Pete flipped the photograph over. After the last family vacation, J.D. had hung a poster in their room that showed Space Mountain at Disney World, and Pete had looked at it every day for almost a year. On the back of the file picture he recognized a familiar name from the poster. Orlando. The man lived in Orlando, Florida.

"Let's try him," he suggested.

J.D. made a face. "Why? He looks too serious."

"He lives in Orlando, J.D. Do you know how many times we could go to the theme parks and ride the rides?"

That settled it for J.D. With a short nod, he said, "Call him."

Mark Bi-shop. Mark Bishop.

Pete pressed in the number. He hoped Mark Bishop would be the one. He was getting nervous and a little scared. If this guy wasn't any good, Pete didn't know what they'd do.

PROFESSIONALLY SPEAKING, it had been one of Mark's more productive days.

After frustrating weeks of stalled negotiations, the Castleman Press acquisition was finally moving forward. The Boston office had settled its thorny personnel issues with the home-delivery drivers. The drumbeating auditors in the accounting department, claiming that the books in the Atlanta office weren't jibing, had settled down at last after two grueling weeks of reviewing every file and statement.

Even Deb was looking happier these days.

Mark had strong-armed her husband into a man-to-man talk that had revealed Alan Goodson was *not* having an affair. He had lost his job and simply been too ashamed to tell his wife. Mark had been so relieved it wasn't an extramarital fling that he'd hadn't even minded when a grateful Deb threw herself into his arms and bawled for ten minutes straight. Now Alan was making the rounds, looking for employment—hardly an ideal situation, but at least Deb was fully involved, right by his side. At least Mark had his assistant back.

He poured himself a glass of Scotch from the mini-bar in his office. It was hundred-year-old stuff, smooth as silk, and he saved it for days like this. Darkness had started its slow crawl up the sides of the office buildings. In a little while there'd be the usual stampede for the time clock.

Hands laced behind his head, he leaned back in his chair, thinking he would call Deb in to share a glass. Through the open office door, he could tell she was still fielding calls on the phone, sounding like the old Deb with a voice that managed to be warm and crisply professional at the same time.

He heard the sounds of the staff closing up shop—drawers closing, the rattle of car keys, workers bidding one another goodbye. In another five minutes there was only silence.

He realized he ought to go home, but he wasn't tired. He felt almost energized. Maybe it was the potency of the Scotch.

"Deb!" he called through the open door. "You heading home?"

She came into his office, stuffing paperwork into her briefcase. "In a few minutes."

"Want a drink before you go?"

She shook her head. "Alan and I are taking the kids to dinner and a movie. We're splurging on a night out for the first time in weeks."

"How's the job hunt going?"

"You know how it is," she said with a shrug. "At Alan's level, jobs aren't that plentiful, and the interviewing process takes forever. But he has some good prospects lined up for next week. I'm revising his résumé." She gave him a smile that was all cheerful determination. "I guess we'll just continue to work through it together."

He didn't doubt her for a moment. Deb was a nurturer. If there was anything she could do to help Alan get through this with his ego intact, she'd find a way to accomplish it. For just the tiniest moment Mark speculated on what it must be like to have that kind of helpmate. He couldn't imagine it. His own parents had never been supportive of each other. If anything, they'd enjoyed tearing each other apart.

"How about you?" she asked. "Do you have plans for tonight?"

He took a sip from his glass. "Actually, Shel's in town. I might see if she wants to have dinner."

"Shelby Elaine?"

"Yep. Didn't I tell you? We patched things up a couple of weeks ago."

Deb looked stunned. "You're back together?"

He chuckled, knowing he'd shocked her. "No. She wouldn't take me back if I were the last marriageable man on earth. But at least she doesn't think I'm the devil incarnate anymore." From the corner of his desk, he lifted the pocket folder labeled "Shelby" and waved it toward Deb. "Besides, we still have joint ventures that have to be dissolved."

"I suppose it would be difficult to remain business partners."

"Probably not a good idea."

"She *is* a little volatile," Deb concurred. "Slapping you silly. Calling you—"

"Don't remind me," he said with a sour look. "I'm trying to forget that day."

That wasn't the only thing he wanted to forget about those few days in New York. Over the weeks he'd told himself that he could hardly remember what Jenna Rawlins looked like. They'd shared a few hours of great sex wrapped around interesting conversation, but nothing more. And certainly, for now, work kept him busy and satisfied.

But sometimes there were moments when he seemed to have no command of his thoughts. He would find himself back at the penthouse, watching the way the moonlight seemed to turn Jenna's flesh to satin, enjoying the sight of that achingly sweet mouth as it quirked in a dozen different ways, all of them tantalizing. And the sex—God, he remembered every second of that. Hearing her breathing change when he touched her, feeling her tremble. Those were the kind of memories that got harder and harder to push away.

He glanced down at his calendar and realized that it had been six weeks. Maybe in another six he'd have put it all behind him. He hoped so.

"You're incredible," Deb said, drawing him out of the past. "Women will forgive you anything."

He grimaced and swallowed more of the Scotch. It burned a path down to his stomach. "Not all of them," he replied.

The telephone rang, and Deb returned to the outer office. Absently Mark rubbed the edge of his glass against his bottom lip while she picked up the call. After a few moments Deb put the caller on hold and stretched to catch his glance.

"It's someone named Peter asking for you," she told him. "Sounds like a kid."

Mark frowned. "I don't know any kids."

"Shall I take a message?"

"No. I'll take it." He punched the blinking light on his phone. "This is Mark Bishop."

"Hello, Mr. Bishop," came a young boy's voice. "I'm sorry to bother you, but I'd like to talk to you for a few minutes."

Sometimes kids showed up at his door selling products to get more school computers or send students on a trip with their school band. But surely the schools hadn't been forced to resort to phone solicitation, had they? "What about?" he asked tentatively.

"Well, first...do you...I mean, are you still one of the South's most legible bachelors?"

The question made him smile. "I guess you could say that."

"You were in a magazine story."

"Yes. Quite a while back."

"But you're still not married?"

"No."

"Or got a girlfriend?"

"Not right now."

There was another voice in the background suddenly. Muffled, but insistent. Mark had to admit he was intrigued. What was this about?

"You're not in trouble with the police?" the boy asked at last.

What the hell? As a kid, Mark had made his share of crank calls. But suddenly this didn't sound like one. "Why are you asking me these questions?"

"Well...my brother and me, his name's J.D., we were thinking that our mom might like to meet you. And maybe you'd like to be...not legible anymore. You know, like married?"

Debra Lee had come back to the doorway. He waved her away, silently mouthing to her that she should go home. On the other end of the telephone, he could hear the sound of breathing, as if the boy knew the magnitude of that proposal and wanted to give Mark a chance to absorb it.

"Let me get this straight," Mark said finally, still feeling amused indulgence. "Are you asking me to marry your mother?"

"Uh-huh."

"Why would I want to do that?"

"Umm...she's very pretty. And she takes baths every day."

"That's a plus."

"She's a good cook. We eat everything she makes. Well, not asparagus. *Nobody* likes that very much, no matter how hard she tries to cover it up with something else."

Mark almost laughed aloud at that, but the boy's attitude was so earnest he didn't dare. "I'm with you there. I hate asparagus."

"She likes animals, too. Except snakes. So you could have a pet if you wanted."

Mark cleared his throat and adopted a more serious tone. "What about your father? Where is he?"

"Mom got a divorce. Grampa says Mom needs Dad like Custer needed more Indians. I don't know who Custer is, but I think that means he's not ever coming back to live with us."

That information was delivered in a very matter-of-fact way, but something in the kid's voice tugged at Mark's heartstrings. He didn't know what had made this boy and his brother suddenly decide to take matters into their own hands, but they were obviously very determined to resolve their mom's marital woes.

"I'm sorry to hear that. It's tough not to have a dad around the house," Mark said, and meant it. He knew all about trying to get by in a home where all-out war had been declared and the dad had made himself scarce.

Again there was muffled conversation between the two boys. Mark waited, swirling the last of the Scotch in his glass. Eventually Peter said, "My brother wants to know if you live near Disney World."

"Yep. Is that why you called me? Because of where I live?"

"Sort of," the kid admitted. "First we called a bunch of others who have really cool stuff, but none of them would talk to me. So we picked you."

"Gee, thanks," Mark couldn't resist saying. He wondered just how far down the "legible" list he'd been, then decided he didn't really want to know. Before he could say anything more, the kid went back on the offensive.

"We wouldn't want to go to the parks all the time," Peter said quickly. "We're not much trouble. Honest. And we wouldn't mind having a new daddy."

It was time, Mark decided, to put an end to this as gently as he could. He hated to burst this boy's bubble, but he wasn't looking for a wife. Certainly not one with kids. "Look, Peter," he began, "I'd like to help you out, but don't you think you should leave it to your mom to pick out a new husband?"

"She'll never do it," the boy said, sounding anxious now. "Grampa says getting Mom to do something she doesn't really want to do is as hard as scratching your ear with your elbow. She's too picky. And she works really hard. She doesn't have time to look. That's why we're helping her."

Mark wished suddenly that he'd never taken the call. How was he going to let these kids down easy? "What kind of work does your mother do?"

"Counting."

"You mean, accounting?"

"Yeah. And she helps Aunt Vicky and Aunt Lauren with the magazine."

"What magazine?"

"It's about weddings. Stuff brides like."

Mark scowled, draining the last of his drink. *"Fairy Tale Weddings?"*

"Uh-huh."

His heart suddenly beat a lot faster. "What's your mom's name, Peter?"

"Mom."

"No, her given name. The name other people call her."

"Jenna."

Mark sat upright in his chair so fast that the ice in his glass sloshed over the rim onto his lap. He was so stunned he hardly noticed its chilly discomfort. "You're Jenna Rawlins's son?" he managed to get out.

"Uh-huh. So is J.D."

Blinking like a man just coming out of a trance, Mark set his empty glass down on his desk and began plucking ice cubes off his lap absently. In a million years he couldn't have imagined Jenna's boys tracking him down this way. They must have come across the magazine article somehow. Or had Jenna mentioned his name to them?

That seemed unlikely. Regardless, if she knew they were playing matchmaker, she'd probably ground them for a month. No, if she knew they'd called *him,* the poor little guys were looking at a life sentence.

He squeezed his eyes shut and pinched the bridge of his nose. This was getting tougher by the moment. "Listen, Peter, it's nice of you two to try to help your mom, but I don't think she'd be interested in me as a husband. Maybe you'd better talk this idea over with her before you call anyone else."

"We can't talk to her," Peter said, a note of annoyance in his voice. "I told you, she's too busy right now."

"Doing what?"

"Getting ready for the new baby."

"What!" If his heart had been racing before, it almost burst out of his chest with that bit of news. "What new baby?"

"Hers. Our little brother or sister. She's gonna have a baby."

"That's impossible!" he said sharply. *No way. Not a chance in bloody hell.* These kids were making crank calls, after all.

"It's *not* impossible," the boy argued back. "Grampa says—"

"Never mind what Grampa says." Damn, he wanted to jam the old coot and his homespun truisms straight down a well. There were things Mark needed to know immediately, and still feeling stunned, he voiced his thoughts aloud. "How can your mother be pregnant?"

Some of his shock must have communicated itself to Peter, because when he spoke, the boy's voice was rushed. "I don't know *how*. No one tells us anything."

"Okay," Mark said more slowly. "Okay." He scrubbed a hand over his face, trying to keep his voice calm, trying to hang on to some illusion of control. Whatever the true situation was or wasn't, there was no point in scaring the hell out of these two boys. "I'm sorry," he added when he could finally speak again. "When is your mother due, Peter?"

"Due for what?"

He ground his teeth. *Patience.* "When is she supposed to have the baby?"

"We don't know that, either. She hasn't even told us about it yet. But I heard Grampa say that by the Superbowl she's gonna look like she swallowed a football."

Mark did a quick mental calculation. *Oh, hell. It can't be.*

He heard a few seconds of whispered confusion between the two boys, words Mark couldn't make out, in spite of straining to hear them. Then Peter said quickly, "I gotta go. I guess the answer's no, huh?"

"Wait a minute," Mark shot back, suddenly afraid the kid was going to hang up. "I didn't say no. I need to think about it."

"We can't wait too long."

"You won't have to. I promise. Just don't call anyone else right now. All right?"

"I guess," the boy agreed. "You should meet Mom. Do you think you'll want to come and see her?"

Mark took a deep breath, trying to hear over the pulse thrumming in his ears. "Peter," he said, "there isn't anything I'd like to do more."

CHAPTER EIGHT

"I'LL CALL YOU tomorrow," Jenna said, hoping she could keep that promise.

The real-estate agent, a friend of Vic's named Kathy Bigelow, nodded as she gathered up the last of her paperwork from the kitchen table. "I'm sorry nothing we looked at this morning pleased you. I was sure one of them would."

"I was hoping it would be easy, too. But I'll know the right place when I see it."

Kathy tilted her head at Jenna, looked hesitant for a moment, then seemed to come to a decision. "I hope you won't mind me saying this, but...are you sure you really want to buy a house?"

That was the last thing Jenna expected the woman to say. "Absolutely. Why do you ask?"

"I've been in this business long enough to know the difference between serious buyers and Lucy Lookers. I also think I know what my customers want. But you seemed so ambivalent about everything we looked at today. Am I misreading you completely, or is it possible—"

"They were lovely houses," Jenna said quickly. "It's just..."

She trailed off, unsettled by the agent's comments. She'd been about to say that none of the houses pleased her, but would that have been a lie? Was she finding fault with perfectly good homes because she didn't really want to move out of her father's house? Because of fear? Surely she'd beaten that monster to a pulp by now.

She wanted her own place. She needed her own place. And so did the boys. No. She wouldn't let herself be filled with doubts anymore. The decision to move was a good one.

Kathy looked uncomfortable with the silence. Jenna gave her arm a friendly squeeze and rushed into speech, trying to put her at ease. "This is probably going to sound silly and dramatic, but the truth is, as lovely as those houses we looked at today were, none of them *spoke* to me. They didn't feel like home. Whatever I choose, the boys and I are going to have to live in it a long time, so it has to be the right place. It doesn't have to be fancy. But it has to *feel* right. And when it does, I'll know it." Jenna smiled at Kathy, hoping she didn't write her off as a nutcase. "I hope that makes sense to you."

"It makes perfect sense," Kathy replied, nodding.

They talked for another minute or so, then Jenna led the woman to the front door. Kathy was just about to leave when she turned back in the doorway. "You know, there's a great Victorian a few miles from here that's been on the market for a while. It needs work, but since your family's in the construction business, they may be able to give you the help you'd need."

Jenna grimaced. "I'd like to keep my father and brothers out of this if at all possible."

She caught Kathy's surprised expression. A single mother on the verge of buying a new house? Who wouldn't be delighted to have a couple of strong men to pitch in? And especially men who knew one end of a hammer from the other.

"They mean well, but they have a tendency to try to take over," Jenna explained.

"I see," Kathy said with a smile. "I only mention it because I think it's the kind of place you're looking for— plenty of trees, an established neighborhood, lots of charm. Because it needs a facelift and the owners are eager to realize some quick cash, the price is in your range."

"Then I suppose I should look at it."

"Tell you what. The owners had to relocate to San Francisco for work, so the place is empty. Why don't I drop off the key, and you can take a look at it in private. See if it sends out the right vibes."

"Thanks for understanding. That sounds like a good idea."

"Great!" With a wave of one manicured hand, Kathy left.

Jenna leaned against the closed door for a moment. She'd been fighting nausea throughout the appointment. Still, she was glad she'd insisted Kathy come to the house this morning when both boys were in school and her father was at his monthly veterans' meeting. This was the first step toward what was bound to create additional tension in the family, but she was not going to back down.

The past few days since she'd told her father and brothers about the baby had been difficult. Had she hoped they'd get behind her one hundred percent? Fat chance. The men in her family were determined to show her that they were behind her *two hundred* percent.

They treated her as though she were made of spun glass. Her father watched her constantly, always ready to jump in and grab a heavy platter or reach for something she had to stretch for.

The family construction company was knocking down a used bookstore, and yesterday her brother Trent had brought home two boxes of maternity books he'd salvaged. Help for a new mother, he'd told her. Very thoughtful. Unfortunately Eisenhower had been in office when these moms were pregnant, and things had changed a bit since then.

Even Christopher, the brother she felt closest to, was driving her nuts. Last night he'd called her from the middle of a crime scene to tell her he'd met a well-known local obstetrician who would be happy to squeeze her into his office schedule. Without asking, Christopher had made an appointment for her. Considering her brother's job, Jenna didn't even want to guess how he'd met the man.

She supposed an outsider might have found their concern sweet and wonderfully supportive. It was. But it was also overwhelming, smothering and downright insulting to her intelligence. She suspected that, as her pregnancy developed, it would only get worse. She still had to get through tonight, when she'd sit the boys down and tell them. She couldn't imagine how they would take the news.

Jenna realized rather abruptly that the doorbell was ringing. She was still leaning on the door, and she turned, swinging the door wide. "Did you forget something?" she asked.

Mark Bishop stood on the porch, looking just as handsome as she remembered him. He gave her a smile, one that didn't quite reach his eyes. "I didn't forget a thing," he said. "Did you?"

His gray eyes traveled over her from head to toe. Nothing in her clothing—a simple blouse and jeans—revealed her pregnancy; it was much too soon. But she felt self-conscious all the same.

"Mark," she began, and discovered that her nerve endings were registering swift alarm. Whatever reason he'd come, it wasn't a social call. Not after the unpleasantness of that last phone conversation. "What are you doing here?" she asked. "I'm surprised to see you."

"I'm sure you are. May I come in?"

"That's probably not a good idea."

He tilted his head, and some trick of the sunlight suddenly made his features seem sharper than she remembered. "I think it is."

"We don't have anything to discuss."

"Does that mean you weren't planning to tell me about the baby?"

The base of her spine prickled. Her heart went into overdrive. So he knew. She stood there a moment, suspended. It didn't matter how he'd found out. All that mattered now was what he was going to do about it.

She stepped aside so he could enter, then turned and went quietly into the kitchen. She heard the front door close and his footsteps as he followed her.

Desperate for some stall tactic, she reached for the coffeepot on the stove. "Would you like something to drink? Coffee? Or iced tea?"

How ridiculous it seemed, offering the conventional sustenance at such an unconventional and awkward moment. He didn't sit down, but leaned against the counter, a dark, presence she couldn't bear to face.

"No. I had my fill of coffee in the airport this morning. While I was mulling over all the different ways I could ask you."

She looked at him then. He stood closer than she liked, no more than five feet away, watching her. His hands were slightly behind him, his fingers curled around the edge of the counter in a white-knuckled grip. He wore black slacks and an emerald-colored polo shirt, which covered a chest that she remembered was matted with dark, curling hair. In spite of his casual dress the overall effect was one of understated elegance.

Many times during the past few weeks she'd wondered how she would feel if she ever saw him again. She wasn't prepared for the urge to simply go to him and lay her cheek against the place where his collarbones met, where she knew his pulse could pound like a thousand drums.

But he hadn't come here for that. He hadn't come here for anything but the truth. And in spite of the fact that she was beating down panic, she owed him that. "Yes," she said softly. "I'm pregnant."

His gaze held hers for a moment. Then, in a surprisingly gentle voice, he said, "That wasn't the question I was struggling with."

She didn't pretend to misunderstand. "Yes," she said again. "It's yours."

"I'm glad to see you're going to skip any retreat into moral outrage," he said in a voice that had a thin border of amusement.

"I know we used protection, but it's never foolproof, I suppose."

He tilted his head, frowning a little. "Foolproof. Is that what you think we were? Fools?"

"Foolish, maybe. I think we were two people who needed something that night. I'm not going to pretend I regretted a moment of it, so it's not necessary for you to pretend it meant anything special."

His frown deepened. "You think you know what I feel? All right. Want to tell me how I feel about discovering that you're pregnant with my child?"

It took her less than five seconds to come up with the answer. "Shocked."

"I think that's a reasonable response."

"Angry."

He shrugged. "Perhaps at first."

"Hoping that I'll decide to…" She felt her cheeks redden and ducked her head. "That I'll get…"

He moved closer to her suddenly, taking her chin in one hand so that she was forced to meet his eyes, and she felt something unknown and frightening zip through her veins. His lips carried the ghost of a smile. "I realize that we spent only a few hours together," he said softly. "But I know you'll keep this baby."

She nodded.

"What else?" he asked, and his hand fell away from her face.

She moistened her lips. Might as well tell it all. "I think you're wishing you could make this situation just disappear as if it never existed."

His eyes, bright as diamonds, held hers in an unwavering scrutiny. Then he moved away from the counter without answering her. She watched him pace restlessly around the kitchen. He stopped at the refrigerator, where magnets and drawings and school photos made a ridiculously sentimental art gallery. Fingering a small photo of her sons, he looked back over his shoulder at her.

"Peter and J.D.?" he asked.

"Yes," she replied in surprise. She didn't remember telling him their names.

"They're the ones who called to tell me you were pregnant."

"What? That's impossible."

He told her about the telephone call the boys had made yesterday.

"I don't understand," Jenna said, shaking her head. "I've never mentioned you to them."

"You didn't have to. You evidently have some file you keep on eligible men?" His mouth quirked wryly. "Something connected with the magazine, I hope, and not your personal hit list."

The file folder from work! It still lay on her bedside table. Remembering the conversation she'd had with Petey about it, everything started to make sense. "I brought the file home because I'm interviewing Rusty Delacruz from the list. He's opening a new resort in the Bahamas."

"I can't tell you if your sons spoke to him or not. I do know that unfortunately I wasn't the first one they tried to market you to."

Mark supplied more of the details. At first she was horrified, then embarrassed, amused and finally worried. Obviously her sons were confused and anxious about the future. She shouldn't have waited to tell them about the baby.

"Don't be too hard on them," Mark advised her. "As plans go, it was rather inventive, and you shouldn't stifle creativity." He crossed his arms and his face turned serious again. "The point is, they called. You didn't. Why not? When were you going to get around to it?"

"I wasn't," she admitted.

"You were never going to tell me? You were just going to have the baby alone?"

"I'm not alone. I have a very supportive family."

"That's not the same thing, and you know it," he said. He pointed a finger at her stomach. "That's my child you're carrying. So I guess the question comes down to, what are we going to do now?"

Jenna lifted her chin. She could feel the tension in the room escalating. "*We're* not going to do anything. *I'm* going to have this baby in the spring. I'll be a good mother—it really is one of the things I excel at, in spite of what you may think. You don't need to worry about anything. I won't make demands of you. I don't expect you to have any involvement at all."

His eyebrows rose in obvious displeasure. "Nice little speech. Only one problem. Suppose I say no?"

"You can't say no."

"Sorry, I think I can," he said with a thin smile. "No."

The sickening sensation of her life plunging downward weakened her knees. She pulled out one of the kitchen chairs and lowered herself into it. "What does that mean exactly?" she asked when she could catch her breath.

"It means I don't intend to be relegated to the position of sperm donor. I can't go back to Orlando and just pretend this baby doesn't exist."

"Yes, you can. He'll be fine."

She saw his eyes narrow. "You know it's a boy?"

"No. It's too soon. I guess I've just been surrounded by so many men all my life that I assumed it's a boy."

His stance relaxed a little. Maybe he realized this whole situation wasn't any easier for her than it was for him. Whatever the reason, he sat down in one of the chairs. Her fingers were knotted tensely on the table, and he placed one hand over them. After a sticky moment of silence, she lifted her lashes to find him looking at her curiously, sympathy behind the dark steel of his eyes.

"What are you so afraid of, Jenna?"

She shook her head. "Nothing. It's just that there's no reason for you to feel that you owe me anything. I'm not asking for financial support." Remembering that last, bitter conversation, she added, "And if you're worried the news will get out, that your reputation will suffer—"

"Don't," he said, squeezing her hands. Without releasing her, he leaned back slightly, as though trying to see her better. His mouth produced a pained twist. "I'd give anything to take back what I said that day. It was so different from what I intended." He gave a little huff of laughter. "You're the first woman I've ever met who leaves me tongue-tied."

It would have been nice to explore just what he meant, but for the sake of the baby, she had to make sure he understood her intentions. "Please don't make this difficult," she said, pulling her hands out from under his. "I don't want anything from you."

"Why? Because you think I can't handle it?"

"Because you don't want to. I have you on record, remember? When I interviewed you, it couldn't have been clearer that kids were the last thing you wanted. I may be a lousy journalist, but that came through loud and clear."

He raked his fingers through his hair. "I won't deny that children were not in the picture I envisioned with Shelby. That doesn't mean I can't change my mind."

"Or that you can't change it back."

She watched his uneasiness suddenly spike with irritation. His expression became cold, pinched. "I have certain rights to be involved with this baby. Morally, ethically…legally I have rights that make a pretty powerful argument."

She felt the blood leave her face. "You'd fight me in court?"

He shook his head, as if he already regretted his words. "It doesn't have to come to that. Why are you being so stubborn?"

"Why are you?" she shot back. "Admit it. This isn't

what you want. When you came here, weren't you hoping to find out that I *wasn't* pregnant? And before I told you the baby was yours, weren't you praying, even just a little bit, that it was somebody else's? Anybody's problem but yours?''

His chair scraped noisily as he slid it back and rose. He stalked away from the table, as though he needed to put distance between them. ''What's done is done,'' he said. ''Neither one of us has the luxury of changing things. But we can come to an arrangement that's agreeable to both of us. Visitation. Joint custody...''

''For how long?'' she asked. ''This baby will have a very loving home with me and with my family. But he also needs stability. Right now you're interested. Maybe you even feel the need to salve your conscience by taking an active role. But what happens when you lose interest?'' She breathed an exasperated sigh, tired of trying to make him see reason. ''You can't flit in and out of this child's life whenever you feel like it,'' she said at last. ''It's not fair to the baby and it's not fair to me.''

The distance of the table separated them. Spreading his hands and planting them on the wood surface he leaned forward to meet her eye to eye. ''Then let's make it fair to both of you. Let's get married.''

Taken aback, Jenna looked at him as if she'd never seen him before. He couldn't be serious. One night's indiscretion couldn't lead to a lifetime commitment for either of them.

''Please don't make jokes about this,'' she finally said on a soft breath.

''Your divorce—it's final, isn't it?''

''Yes, but—''

''Then legally there's no reason we can't. We get married. Give this baby both a mother and a father. A father who doesn't come and go out of his life. Together I think we could make a good team.''

She shook her head. ''It's a preposterous idea.''

"Why?"

Her hand flew out to encompass the kitchen. "Look around you, Mark. This house is a perfect example of the way middle-class America lives. A Leave-It-to-Beaver lifestyle in the 'burbs isn't the kind of life you're used to. Or one that you'd want."

"You're right," he agreed. "Personally I don't think there's anything wrong with having the kind of luxuries money can buy. I don't think being a capitalist should count against me. What's your objection to money?"

As a working mother, she couldn't possibly be opposed to having more income. And Mark would certainly be able to provide it. But she also knew people who weren't one bit happier because they had money. Some of them were downright miserable.

"Money isn't an answer for everything," she told him. "It changes people."

"It doesn't have to. Just consider what I can offer you and this child, Jenna. The best education. Security. The freedom to have the kind of life you've probably only dreamed of."

Her irritation flared. "I *have* a great life right now. I have family and roots and happiness that can't be bought, not even by you."

He tilted a smile her way. "I don't doubt that. But what's wrong with expanding your horizons a bit? You want to raise this kid in a commune, I might have to retract my offer. But surely some middle ground can be reached, don't you think?"

Frustrated, she stood and began pacing the kitchen. "Do you know how many years are involved in raising a child? When the novelty of being a dad wears off and all you're left with is dirty diapers and runny noses and a dozen other problems that can drive any sane person up a wall, what are you going to do then?"

He crossed his arms and lifted one shoulder. "Hell if I know. But I figure you'll have a pretty good idea how to deal with almost anything. I'm a fast study. Give me a chance, and I may surprise you.''

Her jaw compressed. ''Will you please be serious?''

''What makes you think I'm not serious? I don't go around offering marriage to just anyone.''

''Just to women you feel obligated toward,'' she said. ''Ones who happen to have gotten…knocked up.''

He stared hard at her, and she sensed she'd angered him. When he spoke, his voice sounded harsh. ''You think that's how I see you? The little idiot who let herself get caught? Or maybe a sly manipulator looking for a rich husband? I was there that night, Jenna. In spite of everything, I knew what I was doing and so did you. It didn't have anything to do with tricks or stupidity. It had everything to do with two people who wanted to connect in the most basic way. If you hadn't run off the way you did, if I hadn't blown it the next day with that stupid phone conversation, do you honestly think we wouldn't have been inventing new ways to—''

She raised one hand to halt his words, her cheeks flooding with color. ''Stop! Having great sex and falling in love are two different things.''

Again the silence became uncomfortable. He met her intense and blatant scrutiny, but she had no idea what he was really thinking. Finally he said in a tight, quiet voice, ''Who said anything about falling in love? ''

She felt the need to lick her lips. ''You're not in love with me.''

''I've never believed in that sort of romantic foolishness,'' he conceded. ''That doesn't mean I don't care what happens to you. Or this baby.''

She moved away, full of wounded pride and shaky dignity. ''I can't marry someone I don't love or someone who doesn't love me. Who'd want a marriage like that?''

He cleared his throat, as though trying to make sure he sounded reasonable. ''There are a lot of marriages that have been based on less. We could still make a good home for this child. We could find a way to make it work.''

"I can't do it. Not just for me or the baby, but for Petey and J.D. I have to think about them, as well. They're just getting used to their father not being around. What would happen if I married you, made you part of their lives? They'd start to depend on you, to think of you as a real stepfather. Then in a few years, when you meet someone else, or get tired of all the tiresome things that go along with parenting, what then? You just walk out of their lives? I can't let that happen. Not again.''

Clearly clamping down on impatience, he said, "Whatever your ex-husband was like, I'm not that man, Jenna. I don't take my responsibilities lightly. I don't run when the going gets tough.''

"You can't make that kind of promise.''

"If you'd just think about it, this baby needs a father—''

"Please don't say that,'' she cut in sharply, giving him a steely look. "You sound like Dad and my brothers. But I can tell you from personal experience that sometimes a father isn't an asset. There were times when...''

She broke off, unwilling to discuss or explain her ex-husband's relationship with Petey and J.D. Her nerves were quivering with tension, and she put her hands to her cheeks, wondering if her face looked as stiff as it felt.

"Jenna, listen to me—''

Her hands slapped into her lap in a quick, annoyed movement. "I'm so tired of men trying to tell me what's good for me. I'll tell you what I *don't* need. Another man trying to make all my decisions when I'm perfectly capable of making them myself.''

"Then make the decision.''

"I have. No.''

Abruptly he turned away for a moment. Exhaling a deep breath, he swung back to face her. "All right,'' he said calmly. "Let's come at this another way. Your biggest objections to marrying me are that you don't love me and you suspect I won't be there for you in the future. I suppose that's understandable, considering you don't really know me. Is that a fair statement?''

"I…yes.''

"Then consider this. I'll stay in town a few weeks. As it happens, the Atlanta office can use some one-on-one time with me right now. While I'm here, we get to know each other better. We go out to dinner. To a movie. Maybe take your kids on a few outings so they get comfortable with me. I'd like to meet the fellows who were so determined to get their mom a husband.''

"You're suggesting that we date.''

"Exactly. And we pretend that there's no baby calling the shots here. Just two people who've discovered a mutual attraction. I have no idea what the protocol is for this kind of situation, but it can't hurt for us to get to know each other better, can it?''

"As people, instead of lovers,'' she said cautiously, trying the idea on for size.

He smiled as he approached her. When no more than a few inches separated them, he said, "I'd be lying if I said future sexual encounters between us weren't a very appealing possibility. We both know there was a spark, and I'm not averse to fanning it.''

Something in her face must have told him she didn't think that was a good idea. "If you're not comfortable with that, I'm prepared to wait,'' he said. He stroked one finger across the pink-tinged softness of her cheek. "Until you are.''

She tilted her head away from his touch. "It won't work. What happened in New York was an unexpected, lovely accident. But that doesn't mean we can build a future out of it. Not one that will last.''

"Isn't it worth exploring?'' He captured one of her hands. She took a sharp breath, then a sharper one as he laid her hand and his against the flatness of her stomach.

"There's only one guarantee in this whole situation, Jenna." He pressed slightly. "You're going to have my baby. And as far as I'm concerned, that's reason enough to try."

She felt herself trembling, remembering all those lovely hours they'd shared between tangled sheets. This was insanity. She knew her objections must sound profoundly cynical, but couldn't he see how foolish this idea was?

Her gaze leaped to his. "And if I won't agree to this?"

His face was fixed like steel. "Then as much as I would regret it, I'll go home and determine what options I have legally."

SITTING IN THE BATHTUB, J.D. was annihilating plastic Cyberlons by smacking them with the tip of his space cannon. Jenna watched one after the other plop into the sudsy water, sent to a watery grave with all the accompanying battle sounds and expressions of victory that any successful intergalactic cop would employ.

Petey, who was enduring getting his head towel-dried, rolled his eyes at her. He considered J.D.'s never-ending battle with Cyberlons annoyingly passé. His own bath toy, a battleship with a Spiderman action figure inexplicably tied to it, was clutched in his hand.

Seated next to the tub, Jenna stopped rubbing Petey's head long enough to scoop up the floating soap and deposit it closer to her son's body. "J.D., stop fooling around and finish up."

Her back ached. She realized that, even though she'd taken the day off from work, she was exhausted. Bath time with the boys was always a challenge; she'd never seen two kids who could stall and goof around the way these two could. But she felt frazzled and edgy tonight, as well. Was it just the demands the baby was making on her body? Or was it Mark's visit this morning?

Petey pulled his head away from the towel to find her eyes. "You mad about something, Mom?"

She'd been toweling pretty vigorously. She brought her movements down a notch. Smiling at him, she decided that now was as good a time as any to address today's events with her sons. "Any reason I should be?"

J.D. just shrugged. Petey shook his head. "I can't think of any."

She tugged her oldest son closer with the ends of the towel so she could give him a narrow-eyed look. "Not even the fact that you've been calling total strangers in a search to find me a husband?"

J.D. dropped his space cannon, sending water out of the tub. "It was all Petey's idea! I didn't want to do it."

Petey swung toward the tub angrily. "Squealer!" He turned back to his mother. He had the same soft brown eyes as his father, and they seemed even more so now when they were filled with guilt. "We were only trying to help," he said.

Both boys began to argue with each other, throwing incoherent explanations her way whenever they felt the need. She took Petey by the arms and looked sternly at J.D. "Both of you, stop!" she commanded. "It doesn't matter whose idea it was. You shouldn't have done it."

They were immediately contrite. Petey dropped his head, and J.D. began lightly tapping one of the Cyberlons with the tip of his cannon. Mark's version of yesterday's telephone call had been embarrassing enough to hear. She could only imagine what the other men they'd called must think, but considering where she stood now with Mark, it hardly seemed important. Still, the boys needed to be scolded for such outrageous behavior. And threatened with dire consequences if they ever did something like that again.

She lectured them until she sensed they'd stopped listening. Then she said, "I haven't decided yet what your punishment should be." She helped Petey slip into his pajama bottoms. "Maybe no video games for a year."

"A year!" J.D. exclaimed from the tub. "We can't go a whole year. Especially since it wasn't even my idea."

"Loser," Petey muttered.

"I suppose I could put you both on bread and water for a month. That would certainly make mealtime easier on me."

J.D. gasped in horror, but Petey looked at her sharply, realizing she wasn't quite as angry as he'd feared.

She snapped her fingers, as though coming to a sudden decision. "Suppose I make you help Grampa clean out the garage this weekend?"

That really amounted to no punishment at all. The kids knew that her father cleaned out the garage almost every weekend. Or *tried* to. He invariably got tired and ended up in front of the television watching a game or got sidetracked by all the memorabilia he came across that had been sitting in boxes marked in her mother's neat handwriting.

J.D. looked confused. "That's nothing—"

"Whatever you say, Mom," Petey cut in quickly with a comically censoring glare at his brother.

"Then it's settled," Jenna said. She pointed her finger at Petey. "And I don't expect either of you to do something like that ever again. Understand?"

"Yes, ma'am," both boys promised.

She slipped Petey's pajama top over his head. When she could see his face again, she asked, "How did you two find out about the baby?"

J.D. was the one to confess. "We listened on the stairs while you talked to Grampa and Uncle Christopher and Uncle Trent. You can hear everything from there. Sometimes—"

"It was an accident," Petey piped in, shooting a warning glance in his brother's direction. "We hardly ever hear anything. We always go right to sleep."

"Sure," Jenna said. "Perfect little angels."

Petey looked relieved.

"I know I should have told you both about the baby sooner. How do you feel about having another brother? Or maybe a sister?"

Petey shrugged. "I guess it's okay."

"I'd rather have a dog," J.D. said absently. He'd gone back to slaying Cyberlons.

"Are you happy about the baby?" Petey asked.

"Well, I have to admit, I was surprised at first. But having you two is such a wonderful adventure that I'm excited about having another child." She looked back and forth between them. "You boys know, don't you, that this doesn't change the way I feel about you? I won't love this baby any more than I love you."

J.D. frowned up at her. "Can it be a boy so we can play Alien Invasion?"

"Girls can be pretty tough enemies of Cyberlons, too. Remember Queen Persefa in *Alien Advance?*"

He considered that a moment, then gave her the gap-toothed smile that always made her heart go bump. "Yeah, I guess a girl can shoot."

Petey was too quiet, his head down. His fingers plucked at the twine he'd wrapped around his Spiderman on the battleship. Jenna waited, knowing her son well enough to sense a question was forthcoming.

"Is Daddy ever gonna come back?" he asked at last.

Even J.D. went still to hear the answer to that one. After Jack had left, she'd talked to the boys briefly about the changes they'd have to go through. She'd never believed in long-range deception, and she'd thought they took it pretty well. But evidently, not as well as she'd hoped. Particularly Petey, who had been much closer to his father than J.D.

She pulled Petey to her side so she could see both the boys without turning her head. "No, honey," she said. "Daddy isn't coming home."

"Do you want him to come back?" Petey asked.

"No," she told him honestly. "Because I don't think

either of us would be happy if that happened. Someday I'd like him to come back to see you and J.D. But until he does, I think we need to stick together as a family.''

Petey's downcast eyes raised to hers. ''Do you want another husband?''

She didn't want to answer that and decided to settle on something indefinite. ''Maybe someday.''

''Grampa says you raising this baby alone is gonna be harder than pounding nails in a snowbank.''

She agreed it would be difficult, but as usual, that lack of faith coming from her father made her hackles rise. ''That sounds like your grandfather. You all have talked this out, I take it?''

''No,'' said Petey.

''We heard him talking on the phone to Uncle Christopher,'' J.D. volunteered.

Petey opened his mouth to protest but Jenna silenced him with a finger to his lips. ''I know. Just by accident.''

''It was!''

''I think I need to have a talk with everyone about respecting other people's privacy,'' she muttered. For the boys' sake, she smiled. ''You know, your grandfather still thinks of me as a little girl. But I'm much more capable than anyone gives me credit for around here.'' She nudged Petey and dropped her hand into the tub to tousle J.D.'s hair. ''I'm doing all right by the two of you, aren't I?''

''I think you're great, Mom,'' J.D. piped up. ''That's what we tried to tell those guys we called.'' He looked momentarily flustered. ''I mean, those guys *Petey* called.''

Petey gave his brother an evil look, and Jenna had to laugh. ''Oh, I'm so glad I didn't hear those conversations.''

With Petey almost ready for bed, J.D. hopped out of the tub so Jenna could dry him off. His body was soft and pink from the heat of the water. Toweling him quickly, she watched Petey struggle to put toothpaste on his toothbrush.

"You know," she began, "Mark Bishop came to see me today."

"Who?" J.D. said with a frown.

Petey whirled around, his eyes alight with interest. "Orlando, you moron. The theme parks." To Jenna he said, "I knew it! He wanted to meet you. Did you like him?"

She shrugged. "He was nice enough. We're probably going to see each other a few times. Just to see how we get along."

She and Mark had decided that for now, no one was to know he was the father of her child. It was possible that someone, probably Lauren, would make the connection once Jenna told her how far along she was.

She hoped her family wouldn't put it together. After all, during their discussion that night at dinner, when she'd first told them about going to New York for the interview, she couldn't recall even mentioning his name.

And if Mark truly intended to hold her to the idea of dating to see if they were compatible, she supposed it didn't matter just *how* he'd popped up in her life. It was too much to expect her sons to keep their telephone call a secret, but if she was questioned about it, she'd simply refuse to elaborate. How many women wanted to discuss being put up on the marriage block by their own children?

She tried to imagine Mark interacting with the men in her family. They could be brutally protective of her. Embarrassingly intrusive. How would he react to the McNab version of the Inquisition?

Even more than that, how was *she* going to manage having Mark in her life? She must have been crazy to agree to his plan. She could think of a dozen reasons it wouldn't work. She resented his threat that she might have a legal battle on her hands. But how was she going to keep him from exploiting the fact that, every time he got near her, her senses skyrocketed? Damn good-looking men and the foolish way they made women act and feel!

Petey had finished brushing his teeth. He turned toward her. "You should invite him to Aunt Penny's party. He could meet the whole family and see what we're like."

Aunt Penelope, her father's oldest sister, was turning eighty the day after tomorrow. Her daughters had decided that a reunion of every McNab in the country was just the thing to mark the occasion. They'd planned a covered-dish barbecue, complete with hired entertainment, at a local park. McNabs, being firm believers in family, would be turning out in droves. It was bound to be a crowded, exhausting and long day.

She had to hide a smile at the thought of Mark joining them. He'd been an only child, no doubt sheltered and the full focus of his parents' attention. She could imagine the kinds of parties he'd gone to as a kid—sedate, tidy little affairs that began with engraved invitations. There probably hadn't been a piñata within a hundred miles of a Bishop-family function.

He thought he was prepared for family life, but how would he manage surrounded by noisy kids and spilled punch and rubbery hot dogs? She'd bet that being subjected to a mega McNab-family gathering would send him running to the airport. Maybe it was an opportunity too good to miss.

She flicked her oldest son on the nose and grinned at him. "You know, Petey, inviting him to Aunt Penny's party is a pretty good idea."

CHAPTER NINE

THE DAY OF Aunt Penelope's party at Bear Hollow Park, Kathy Bigelow dropped off the key to the Victorian fixer-upper. Jenna was so eager to see it she convinced her father to take the boys to the celebration without her. Later, after running a quick errand, she could meet them at the park, she told him.

She hated circumventing the truth, but she wasn't quite brave enough to confess her plans. Not yet. Why bring up a sore subject if the house turned out to be completely hopeless?

She wasn't expecting miracles, but she meant what she'd said to Kathy. The house didn't have to be especially grand. But it had to have some indefinable *something* that called to her, that told her it could be a place she could turn into a real home for her family.

With the key in her purse and the address clutched in one hand, Jenna finally found it. It was in a neighborhood filled with older homes. Not Historic Registry material, but houses that didn't have a cookie-cutter sameness. Loads of potential. The trees were wonderful, and though the sidewalks were giving way to root invasion, there were signs that children played here. Bikes tipped over on lawns. Basketball hoops over garages.

Jenna stepped out of the car, then stood staring up at the house while her heart did a nervous little back flip.

The Victorian had lots of personality in its curved archways, bay windows and wide front porch. It was asymmetrical, columns on either side of the entryway, matching chimneys along a low, shingled roof.

The exterior was lovely. And it needed a lot of work.

She approached slowly, and as she had with every house she'd seen so far, she tried to envision living here. Watching Petey and J.D. play in the front yard shaded by big magnolias. Imagining herself planting azaleas in the garden that now looked overgrown and lifeless.

Could she and the boys and the baby build a brand-new life around this home? Or was buying a house right now the ultimate in biting off more than she could chew?

If she did buy it, would Mark come here to visit his son?

That was a foolish thought. She shouldn't be thinking along those lines. Everything involving Mark was still so up in the air.

But once she made the break from her father's house, there would be no turning back. The boys felt abandoned by their father. They needed to feel safe and secure again, in a house that made them *all* feel safe and secure.

Was this house the one?

The front door was massive. Jenna fit the key into the stubborn, corroded lock and fiddled with it for a moment or two. Then suddenly she was in.

An impressive staircase wound up to the second floor. To the right a wide, curved archway opened into the front room. To the left another archway opened to a smaller room clearly designed to be a study or den.

She wandered slowly through the downstairs rooms, stroking the smooth, aged rosewood that glowed warmly in spite of recent neglect. The broad, wooden floorboards creaked under her weight, but it was a nice, homey sound. The high ceilings would make the rooms difficult to heat, but there were touches of whimsy along the crown moldings, and the charming fireplaces would give the rooms a cozy, friendly ambience.

The room she envisioned as a den made her heart beat

faster. As much as she enjoyed her involvement with *FTW,* she had always dreamed of opening her own office as a CPA. With massive built-in bookcases and multi-paned, beveled windows that offered great light, this room was ideal.

Actually the room was big enough for two good-size desks. Before she could wonder what had spurred the thought, she pictured Mark sharing this space with her, their desks facing each other. She could imagine them working quietly together, neither one disturbing the other, but every so often, they'd look up, connect without words, content just to be in the same room.

The fantasy stunned her a little. Since Jack's departure, she'd managed to keep her head out of the clouds. She didn't indulge in daydreams involving men anymore.

Until now. Until Mark.

She rubbed her hands vigorously up and down her arms as if she needed warming. She mustn't slip this way. Mark didn't fit in this picture at all. He'd probably hate a house like this.

She turned her back on the den and returned to the central hall. The stairs beckoned, curving and graceful. The newel post caught her attention. Carved from solid oak, it depicted a surprisingly delicate-looking bird, wings caught as though poised to take flight.

It could have been any number of bird species, but right then and there Jenna decided it was a phoenix. Rising from the ashes. She didn't mean to romanticize it. It just fit somehow.

So the house is a beautiful, slightly faded lady, she scolded herself. *That doesn't mean you can make it yours. That doesn't mean it's the place.*

But the moment she wrapped her fingers around the newel post, she knew that it was. The wood was warm and welcoming under her hand, and all she could think was *Yes. Oh, yes.*

This is home.

BEAR HOLLOW PARK was the kind of park made for family get-togethers. Acres and acres of wooded trails to hike, a pretty lake good for boating, ball fields for impromptu games. Today a clear blue sky promised to make the day perfect.

Unfortunately, by the time Jenna left the Victorian and made it to the park, it didn't look as if she would get to enjoy much of it. On her way toward the covered pavilions, she was strong-armed by one of Aunt Penelope's daughters and talked into setting up the food tables.

Jenna had immediately realized that the job called for reinforcements. Now, while she set out stacks of napkins, utensils and cups, Trent's girlfriend, Amanda, and Jenna's second cousin Louise were sorting through various bowls, plastic platters and foil-covered pans. By noon every McNab within hollering distance would be heading their way.

A shaggy-headed teenager—was he one of cousin Alice's boys?—handed her a covered pan with no explanation and trotted away to join the Frisbee tournament in the nearby field. Jenna lifted one corner of the foil and frowned. She couldn't tell if it was a dessert or a main dish.

"There're so many of them," Amanda said behind her.

Jenna nodded, giving the pan a sniff. "Most of the McNab women are good cooks and they like to share. We'll have plenty to feed the hungry hordes."

"I meant, there are so many McNabs."

Turning, Jenna saw that Amanda was surveying the area around the covered shelters. Everywhere you looked were McNab relatives, the older folks gossiping and laughing in folding chairs, the men swapping stories around coolers of beer and soda, the kids squealing with delight and excitement as they watched the clown who'd been hired to keep them from driving the adults crazy.

Even if you hadn't known this section of the park had been reserved for the McNab reunion, you could probably have picked them out, anyway. The McNabs were more healthy-looking than beautiful, but they tended to have the same physical characteristics. Good tans. Lean bodies. Light, dancing hair. And what her father referred to as "the McNab muzzle"—a wide, expressive mouth.

Christopher had told her that he and Amanda were starting to talk about getting married. Seeing the woman's astonishment, Jenna could imagine that Amanda felt slightly intimidated by the thought of being part of such a large family. It was the same reaction she hoped to get from Mark when he showed up. *If* he showed up.

"They *can* be overwhelming," Jenna agreed. "Taken in small doses, they're pretty harmless. Only about a hundred of them live around Atlanta."

Judging from the look on Amanda's face, she might as well have said a thousand.

Jenna squeezed her hand affectionately. "Don't worry. Christopher's one of the saner McNabs. He'll only drive you crazy *half* the time."

"That's funny," Amanda replied with a smile. "That's what he says about you."

Louise, whom Jenna had always considered a bit of a complainer, made a show of squashing a stray ant unlucky enough to take a shortcut across one of the tables. "I hate bugs. Why can't we all go to a restaurant and be waited on like civilized people?"

Jenna handed Louise a stack of plastic tablecloths. "Because Aunt Penny loves the park, and since it's her birthday, she got to decide."

Louise jerked her head toward a nearby clearing, where two men were unloading a large cage from the back of a pickup truck. "That's her idea, too, you know?"

Jenna nodded, but Amanda shook her head.

"It's a dunking booth," Jenna explained. "You see, Aunt Penny loves animals and—"

"Cat crazy," Louise jumped in. "You know those old

women who live with a zillion cats and spend all their time talking to their tomato plants? That's Aunt Penny.''

"Four is hardly a zillion," Jenna said, giving her cousin a look she usually reserved for the boys. Aunt Penelope was one of her favorite relatives, and she felt compelled to defend her. ''She's a big supporter of the Humane Society. Instead of birthday gifts, she wanted a dunking booth where we could pay a dollar for the chance to dunk some poor, unsuspecting relative. I think it's a great way to make money for a worthy cause.'' She watched as the tank was maneuvered into place, the workmen surrounded by a dozen excited children and adults. ''The kids are going to love this. And I heard Dad trying to talk Uncle George into taking a turn in the tank.''

Louise brightened. ''I should have brought my checkbook. I'd pay a week's salary to dunk that smelly old goat.''

Jenna had to agree with her. Uncle George had the annoying habit of ogling any woman who came within ten feet of him. Admittedly, if it was Uncle George perched on the dunking-tank ledge, she might have to come up with a few bucks herself.

She began shifting plates to make more room at the tables.

''Wow,'' Amanda said beside her. ''What branch of the McNab family tree is *he* from?''

Jenna straightened and followed Amanda's gaze toward the parking lot.

Mark Bishop had just gotten out of an expensive sports car that looked very out-of-place among all the SUVs and minivans. Spotting her, he headed in her direction, walking in that loose-limbed, yet elegant way that made her think his hips were somehow connected differently from everyone else's. He wore designer jeans and tennis shoes that looked as if they'd just been taken out of the box.

''He's not a McNab,'' Louise declared. Louise measured McNabs in terms of wealth, and while a few members could be considered well-heeled, most were decidedly middle-class.

Jenna watched him approach. That long body so beautifully proportioned. The dark hair that sifted carelessly across his brow. She remembered how soft those wayward strands felt under her fingers, the way... Rats! There she was again, indulging in that despicable thing she'd promised herself she would stop doing—shivering with expectation and longing for something she couldn't even put a name to.

He smiled and waved at her.

"Actually," Jenna said, "that's my date."

Both women gave her a look that was too surprised to be considered polite. She was glad she'd decided to call him at his Atlanta office yesterday to invite him to this party. She still wanted him out of her life quickly, and this occasion might really do the trick. If he took one look at all this family togetherness, turned his back and walked away forever, she'd be delighted.

But in the face of all the McNab inquisitors who had started to openly offer suggestions for ways to change her divorced status into something more acceptable to the family, it was rather nice to have a good-looking man to claim as her own today.

"You made it," she said as he reached her side. He didn't try to kiss her, but he squeezed her upper arm in a friendly welcome that made her breath catch a little.

"I wouldn't have missed it for the world," he replied, though he didn't sound completely sincere. "Sorry to be late."

You'd never know he'd left her house the day before yesterday amid rock-solid tension. His declaration that he might seek legal means to resolve the issue of the baby had left her feeling sick with anxiety, but she was determined not to show it. He wasn't the only one who could put on a good show for outsiders.

She introduced him to Louise and Amanda. He had

impeccable manners, an easy way of engaging a person in conversation when he chose to, and a wonderful laugh. In less than five minutes he'd won them over.

"Anything I can do to help?" he asked.

She held up the pan of unidentified food and a plastic fork. "Tell me what this is. Does it go with the desserts or the main dishes?"

He allowed her to poke a good-size chunk of it into his mouth. He chewed for a moment. "Chicken," he claimed. A few more chews, then he grimaced. "And some sort of…marshmallow topping. Tell me this isn't what we're having for lunch."

"Not unless you get in the food line last," she told him. "Come on. We'll get you a beer to wash the taste out of your mouth. And you'll want to meet the family."

She headed in the direction of a small group of men watching two of her cousins fire up the barbecues. Not surprisingly, her father was among them, offering unsolicited advice.

Walking beside her, Mark gave her a sideways glance. "What did you tell them?"

"I told them about Petey and J.D. calling prospective husbands—no point in lying about that since neither of the boys can be trusted to keep a secret—and that since you were in town, anyway, we agreed to meet. You were all alone for the weekend, so I took pity on you and invited you to the party."

"You think they believe that?"

She shot him a tight smile. "I guess we're going to find out."

PETE LOOKED DOWN at the hamburger on his bun and thought he was gonna barf. His mom's burgers were big, thick and juicy, but cousin Larry had cooked this one. It looked like a burned-up Frisbee. No way could he eat it.

Seated at one of the tables under the picnic shelter, he

kept staring at the burger, wondering what to do. All around him bowls were being passed back and forth, but he wasn't interested in potato salad and yucky deviled eggs. He just wanted a good burger. But his mom was still busy at the food line, making sure everyone got something to eat while her own son starved to death.

He felt a nudge against his shoulder. "Try this one, instead," Mark Bishop said from beside him, and before Pete could blink, the man had switched his own burger for the burned one.

While Pete watched, Mark topped the burger with enough ketchup to choke a horse, added lettuce, tomato and cheese, then took a big bite.

"Is it gross?" Pete asked, frowning up at him.

Mark shrugged. "It sure beats chicken with marshmallows."

Pete didn't know what that meant. Probably some grown-up thing. Relieved, he started in on his own burger.

Everything was going pretty good today, and he knew it was 'cause of him. Calling Mark Bishop had turned out okay. He had a cool car, even if it was a rental. He didn't seem to mind J.D. yammering about Cyberlons all the time. Even Grampa and the uncles seemed to like him, although maybe not Uncle Chris so much. Being a detective, Uncle Chris was suspicious of everyone.

His mother finally showed up at the table with a plate of her own. It didn't have much food on it. Finding an empty place on the other side of Uncle Chris, she smiled over at him.

"If I'd known I was going to be drafted for kitchen detail, I'd have brought an apron. How are the burgers?" she asked as she wriggled her hips to make room on the bench.

"Great," Mark said, and when he caught Pete's eye, he winked.

"Thanks for watching the boys for me."

"No problem."

"Mom," J.D. piped up, "Mark knows Captain Treadway. Honest! Can I be excused?"

"*May* I be excused," their mother corrected automatically, and nodded.

J.D. hopped up from the picnic table and headed toward the end of the pavilion where the clown, with a little monkey sitting on one of his arms, was entertaining a bunch of people.

"You told him you know Captain Treadway?" Pete's mother asked. Her raised eyebrows said just how little she believed that claim. Captain Treadway was really a famous movie star, and how many people got to meet movie stars?

"Some of the last *Space Warriors* movie was filmed in Orlando," Mark explained. "I met him at a party. He seemed more interested in the open bar than in tracking down Cyberlons."

Pete, who considered himself much too old to still believe in the space adventures of Captain Treadway, tugged on Mark's sleeve. "Don't tell J.D. He thinks those movies are real."

Mark frowned. "And have him think I'm a traitor to the Federation? No way."

They laughed, and he noticed that his mom was watching them in a funny way. He wondered why.

People were starting to head back to what they'd been doing before lunch. Pete would probably get stuck playing softball, which he hated because he sucked. Maybe he'd hang out at the dunking booth. Everyone wanted to see that.

He glanced across the table at Uncle Chris, who was now holding hands with Amanda while he finished off the last of his soda. "Are you or Uncle Trent gonna take a turn in the dunking tank?"

His uncle shook his head. "Not a chance."

"All the money raised goes to a worthy cause," his mom reminded Uncle Chris.

Beside him, Mark Bishop looked at Uncle Chris and said, "Write a check. It'll be easier on your wardrobe."

Pete had the feeling his mother didn't really like that suggestion. She turned her head to stare at Mark Bishop. "Anyone can throw money at a problem. I think Aunt Penny was thinking it would mean more and produce better results if everyone had some personal involvement."

Her voice sounded okay and she didn't look mad, but Pete knew better. He glanced up at Mark, but the man just kept on eating the last of his burger. Pete guessed he wasn't so good at telling what his mom was thinking.

Across from them, the clown was coming down the row of tables. Pete noticed that, instead of the monkey, he now had a big snake wrapped around him like an old lady's shawl. Lots of people had come up to touch the monkey, but no one looked like they wanted to get near the snake.

The clown stopped in back of Pete's mom. "Hello, folks," he said. "Meet my friend, Cricket. Cricket, meet the nice lady."

Before Mom could turn around, the clown lifted each end of the snake over his head and put it on her shoulders. His mother went real still and white, and Pete felt suddenly sick to his stomach. His mom hated snakes. Even little ones they found in the backyard.

"Cricket is a Burmese python," the clown explained. When Pete's mother still didn't move, he added, "Go ahead, pet her. She's very friendly."

Pete didn't know what to do. His mother looked like she was hardly breathing. He should do something to help her, to protect her, but what? The snake was almost as big as he was, and Pete was a little afraid of it himself. He glared at the clown, wondering if anyone would be mad if he jumped up and…and what?

Mark Bishop stood all of a sudden and went around the picnic table. "Mind if I take a closer look?" he asked Pete's mother, and without waiting for an answer, he lifted the snake off her.

She barely nodded. She didn't say a single word, but he could tell by the look in her eyes that she was glad it was gone.

Mark made a big fuss over the snake, petting its head and looping it around his arm. Then he handed it back to the clown, who wandered in the direction of a group of silly McNab girl cousins who squealed and made faces as the snake got nearer.

"You all right?" Mark asked Pete's mom, bending toward her so that nobody else at the table except Pete could hear him.

His mom looked okay now. She nodded again and turned her head to look at him. "How did you know?"

He glanced across the table at Pete. "When Pete interviewed me as a prospective husband and father, he said you liked animals. Except snakes." He grinned. "Besides, it was pretty obvious. You went white as a sheet when that idiot put it around your neck."

His mother laughed in sort of a shaky, uneven way and thanked Mark. He didn't act like it was any big deal. Pete looked at the man and thought for the first time that it might not be so bad to have someone like him around. Someone who could look after his mom in ways that he couldn't.

He wasn't Daddy. But he was here.

AFTER LUNCH Mark got corralled into playing horseshoes with a bunch of old coots who wouldn't take no for an answer.

He hated horseshoes. He hadn't played the game since he'd been a kid at camp, and he hadn't missed it. It was boring and, as far as he could tell, didn't require much skill. Which made it really irritating to be losing by such a big margin to guys who didn't look like they could *pick up* a horseshoe, much less throw one.

He tossed his second horseshoe. It thudded so far from

the stake that all the old fools watching him laughed until they were wheezing.

Jenna's uncle Toddy clapped Mark on the back and shook his head sadly. "Son," he said, "the horse that wore those shoes could throw better than you."

Mark just smiled. He wished Jenna would come and rescue him, but she'd deserted him in favor of indulging in a gabfest with a bunch of the women. Probably on purpose, just to avoid him. So far today she'd been pleasant, but he suspected she was still feeling fragile about his offer of marriage. Scared, maybe. Ready to fight if she felt cornered. Ready to break under the burden she carried.

He looked around, trying to spot her. Instead, he saw Lauren Hoffman just getting out of her car. Since the other two partners of *Fairy Tale Weddings* had grown up in the same neighborhood and knew so many of the McNabs, Jenna had told him that Lauren and Vic had been invited to stop by and say hello. As Mark watched, the photographer for the magazine greeted several members of Jenna's family, stopping eventually beside Jenna's brother Trent.

Mark tensed. This could be trouble. Lauren might not know about the baby yet, but Jenna had told him her friend knew they'd been intimate in New York. How much might she divulge to Trent McNab, or anyone else, for that matter?

He forced himself to continue interacting with the older men, his movements mechanical and distracted. He was probably overreacting. The male members of Jenna's family were understandably protective of her, but they'd been cordial enough today. Well, with the possible exception of her brother Christopher. Maybe all those long silences and close looks came with the territory when you were a cop. Trent, on the other hand, seemed easygoing, big, but nonthreatening. In the cutthroat, dog-eat-dog world Mark inhabited, challenges like Trent McNab didn't scare him much.

And then, ten minutes later, Lauren detached herself from Trent's side and sought out William McNab. Trent frowned in Mark's general direction and began walking toward him.

Take it easy, Mark told himself. *Stay cool.*

He stepped away from the horseshoe game and pulled a cold beer from one of the coolers. He took a couple of swallows and nodded at Trent as the man came up beside him.

"Enjoying yourself?" Trent asked.

Mark motioned toward their surroundings. "It's a beautiful day. The beer's cold. Everybody's friendly. What's not to like?"

"You probably don't go to many of these, do you?"

"Picnics? Or family reunions?"

"Both. Not exactly your usual stomping grounds."

Mark turned toward Trent. He could feel the hostility coming off the guy in waves. Big brother had some ax to grind, but he wasn't willing to just come out and say it. "I'm more comfortable in a boardroom, if that's what you mean," Mark replied. He gave the man a twisted smile. "But I've been adept at social conversation for several years now."

Trent inclined his head toward an old man seated in a folding chair that appeared to have swallowed him whole. "You might want to avoid Uncle Fred over there. He never stops talking about the war years." Then he motioned toward a trim, older woman fanning herself with her sun hat. "And don't let Aunt Wanda get you cornered. She does astrological charts as a hobby, and she won't rest until she's told you every gruesome detail of your future."

"Good to know," Mark said, trying to keep the conversation light. "Although I could use a little insight about the future."

There was a long, uncomfortable silence then. From the corner of his eye, Mark watched the man rock back and forth on his heels. He had a feeling that subtlety wasn't one of this guy's strengths. Growing impatient, Mark took another swallow of beer, then turned to look at Jenna's brother again. "Have I done something to upset you?"

Trent got out a sound, vaguely annoyed. "Not yet. Are you going to?"

"Hadn't planned on it."

"Good."

"You seem a little uneasy."

"I was talking to an old friend of the family earlier. Lauren Hoffman."

At last, Mark thought. *Now out with it, big guy.* "I noticed she was here."

"Yeah, she's tight with my sister. They watch each other's backs."

"Nice to have a friend like that."

"Uh-huh. She told me something interesting. She said you and Jenna actually met in New York. That you were the one my sister was supposed to interview several weeks ago."

"That's true. Jenna and I spent a few hours together. We seemed to hit it off."

Trent McNab's jaw went steel-tight for a moment. "Was that before or after your fiancée threw her diamond ring in your face? Just for the record."

"Just for the record?" Mark said with a raised brow. He felt his heartbeat accelerate. He knew he had to be careful. Very careful. "I wasn't aware I was being interviewed."

Trent made a dismissive motion with his hands. Mark couldn't help noticing that they were big, too, big enough to crush a man's windpipe, no problem. "No need to get defensive. Just talking guy to guy, it must have been rough to lose a high-profile woman like Senator Winston's daughter."

"Shelby would be a catch for any guy."

"So would my sister."

"There's something we agree on," Mark said, his tone placating.

Trent moved closer, ready to get to the point. "Seems like you went pretty quickly from Shelby Winston to my sister. You know, I'm not sure I like the idea of—"

"Trent McNab!" a high-pitched female voice broke in. A moment later the family soothsayer, Aunt Wanda, had pulled Trent around. "I had a vision about you last night. Very dark stuff, let me tell you."

And she did, rushing into dire predictions and mysterious suppositions that left no room for interruptions. Mark almost felt sorry for Trent, who listened patiently and nodded in all the right places.

Mark excused himself, wondering if he'd have any more bullets to dodge before the day was through.

"YOU DON'T HAVE to do this," Jenna said for the third time.

"Sure I do," Mark replied. "You made it pretty clear how you feel about charity and cold, hard cash."

"That doesn't mean you have to take a turn in the tank."

Mark, Jenna and Pete were standing beside the dunking booth. Mark was getting ready to climb onto the ledge. He'd made the decision to do it suddenly, egged on by the men in Jenna's family and the memory of her face as she'd told him just what she thought of his usual method of making charitable contributions.

"Relax, Jenna," Mark said with a grin. "I've seen most of your family play softball today. They can't hit the broad side of a barn."

Pete squinted up at Mark. "Uncle Chris throws good. He coaches me on my pitches."

"I'll take my chances," he told him. After sidestepping Trent McNab's aborted grilling, he was feeling lucky.

Pete moved back toward the pitching line. When he was out of earshot, Jenna turned toward Mark.

"You're doing this just to annoy me, aren't you?"

"Doing what?"

"Being agreeable. You're just trying to prove a point."

"What point would that be?"

"That you can fit into my world."

He laughed. "I'm not from another planet, you know. I *have* been to functions like this before. Once I even made an appearance at a company picnic."

"And did you enjoy it?"

He considered lying, then decided against it. "Actually," he said, "no. But only because I didn't have someone like you to make sure I had a good time."

"I don't care if you have…" She stopped and stared at him, clearly frustrated. At last she said, "Fine. Think what you like. *Do* what you like. When you end up soaking wet, don't say I didn't warn you."

Before she could turn and walk away, he grasped her forearm, squeezing lightly as though testing the muscle. "Think you can knock me off that seat?"

She shook her head. "As attractive as that idea sounds, I'll leave it to the rest of the family. I figure I owe you one since you saved me from that monster."

"He was just a harmless clown," Mark said, pretending not to understand that she meant the snake. She laughed at that, a light, tinkling sound that floated away on the breeze. Then he added, "I suppose having you in my debt is one way to jump-start our relationship."

"Trust me," she replied with a skeptical look, "it's not going to help."

He made a scornful sound deep in his throat, but he suddenly thought he finally understood what Madison Avenue admen tried to convey with their multimillion-dollar beauty campaigns. In the afternoon sunlight Jenna was all peaches and cream. That thought slipped past the unguarded part of his mind, and all he wanted to do was prolong this moment forever. Forget carnival games and nosy relatives and burned hamburgers. Damn, his blood had turned to hot oil.

She left him to return to the others. He toed off his sneakers and socks, then climbed the short ladder to the ledge. If he was unlucky enough to go up against a McNab who could actually throw, he was relieved to see that the water was no more than chest high.

The day was winding down, and frankly, Mark would be glad when it was over. What he'd told Jenna was true. He wasn't used to this kind of gathering, this lazy, jovial, close-knit interaction among people who'd known you all your life. Today there seemed to be no hidden agendas. No political maneuvering. No need to see and be seen. Jenna's relatives appeared to be decent, hardworking families with a couple of oddballs thrown in the mix to make it interesting.

Still, he knew he must seem like the alien invader in her immaculate universe, and she didn't really want him here. Her agreement to his plan to date each other had come grudgingly and soaked in pessimism. Watching all the kids today with their parents had almost made him concede that she was right. Parenting looked like a lot of work. But surely if it was impossible, people wouldn't keep doing it, he reasoned. *Time to adjust,* he thought. *That's all I need.*

Trent McNab took the first turn. He hadn't sought Mark out again since Aunt Wanda had interrupted them, thank goodness.

Okay, big guy. Bring it on. Let's see what you got.

Half-a-dozen throws later, Mark was still sitting high and dry. Losing interest quickly, Trent shrugged and headed off in the direction of the beer coolers.

No competitive edge, Mark thought as he watched the man walk away. *I go up against softies like you all the time.*

A few others took a turn. Jenna's father. Even Petey and J.D. No one came close to sending him down. Fol-

lowing his predecessors, Mark came up with a few playful
taunts to egg them on, but that just made the throws wilder. He began to get bored. Maybe it was time for someone else to take a turn on the ledge.

Then Christopher McNab came up to the pitcher's
plate.

If Lauren Hoffman had said anything to Christopher
McNab, Mark could just imagine the detective pressing
her for more information. He'd be more skilled at it than
his brother. He'd also been eyeballing Mark all day, and
there'd been no disguising his look of resentment when
both Petey and J.D. had chosen to sit next to Mark, instead
of their uncle.

Mark glanced at Jenna. Her hands were clasped tightly
in front of her, and she looked pleased. He took that as a
bad sign.

May as well go down fighting, Mark thought. *No sense
letting the guy think he has me running scared.*

He whooped loudly. "Let's go, Detective," he shouted.
"Knock me off and then you can head for the doughnut
shop."

He could practically hear Jenna's gasp from the distance that separated them. To his credit, Christopher
McNab didn't rile easily. He just smiled.

He threw his first pitch. It hooked to the left. Mark
started to relax a little. Evidently the entire McNab clan
didn't have one good pitching arm between them.

"You do *see* the target, don't you, Detective?" Mark
shouted.

He waved at Jenna, giving her a look of mock terror.
She smiled back at him broadly.

Mark barely had time to register that fact before he saw
the next ball coming his way. He heard it clang against
the target. The ledge folded underneath him and he went
down. The water was so cold it made him gasp. He came
up sputtering and slinging water away.

He clung to the side of the tank, listening to the applause and whistles of Jenna's relatives as they reveled in his fall. When he opened his eyes, he saw Jenna approaching, a beach towel clutched in one hand. She passed it to him when he climbed out, her expression one of satisfaction.

Mark pressed the towel against his face. "I'll bet your brother would have gone through his entire paycheck to knock me off."

"I tried to warn you," she said smugly.

"I don't think Trent likes me. And Christopher doesn't bother to hide his feelings."

"You men act like gorillas beating your chests."

He stopped toweling his hair to look at her sharply. "Anyone else in the family I ought to know about?"

"You'll have to find out for yourself." She smiled back over her shoulder as she walked away. "But maybe it's really the McNab women you need to watch out for, not the men."

A few moments later Christopher approached him. It occurred to Mark that if he wanted to make points with Jenna, he might need to have her brothers on his side.

"Nice throw," he told the man.

The detective's lips twisted in amusement as his eyes took in Mark's soggy appearance. "You okay?"

"Nothing an hour in the sun won't take care of."

Christopher started to walk away. Mark called to him, and he swung back around with an expectant look.

"You know," Mark said, "I don't have any intention of hurting your sister."

"That's good," Christopher replied. "Because if you did, it wouldn't matter how much money you have or who you know. I'd take you apart with my bare hands. I don't spend all my time at the doughnut shop. Sometimes I'm at the gym. You understand?"

"I believe I do."

Seemingly satisfied, Christopher nodded and left him. An hour later Mark's clothes were still damp, but at least he wasn't cold any longer. He probably looked like hell, but no real damage had been done.

Most of the family had headed home—tired and happy, with lots of kisses and hugs for their relatives. Mark had felt slightly uncomfortable witnessing their goodbyes. In his entire life he could count on the fingers of one hand the number of times he'd seen his father and mother kiss in public. There were some things you just didn't do in the Bishop family, and showing affection openly was one of them.

Jenna had stayed longer to help with the cleanup. When it was finally time to go, Mark walked her to her car carrying a soundly sleeping J.D. in his arms while Pete shuffled tiredly in front of him.

J.D.'s head lolled awkwardly against his shoulder. Mark repositioned the boy more comfortably, thinking that this was probably one of the better moments of fatherhood. He wondered how it would feel to hold his own child like this. If Jenna could only be made to see reason...

She looked sideways at him. "Is he too heavy?"

"He's fine."

They reached the minivan, and he placed the boy into the car seat. Mark held the kid's space cannon and let Jenna buckle him in since he didn't have a clue how the child seat worked. On the other side of the car, Pete was already crawling into the back seat. He looked half-asleep.

J.D. roused a little as his mother finished, and his eyes found Mark's face. His smile could have melted the heart of a stone dragon. "Will you come to see us again?"

"Sure will."

The kid dropped back to sleep instantly. With a glance at Pete to make sure he, too, was buckled in, Jenna closed the car door and leaned against it. They stood there quietly for a handful of heartbeats, caught in the awkward moments of goodbye.

''Nice day,'' Mark said at last. She stood so close he could see every freckle across the bridge of her nose.

''Very nice,'' she agreed with a soft sigh.

''I like your family.''

''You were a good sport today.''

''You don't have to sound so surprised. I've got quite a few good qualities.''

She grinned. ''Evidently modesty isn't one of them.''

He inclined his head toward J.D. ''Your son thinks I'm pretty cool.''

''He's young and easily impressed. Anyone who's met Captain Treadway gets his vote. The rest of the family is a lot tougher.''

''I noticed. I thought your brother Christopher was going to ask for fingerprints.'' She blinked rapidly, and he realized that she thought that wasn't beyond the realm of possibility. With a quick laugh he added, ''I'm kidding, Jenna.''

She laughed, too, and seemed to relax. A honeyed breeze had tossed a few strands of silky brown-gold hair against her temple. He reached out and stroked them back into place, then let his forefinger gently brush the curve of her cheek. She didn't move, didn't turn away, but beneath his touch, the skin pinkened.

''You got some sun,'' he said.

She nodded and looked at him in that nervous, quick way that told him she didn't trust him at all. ''Too much exposure is such a risk. I'll have to be more careful. ''

He ignored that vague warning. He was bone-weary. The day had been as demanding as negotiating the deal for Castleman Press. Surely he deserved some reward, didn't he?

The possibility was too tempting to be postponed a moment longer. He pulled Jenna closer and lowered his head, eager to connect with her firm, sweet-tempered mouth.

She didn't resist. In fact, he saw enough in her face to

compel him to continue. *Just one,* he thought. *Just a good-bye kiss.*

But in the next moment, there was a fretful sound from J.D.'s side of the car. ''Mom! Where's my blaster?'' the little boy asked worriedly.

''Right here, pal,'' Mark replied and placed the cannon in the boy's outstretched arms.

Jenna gave Mark a small smile. Missed opportunity, that smile said. His mind rebelled, rejecting it. But he knew as well as she did that the moment had passed, so he bullied himself into acceptance. His hand shaped itself around her cheek again, and then dropped lightly to his side.

''I'll be in touch,'' he said, then walked away before he could change his mind.

CHAPTER TEN

JENNA WAS STILL THINKING about that near-kiss two days later.

She and Lauren were seated in Vic's office, and she tried to concentrate on what her friends were saying, but every time there was a lull in the conversation, her resolution slipped. She was back to revisiting those hours at the park, and in particular those moments by the car. She couldn't help it. It wasn't every day a handsome, powerful man who just happened to be the father of your baby pulled you into his arms and made your senses crumble like a wall of sugar.

Of course, the really thorny part was that kisses from Mark Bishop were the very things she should be trying to avoid. She didn't want him in her life. She didn't want complications. She certainly didn't want to get involved with a man who might find all this new-father stuff an interesting diversion right now, but who would inevitably be bored to tears by the time the first baby pictures were in an album. Staying power. That was what she needed in a man if she was ever going to get married again. Not someone who could slap the breath right out of you with the promise of a kiss.

"So we're in agreement?" Vic's voice dragged her back to the present.

Jenna knew vaguely that Vic had been discussing the details of a new advertising client the magazine had signed—Treasures, a manufacturer that specialized in wedding attire. She'd been going on and on about how the president, Avery Lundquist, was getting ready to make a huge market push nationwide and *FTW* would be ideal to showcase their fashions.

"Absolutely," Jenna said brightly. "Whatever you say, Victoria."

Lauren made a small tsking sound. "She wasn't listening to a word you said, Vic."

"Too late," Vic said flatly. "We're all going."

Apprehension flared in Jenna's stomach. Oh, dear, what had she agreed to? She sat back in resignation. "All right, I wasn't listening," she admitted. "Where are the three of us going?"

Vic, who'd been pacing the room with her usual restless energy, swung around. "Don't try to back out now. Avery is hosting a party tonight to kick off their new campaign and we're all going."

"Oh, all right," Jenna said, relaxing in her chair again. She wasn't fond of big company parties, but sometimes she had to make the effort for the sake of the magazine. Time to dig out her only cocktail dress from the back of the closet.

"Avery?" Lauren said with a raised brow. "When did you get on a first-name basis?"

"It seemed time," Vic replied with unaccustomed vagueness. "After all, he's agreed to take out a huge spread in the next issue." Vic threw a pointed look in Jenna's direction. "That ought to make you happy, since you've been harping about signing bigger clients."

"Not bigger," Jenna said. "Just more punctual about paying their bills."

"Avery Lundquist has deep pockets. He's charming. Well connected. His involvement with *FTW* means more exposure. He'll be good for us."

"Are you sure it's just *FTW* you want him to take an interest in?" Lauren asked.

"I haven't decided yet, but promise me, both of you, you'll wear something tonight that will knock everyone's socks off. We need to look professional, but sophisticated. Even sexy.'' She cast Jenna a warning look. ''Don't you dare wear that boring little blue thing you trot out every time we have a dinner to go to.''

''I'm an accountant,'' Jenna protested. ''I'm not supposed to attract attention.''

''Well, do it, anyway,'' Vic said. ''An association with Avery's company could help propel us into the big time. The right people are going to be there tonight.''

Lauren caught Jenna's eye and winked before she spoke to Vic. ''Too bad it's not a business lunch, instead of dinner. Jenna has a great red suit that really catches a man's attention.''

TEN MINUTES LATER Jenna was back in her office, wondering how she was going to fulfill Vic's request on a budget that didn't allow for many extravagances. Vic went to a lot of these shindigs for the sake of the magazine, so she had a closet full of dresses, but Jenna didn't, and she hated spending money on something she'd get so little use from. Darn it, she wished she had more spine! She needed it to stand up against her best friend's persuasive ways.

She picked up a handful of pink message slips, wondering if she'd have time to duck out of the office early and visit the boutique on the corner. She really didn't want to go to this thing tonight. She wanted to sit down with a pad and pencil and figure out the best financing she could hope to get on the Victorian.

Her secretary buzzed her, saying Mark Bishop was on hold. The perpetual serpent in her Eden. She punched the button and answered in her most professional office voice.

''You sound angry,'' he said.

''I am.''

''At me?'' he asked, and she could hear the ribbon of a smile in his voice.

"No. It's a work thing. You I just find a pesky annoyance. Like a mosquito in your bedroom at night."

"Jenna," he said in a throaty whisper that made her giddy, "you know, don't you, that your bedroom is just where I'd like to be? Is that an invitation?"

She was glad he couldn't see her face. Her cheek felt like fire when she pressed her hand against it. "Did you have a specific reason for calling?" she asked. "Besides being obscene?"

He laughed, a sound that could wrap around a girl's heart. "Actually, I did," he said. "I know it's short notice, but I'd like you to go out with me tonight."

"I can't. I have plans."

"A date?"

Did he sound disappointed? She couldn't be sure. "A business thing," she told him. "I'll be bored to death, I'm sure, but you know how these required appearances are. I'll bet they won't even have a dunking tank."

"Blow it off," Mark said. "I have something much more interesting in mind."

"Can't. I'm committed."

She heard him sigh heavily. "Tomorrow, then?"

"If I say no, will you think I'm trying to avoid you?"

"Yes. And I'll just redouble my efforts."

"In that case…yes. Tomorrow night. You can join me and the boys. It's two-for-one pizza night at Pepino's."

"That wasn't exactly what I had in mind."

She smiled into the receiver. She'd just bet it wasn't. "Sorry," she said. "You wanted to be part of my exciting life, and this is it. I've had this date set with J.D. and Petey for a week, and I don't want to disappoint them."

"I'll pick you up," he said, and didn't sound a bit discouraged.

After they hung up, Jenna speculated about tomorrow. Aunt Penelope's party had been full of other distractions, with no time for intimate conversation. Even though the pizza parlor was noisy and bound to be crowded with kids, it would really be like a first date with Mark. What would they talk about? They seemed so far beyond the usual mundane conversations already. She glanced down at her stomach. They could talk about the baby....

What if he tried to kiss her again? Allowing that would definitely be a mistake. She realized that her fingers had unconsciously gone to her bottom lip, as though she could actually feel his mouth on hers.

"Idiot!" she scolded herself.

SHE WAS LATE getting away from the office, so that by the time she reached the dress shop, it was nearly closing time and she let the saleswoman talk her into buying one of the first things she tried on.

Then, to make matters worse, everything at home was chaos. She'd forgotten her brothers were coming over to pack up her father's truck for the trip to North Carolina tomorrow morning.

The men in her family were heading off on their annual trek to the McNab-family cabin. The two-bedroom log home had served as a weekend and vacation retreat for four generations, and every year her brothers and father set time aside to drive up and winterize it. Now that her mother was gone, it was Jenna's job to guarantee that the men got up there with enough comfort food and warm clothing to make the trip enjoyable. While the boys dawdled over a quick dinner of leftovers, Jenna rushed through packing the grocery box and making sure her father's duffel bag had enough warm clothes. Christopher and her father were still arguing good-naturedly over whether there was room in the truck to take extra lumber. Trent was trying to sneak chocolate-chip cookies out of the plastic container she'd just set on the kitchen counter.

Jenna smacked her brother's hand. "Get out of there," she ordered. "Those are for the trip."

"Why can't we go?" Petey complained from his place

at the dining-room table. It was about the fifteenth time he'd asked the question.

"Because you have school," Jenna answered for the fifteenth time. In another hour she had to be at the dinner party, and she hadn't even showered yet.

Her father walked past the table and ruffled his grandson's hair. "Besides, you and J.D. have to take care of the womenfolk."

Petey looked up at him as though his grandfather was getting senile. "There's only Mom."

"Yeah, but she's more contrary than half-a-dozen women," William McNab said as he ventured into the kitchen.

"Very funny," Jenna sniffed. She wiped her hands on a kitchen towel, then pointed a warning finger in her father's direction. "*Don't* bring back any fish for me to clean. You catch 'em, you clean 'em."

Her father looked affronted. "We're going to work, not fish. We'll be slaving round the clock."

"Uh-huh. Then how come I'm packing beer and you've already stowed your fishing tackle?"

The phone rang, and while her father answered it, Jenna flew upstairs to take a quick shower. By the time she finished doing her makeup and hair, she was down to thirty minutes left before the party. Hurriedly she pulled the sleeveless, black-beaded cocktail dress out of its protective bag, stepped into it and looked at herself in the mirror.

From the front, the halter-style standup collar flattered her neck and made her look taller. The dress was tight, but slimming, and she certainly didn't look pregnant. But as soon as she turned... What had she been thinking? She'd been in a hurry at the shop, but surely she should have realized that the back of the dress, with its keyhole opening cut down to her waist, was more daring than anything she'd ever worn.

Well, it was too late to change things. Vic had wanted

elegant, professional and sexy, and she was going to get it. Now all Jenna had to do was carry it off. Slipping on her heels, she straightened her shoulders and smiled at her reflection in the mirror. *Too broad and fake,* she told herself and took the grin down a notch.

She went back to the living room, where the last of the supplies covered the couch and the men were discussing what time they should leave in the morning.

"Wow," Christopher said as she walked past him.

"I'll take that as a compliment," Jenna replied as she bent over the duffel bag to tuck her father's extra pair of glasses into a safer compartment.

"Hey, someone stole the back of your dress," Trent teased.

She rose and gave her brother a warning glance. "Don't start with me." She caught her father frowning at her. "You, either, Dad. What I'm wearing is not up for discussion."

"Never mind what you're wearing," her father said. "Who's Kathy Bigelow?"

Uh-oh. She'd rather have gotten into an argument about her dress. But buying a place of her own? She wasn't ready yet for that discussion. But here it was before her and no way out.

"She's my real-estate agent."

Trent and Christopher went still and stared at her.

Her father looked stunned. "Your real-estate agent? What do you need a real-estate agent for?"

"We've discussed this, Dad," Jenna said warily. "Was that Kathy on the phone?"

He nodded. "She wanted to know what you thought of the Victorian. I take it you're looking at houses to buy. We have most certainly not discussed *that.*"

"You're still thinking of moving out?" Trent asked.

Christopher shook his head. "Jen, that's crazy—"

"Whoa! Stop," Jenna said, holding up her hand. "We are not going to get into an argument over this now. I don't have the time, and neither do you. Especially since I've made up my mind.''

"Then I think you should consider *un*making it," her father said tightly. "There is absolutely no reason for you to move out of this house. The boys are happy here. I like having you around. Why do you want to mess with that?''

Jenna tossed a quick glance toward the dining room. Petey and J.D. weren't showing any interest in their conversation. "Dad," she said in a low voice, "you know perfectly well why I want my own place. I need my independence again. The boys need to feel as though they have a home of their own, that they belong somewhere. That they're not just visitors there.''

Her father made a face. "For pity's sake," he grumbled. "They're my own flesh and blood. How can they be considered visitors?''

"Stop being obtuse. You know what I mean.''

"I won't have it. The answer is no. You are not moving out.''

Christopher winced. Trent stared at his father, openmouthed. Even they knew he'd overstepped. Jenna tried not to let anger take over. She went to him, gave him a quick hug and planted a kiss on his cheek.

"I love you, Dad," she said softly, "and I don't want to hurt you. But this isn't your decision, it's mine. And it *is* going to happen.''

William McNab stood stock-still for a long moment. She sensed some kind of chain reaction taking place in the older man's mind. He looked as if he'd swallowed broken glass.

Finally he moved away to sling one of the duffel bags over his shoulder. "You do what you want," he said to her. Then he turned toward her brothers. "Boys, let's finish loading the truck.''

THE PARTY WAS being held at one of Atlanta's oldest, grandest and most lavish residences. A lovely, sad relic of days gone by, Misthaven had once been a Georgian-style plantation surrounded by magnolias, peach trees and mossy, towering oaks.

But then progress had come along.

Now it was the centerpiece of the Misthaven Country Club. All those lovely trees had become thirty-six holes of championship golf, and the only place to sit and sip mint juleps on a summer day was on the patio overlooking the tennis courts.

Victoria, Lauren and Jenna entered the ballroom, and Jenna immediately realized that Vic hadn't been kidding. Avery Lundquist did have money. All the stops had been pulled out tonight to make Misthaven look and feel even more special than it was. There were flowers and champagne fountains everywhere. Waiters circled the room, offering appetizers that looked more like works of art than food. At one end of the room, a full orchestra enticed couples onto a parquet dance floor.

One unexpected touch made both Lauren and Jenna do a double take. Several couples in costume passed them—Cleopatra and Marc Anthony, Romeo and Juliet, even Lucy and Ricky Ricardo.

Lauren leaned toward Vic. "What's with the costumes?"

Vic held up the invitation she'd shown the doorman. "The theme tonight is 'Lovers Throughout History.' Avery plans to do a retro line for couples who want something a little unusual for their weddings." She squinted toward a couple in medieval dress. "Is that Guinevere with Lancelot? Or Arthur?"

Avery Lundquist met them near the door. He was obviously quite taken with Vic. After catching her up in a hug that crushed the red satin of her dress, he couldn't seem to take his eyes off her.

Jenna and Lauren were introduced to him, then largely ignored. They stepped farther into the room. Lauren snagged two glasses of champagne from a passing waiter, then handed one to Jenna. "I'm going to need a lot more of these before the night is over," she said, her eyes flitting around the room.

Jenna watched Avery Lundquist laugh at something Vic had said. He was a handsome man, but didn't seem to be Vic's type. "I think Vic only wanted us to come so she wouldn't have to face Lundquist alone. Should we try to save her, do you think?"

"I say let her stew in her own juice," Lauren said. She tipped her head toward the champagne glass in Jenna's hand. "Drink up. It could be a long night."

Jenna made a face and placed the champagne on a nearby table. Now that she was pregnant, alcohol was definitely out. "I'm not in the mood," she said. "I hate these things. You and Vic are so much better at them than I am."

"You'll do fine," Lauren remarked as she glanced around. "No, in that dress, you'll do better than fine. Set your sights on one of these guys, Jen. There are a lot of possibilities here tonight, and we should both explore them."

"Still holding Brad off, I take it?"

Lauren shrugged. "Just giving our relationship a rest. Now let's see, which one of these prominent Atlantans needs to meet you?"

Together they surveyed the room. Lauren was right. A lot of Atlanta's finest were here tonight. The mayor and his cronies. Local politicians were circling like hawks, shaking hands and telling jokes to make any possible constituents feel welcome. Bankers. The press. Avery Lundquist had certainly done his homework on the guest list.

"I don't need to be fixed up. I'm perfectly capable of finding someone on my own." She scowled. That didn't come out right. "Not that I'm looking."

"Your judgment is suspect," Lauren said.

"What's that supposed to mean?"

"That was a bit of a surprise, seeing Mark Bishop at

your family's picnic. I didn't realize he was in town."
She hadn't been looking at Jenna, but now she turned and
looked her in the eye. "You didn't tell me you two were
dating."

"We're not. I mean, we're just...friends."

"You might want to look that word up in the
dictionary. Friends usually don't sleep together, and not
when they've known each other less than twenty-four
hours."

Jenna shrugged a little, wondering what Lauren would
have to say if she knew what those few hours had resulted
in. "You're the one who told me I needed to be more
adventuresome. That I needed to have more fun."

Her friend frowned. "Yeah, but since when did you
start taking my advice?"

The orchestra began playing a waltz. Several couples
stepped out onto the dance floor, including Vic and Avery
Lundquist. The smile Vic gave Jenna and Lauren seemed
genuine. As a couple, they looked good together.

In a flash of jeweled color, an attractive blonde in blue-
striped satin went by on the arm of a tuxedo-clad man.
Her head was thrown back, and she laughed as he whispered something close to her ear.

Jenna drew a sharp breath, unable to smother a gasp of
surprise. "Oh, my God!"

"What's the matter?" Lauren asked, then seeing the
direction of Jenna's gaze, she made a small sound of ap-
proval. "Oh, my," she observed. She squinted to take a
closer look. "Wait a minute. Isn't that...?"

It certainly was, though Jenna was too stunned to answer. The man wheeling the good-looking blonde around
the dance floor was Mark Bishop.

Silly, she thought. That little jolt of resentment at seeing
the blonde in Mark's arms had no business interfering
with the beat of her heart. He certainly had a right to do
as he pleased, and since she'd turned him down, who

could blame him for seeking female companionship elsewhere? Or had this been where he'd intended to take her?

She frowned, trying to remember the conversation, then determinedly putting it out of her head. It didn't matter. He was here and so was she, but not together. No jealousy. Just a little discomfort.

"Who's that brassy blonde he's dancing with?" Lauren asked. "And do you think he knows you're here?"

Jenna shook her head to indicate she had no idea. Lauren was just being catty—the woman wasn't brassy. She might be on the far side of thirty, but with that bone structure and reed-thin body, she was beautiful. Paired with Mark, who looked so tall and elegant in that tuxedo, they made a striking couple.

She saw with knee-weakening relief that Mark had twirled her toward the far end of the dance floor. Maybe it was inevitable that their paths would cross before the night was over, but not right now. Not while she could feel color still creeping up her exposed neck.

Fresh air, that was what she needed. Not too far away were double doors that led to the patio. She was through them before Lauren even noticed she'd left her side.

MARK PINNED Catherine Mevane with his gaze as he steered her safely away from a couple struggling to make their waltzing look effortless. "What do you say, Cath? You know you owe me one."

"For your help with the Doolittle merger?" she asked with an easy smile. "I've more than evened the score for that little nugget."

"Then do it because I'm asking you to. For old times' sake."

She lifted a speculative brow, clearly wondering why he found this favor so important that he was willing to trade on their past relationship. They'd been business associates and lovers once, but that had been a long time ago.

"Are you in love with her?" Catherine asked.

"Hell, no!" Mark replied. Then he added indignantly, "And what kind of question is that? She's married."

Catherine shrugged. "I have no reason to think that would stop you."

"I never mess around with the women who work for me. Bad business. Besides, Deb's crazy in love with her husband."

But he thought of how depressed Deb had sounded when he'd called the Orlando office this morning. So down in the dumps that he'd been leery of asking what was wrong. Eventually she'd told him. Alan's interview with one of the big contractors—his best hope for employment—had gone badly. The job had already been filled.

Mark had done his best to offer encouragement, saying things he wasn't very good at and recognizing that Deb didn't believe a word of it. But when he'd come to this party tonight, he'd spotted Catherine right away and realized that maybe she could help. Catherine Mevane owned a nationwide chain of copy centers based in Orlando, and Alan Goodson's talents could be just what she needed.

"Are you sure he's good?" she asked as he swung her into a wide turn.

"I talked to his former boss. Checked out his résumé. He's tops in his field, but the company just filed Chapter Thirteen with the courts to reorganize their debts."

"Then why don't you find a spot for him?"

"I can't hire him. Deb would see it as charity and eat me alive."

"So what do you want me to do, exactly?"

"All I'm asking is that you have the head of your I.T. department call him in for an interview. Alan's sharp. He'll sell himself. If he fills the bill, hire him."

"That's all?"

"That's it. I don't have any ulterior motive here, Cath.

An interview for the guy, that's all I'm asking. You look at me like I'm trying to sell you swampland in Florida.''

She laughed, more than the comment was worth, and he noticed that her eyes were shining. The smile she gave him was poignant and tinged with regret. "You know, it's a very good thing I'm so in love with my husband. If you'd have been this sweet when we were dating, I'd have done anything you wanted."

He frowned, recognizing the need to keep the conversation away from the past they'd shared. "Deb's the best assistant I've ever had. Until her husband's career gets back on track, she'll find it difficult to give me one hundred percent at the office. It's not being sweet. It's being practical."

"Ah. Practical," she said with a tight nod. "I should have known." She tilted her head at him questioningly. "Tell me something, Mark."

"Whatever you want, Cath."

"Four years ago we couldn't make a go of our relationship because you didn't want someone who would make demands on you emotionally. You told me you came stag tonight. Does that mean you're still holding out for the impossible?"

"It's not impossible," he answered matter-of-factly. "Difficult, maybe."

She shook her head and grinned. "How can such a smart guy be so dumb?"

"Aren't you glad you didn't marry me?" he countered. "Think how frustrated you'd be by now."

Before she could respond, the waltz ended. Catherine's husband was suddenly there to whisk her away. Watching the two of them, it was clear they were nuts about each other.

Mark left the dance floor. He scanned the room. What was he doing here? Being with Jenna might have made it bearable, even fun, but alone he felt emotionally isolated. People were here to be fawned over and wooed. To see and be seen. He'd been to so many of these functions in the past that they couldn't hold his interest for long.

He thought suddenly of the McNab party in the park. Laughter that had not been forced or faked. The breeze that drifted through the trees, bearing the scents of wildflowers and freshly cut grass. How quiet and peaceful the park had seemed at the end of the day when he'd stood beside Jenna at her car. He'd come so close to kissing her....

The band played a few quick notes to grab the guests' attention. Taking the stage, Avery Lundquist welcomed everyone and thanked them for coming. In a few minutes he launched into a speech that was heavily self-promoting, and the captive audience stirred restlessly.

God, I don't need to hear this. Mark pushed his way through the crowd. He escaped out one of the side doors into night air that felt crisp and reviving.

He had hoped to be alone, but he saw right away that he wasn't. Somewhat hidden in shadow, a woman stood leaning against one of the white columns.

Her short, black dress was cut very low in the back, revealing a slim, straight spine. There was something oddly familiar about it. And that graceful neck.

His gaze rested there, and then his breath caught. A small sound, but she must have heard it, because she turned her head in his direction.

He finally found his tongue. "Jenna?"

There was a small silence as they looked at each other. Her eyes flickered with a moment of uncertainty. Soft light issuing from the ballroom lay in yellow slabs across the stone patio, and Mark stepped through them to reach her side. "My God," he said when he stood in front of her. "It *is* you. You look beautiful."

He meant it. Angled moonlight lifted honey tones from her hair. The black dress exposed a tempting amount of creamy skin, and since she couldn't have been wearing a bra under it, he wondered if some wire construction in the bodice was responsible for lifting her bosom. It would be nice to find out.

Don't even think it, he warned himself.

Stray compliments clearly embarrassed her. Even in the shadows he saw her blush. "Thank you. I don't generally come to these things, but Vic insisted, since Avery is a new advertiser for the magazine." She motioned at Mark's tuxedo. "You look very handsome yourself. What are you doing here?"

"Lundquist hopes my papers will give him lots of free PR. If I'd been in Orlando, I wouldn't have bothered to come, but since I was here, I thought I'd make an appearance. And actually I've run into quite a few people I know but seldom get a chance to see."

"Like the woman you were just dancing with."

He looked at her sharply. It would have been nice to think she cared one way or the other. "Catherine Mevane," he told her. "Yes, she's an old friend."

"She's very pretty."

"Yes." Some perverse instinct kept him from elaborating.

"You looked good together. Dancing, I mean."

"Would you like to dance when the orchestra starts up again?"

"Not in these shoes."

There was a sudden burst of applause from the ballroom. They both turned to look through the multipaned windows. On the stage Avery was acknowledging all the costumed models who'd been wandering through the ballroom as lovers. A very dour and dangerous-looking Heathcliff from *Wuthering Heights* took a bow next to a pretty Cathy. Then another attractive couple, dressed in early-twentieth-century clothes came forward.

"Who are they supposed to be?" Mark asked.

As Jenna shrugged, they heard Avery Lundquist announce to the audience, "Jay Gatsby and Daisy!"

"Oh, brother," Mark muttered.

Jenna glanced his way. "You don't like the lovers-throughout-history angle? I think it's eye-catching and clever."

"I suppose people will remember it. But I think they should have given this idea more thought. Lundquist is trying to sell wedding attire. Do you realize that most of these 'lovers' didn't have happy endings? They're star-crossed or tortured or... Hell, Gatsby ends up facedown in his swimming pool! Not exactly wedded bliss there."

"Such a cynic," Jenna tsked. They watched as one of the couples went past the windows, heading for the stage. "What about them?" Jenna pointed. "Scarlett O'Hara and Rhett Butler represent true love."

He turned his head to give her a skeptical glance. "Did they end up together?"

"Of course."

"No, they didn't. Not in the *Gone with the Wind* I remember."

"But it's understood that they will get back together."

"Not by me it's not."

"Did you even *read* the book?"

"No."

"How many times have you seen the movie?"

"Once." He frowned at her. "How many times would I see *any* movie?"

She shook her head. The expression on her face told him she clearly thought he was hopeless. "I'm not sure I could ever trust anyone who doesn't get *Gone with the Wind.*"

"I take it you're a big fan?"

"Not that big. In fact, I think it's rather overrated. Scarlett's so annoying. I've always identified more with Melanie. She certainly put up with a lot."

"You're not at all like Melanie. She blends into the woodwork. That's something you could never do."

She gave him a quick, uncertain glance, then returned

her gaze to the stage. A scowl marred her delicate profile as she watched Scarlett and Rhett take their bows.

Finally she said, "I'll admit, they seem destined to be at odds forever. But clearly, in the end, Scarlett realizes that Milquetoast Ashley isn't the man for her, and she'll never be happy unless she goes after Rhett."

"I have to agree with you there. After all, Rhett has power, money, sex appeal—everything Scarlett wants and needs."

She gave Mark a narrowed sideways glance. "Spoken like a typical guy and a truly unromantic male. Is that what you think the book and movie is about? What Rhett can do for her?" She shook her head again. "You just don't get it. Don't you realize that it's really a love match between them? Rhett is Scarlett's emotional, sexual, intellectual twin. They're soul mates."

"Hogwash," he snorted. "He's better-looking than pasty-faced Ashley. He's got charisma. When Scarlett has sex with him, she sees stars."

She sighed heavily. "No wonder you're single."

The remark was only a playful insult, softened with a ravishing smile. Mark discovered that he wanted to keep that look on her face. He felt his heartbeat quicken. Sometimes she had that effect on him without any effort at all. "I thought we were talking about Rhett and Scarlett. But if you want to talk about us, I'm game."

"Oh, never mind," she said.

She turned away from the windows. Clasping her hands behind her back, she leaned against the white column again. He swung to face her, placing one hand just above her head and leaning forward slightly.

"You know," he began lightly, "Scarlett's problem isn't that much different from that of a lot of women I know. They think they want something or they go after the wrong guy, when all the time what they really want and need, the guy who's perfect for them, is right under their nose. But they can't—or won't—see it."

Jenna's chin lifted. "You're referring to me, I assume. And the perfect guy, that would be you?" Her smile was mischievous now. "Do you ever get back strain from carrying around that enormous ego?"

"No more than you do by carrying all that protective armor," he shot back with a grin. He had a feeling he shouldn't have used *Gone with the Wind* as a metaphor for their relationship. What did he know about such romantic foolishness?

Jenna had dipped her head. He brought it back up with a finger under that strong, determined chin, and watched her throat work as she swallowed. "Stop fighting this so hard, Jenna," he said softly.

Her eyes captured him, froze him in place for a moment. Then he continued, "You know we'd be good together. Like Rhett and Scarlett without the corny accents."

"I already know what we're like together *that* way, and I won't deny it was…lovely. But good sex doesn't make a good marriage."

"It doesn't seem like a bad place to start." He arched a brow. "And frankly, my dear," he said in his best Rhett Butler voice, "it wasn't good sex. It was *great* sex."

She sighed dramatically. "You overestimate yourself, Rhett."

"I didn't overestimate your response," he said, suddenly serious. His fingers moved slowly down her throat, drawing a lazy pattern. "When I touched you here, you gasped." He let his hand move lower, across the soft slope of her breasts. She didn't move, didn't even draw a breath, as though captured in that hypnotic, idling descent. "When I kissed you here, you moaned." He bent his head and nuzzled the soft skin beneath her ear. She'd put some perfume there, and its scent stole into his senses. "And when I put my tongue in your mouth, you didn't shy away." He lifted his head just long enough to find her eyes. "Did you?"

"No," she admitted on a shaky whisper.

"You don't have to be afraid of experiencing all those things again, Jenna. I'd never hurt you."

"I don't think this—"

In the pure light of the moon, her delectable mouth was an invitation he was weary of refusing. He pulled her closer, and she felt good in his arms. Better than good. "Don't think, Jenna. Don't move. You can hate me later. Right now I just want to kiss you."

He touched his lips to hers in a warm and deliberate way designed to encourage her, gently at first, waiting for her response to bloom. And it did. Her lips parted. He felt the brief touch of her tongue against his. A soft moan, a deepening breath. Then she kissed him back as if she'd been wanting to do this every bit as much as he had.

She clung to him, pressing her breasts against his chest. He slipped a hand inside her gown and stroked the soft swell lightly, until he felt her push against his palm for more. He touched her nipple and found it swollen and hard, a delight he wanted to spend more time with.

"Mark…" she breathed.

And then everything changed abruptly. She stiffened in his arms, and that meager glimpse of paradise disappeared completely. Pulling her lips from his, she lifted candid, troubled eyes to him.

"Mark, we can't do this," she said with unsteady conviction. "We're outside…"

He'd seduced women in far more unorthodox places than these obliging shadows. A little longer, and he knew he could have taken her over the edge. But in spite of that one, wild night in New York, he knew that Jenna was the kind of woman who'd spent her whole life playing by the rules. Seducing her now would serve only to intensify her unhappiness and destroy the tiny, fragile trust they'd begun to build. Mark found he didn't want to risk losing it.

He straightened and released her. He stepped back while she pulled at the top of her dress. He followed that action with open admiration and longing. He couldn't look repentant when he regretted nothing.

When she finished, she looked up at him. In her eyes he could see everything she was feeling—confusion, regret, wanting. Her body had been in rebellion against her mind.

"I want to go back inside," she said quietly.

He nodded, determined to ignore the tight, throbbing heat that still engulfed him. Instead, he took her hand and bent low over it. He touched her fingertips with his lips.

Lifting his head, he gave her a smile. "Good night, Scarlett."

CHAPTER ELEVEN

BY LATE AFTERNOON of the next day, after hours of trying to balance the books and do the accounts-payable monthly report, Jenna had a headache that wouldn't quit. Luckily the task was so annoyingly unwieldy that it left little time to think about difficult parents, unexpected pregnancies or moonlight kisses that could make a person feel endangered and spellbound both at the same time.

Vic showed up at Jenna's office, later than Jenna had expected her. But Vic evidently had more important questions in mind than why Jenna had left the party early. "Why didn't you tell me you were dating Mark Bishop?" she accused from the doorway.

Jenna put down the computer report and made a show of pretending to think. "Hmm, let's see…" She snapped her fingers. "Oh, I know! Because it's no one's business but mine?"

Vic ignored that defense of course and strode into the office. "Don't be ridiculous. Anyone dating one of the South's Ten Most Eligible has to expect to explain herself."

"I don't see why," Jenna said mildly.

"This is Mark Bishop we're talking about. A multimillionaire. A multimillionaire who just broke up with a senator's daughter under very mysterious and confusing circumstances."

"Vic, really. This is none—"

"You and Lauren claimed he was the most unromantic male since Attila the Hun. Now you're dating him? Lauren was uncharacteristically oblique when I tried to get something out of her last night, so I'm coming to the source. Explanations are in order. Start talking. You know I won't leave until you do.''

That was true. Resigned, Jenna asked, ''What makes you think we're dating?''

''Because Mark Bishop told me you were. I almost choked on my shrimp puff when he dropped that little bomb.''

Jenna sat up straighter. ''When did you talk to him?''

''At the party. He said you were going out tonight.''

''He's joining the boys and me for pizza. That's hardly a date.''

''Close enough. Now what's all this about? I tried to get the scoop from him, but he wouldn't furnish details.''

Vic levered one hip on the corner of Jenna's desk, prepared to listen. Evasion with Vic was out of the question. Jenna sighed and sat back in her chair, trotting out the amended story she and Mark had agreed on. She made no mention of what had happened in New York or her pregnancy. Just J.D. and Petey's efforts to find her a husband. It was close enough to the truth, and Jenna had repeated it so many times for various McNab relatives that it no longer made her uncomfortable to tell it.

''Satisfied?'' Jenna asked at last.

''No. There's something more you're not telling me.''

''There isn't. Now can I please get back to work?''

Vic tapped her chin thoughtfully with one red fingernail. ''You know, something he said last night makes me think there's more to this than just a little casual dating.''

Jenna couldn't help it. Against her will, her heart bucked. ''What did he say?'' she asked.

''Tony Landon was at the party,'' Vic told her in a voice primed for confidences. ''I mentioned to Mark that I'd been trying to get an interview with him for two years.'' She waved her hand dramatically. ''The next thing I know, Mark's bringing him over for introductions, and the guy's asking when we can meet. Mark had convinced him. I was so stunned I almost fell off those ridiculous red heels I bought. When I tried to thank him later, he just winked at me and said, 'Tell Jenna. With her, I need all the good press I can get.'"

Jenna felt a flicker of amusement. That sounded like something he'd say.

She must have started to smile, because Vic narrowed her gaze. "Why is he trying so hard to get in your good graces?"

Jenna hardened her features, along with her posture. "Because I represent something he's never run up against before. A woman who's not interested in him."

Vic gave her an incredulous look. "Well, for heaven's sake, why wouldn't you be? He's one of the South's—"

Jenna cut her off with a sharp movement of her hand. "Don't, Vic. I don't want to talk about it anymore."

"Very well," Vic said with a disappointed sigh. "Let's talk about something else. Debra Lee called today. She was on cloud nine. Her husband may finally have found a job."

"Wonderful!" Jenna replied, knowing that Vic had been very worried about her friend's recent problems. "Something in his field, I hope."

"Head of development for some big copy-center chain. Mevane Corporation, I think. She said it was completely out of the blue. Nothing definite yet. But I think the poor girl feels she can finally stop worrying."

Jenna frowned. "Mevane? Where have I heard that name before?" The answer was just out of reach, but something about the name struck a chord. And then it hit her. "Is Catherine Mevane the CEO?"

"Haven't a clue," Vic responded without much interest. "Why?"

"She was at the party last night. I saw her dancing with Mark."

One of Vic's finely arched brows lifted. "Well, well.

What a small world. I wonder if he had anything to do with setting this up for Deb's husband. And if he did, I wonder why he didn't mention it.''

Jenna wondered that, too. There had certainly been opportunity when she'd pointedly questioned him about the blonde he'd been waltzing with. It seemed too much of a coincidence that the night after Mark had danced with Catherine Mevane, his assistant's husband would get a job interview at her company. But if that was the case, why hadn't he bragged about his good deed? He'd wanted Vic to sing his praises to her about setting up the Landon interview. He'd have to think that helping an old friend like Debra Lee would go a long way toward melting Jenna's defenses against him.

Generous. Unselfish.

Mark Bishop was even more dangerous and diabolical than she'd thought.

MRS. WEATHERBY dropped Petey and J.D. off at Jenna's office shortly before five. They were keyed up, noisy and rambunctious. She made a mental note to speak to the older woman again. She was a godsend as a sitter, but she tended to get Petey and J.D.'s cooperation by bribing them with candy bars.

By the time Mark arrived to pick them all up, Jenna was almost looking forward to the evening. Work that day had been its most frustrating and tedious, her back ached, and the boys had been driving her crazy.

"Ready to go?'' Mark asked as he entered her office.

J.D., who had been running around the room looking for someplace to hide from Petey, bumped into Mark's legs by accident, then evidently decided he might need an adult to help him out.

"Don't let him get me!'' J.D. squawked dramatically. "He'll turn me into plasma-burgers!''

Petey was doing a passable imitation of a Cyberlon, all menacing growls and swiping claws. Suddenly surrounded, almost unbalanced by J.D.'s grip on his knees, Mark had become the only barrier that stood between Petey and J.D.'s annihilation.

He glanced up at Jenna, and it was the first time she'd ever seen him look uncertain. He clearly didn't have a clue how to handle two energetic young boys who were determined to make him part of their playacting.

"Too much sugar after school," Jenna told him as she pulled her purse from one of her desk drawers.

Ahh, of course, Mark's nod seemed to say.

In that moment she could almost feel sorry for him. The boys were going to be a handful tonight. Mark claimed he wanted to experience family life up close, and he was going to get the full treatment by two little experts.

When they were both like this, there were times when even *she* wanted to run away.

Jenna came around the desk. The lower half of Mark's body looked as if it had grown two pint-size attachments, but she ignored the plea she saw in his eyes.

"All set," she told him. "Let's go eat pizza." And then, because she could hardly hear, thanks to Petey's roars and J.D.'s squeals of terror, she added sternly, "Boys! Settle down."

They stopped immediately and ran ahead to fight over who was going to push the elevator button. Jenna smiled as she watched them charge down the corridor. Her secret weapons.

"Are they like this very often?" Mark asked as he tucked the tail of his khaki shirt back into his pants.

She thought she heard disapproval in his voice, and he definitely frowned as he spied evidence of a small, grubby handprint on the leg of his pants. No way to remain elegant around her two hooligans.

She grinned at him. "No. Usually they're much worse."

PEPINO'S PIZZA and beer weren't the finest in Atlanta, but the place did offer one of the best perks any parent could wish for. An extensive games room complete with indoor playground.

After polishing off a large pizza and two pitchers of soda, Petey and J.D. tore off in the direction of the ball-crawl cage, while Jenna and Mark were left alone at the table. They were seated on bench seats across from each other, and once the boys were out of sight, Jenna turned her attention to Mark.

"Would you mind answering a few questions for me?" she asked.

He cocked his head at her. "You sound like your brother Christopher. But go ahead."

"Were you really an only child?"

"Yes."

"Have you been studying up on how to handle children?"

"No."

She frowned.

"What's the matter?"

"I was watching the three of you during dinner while you were telling the boys that story about the burglar who got stuck in the air-conditioning duct. You had them… enthralled."

He looked pleased, but a little embarrassed. "Well, that's really not too surprising, is it? It's a funny story. What kid wouldn't enjoy it?"

"No, I mean it," she said, realizing that she couldn't begrudge him an honest compliment. "You were very natural with them." She dropped her glance for a moment, then brought her eyes back up to meet his. "Much better than I expected."

"Thanks."

They sat in silence for several long moments. The room was noisy with customer chatter, and he leaned across the table so that she could hear him better. "You know, it would do my ego an enormous amount of good if you'd stop sounding so amazed when I do something right."

Her cheeks felt blazing hot. "I'm sorry. I think I must be a suspicious person by nature."

He grinned and leaned back. Suddenly he rose. "Want anything?" he asked, gesturing at their empty soda glasses, and when she shook her head, he added, "Then sit here and be repentant. I'll be back."

She watched him make his way to the order counter. He was every woman's dream. Handsome. Powerful. Confident. But more important on her list of priorities were qualities that made him seem like the kind of man she could admire. He cared about his employees. He didn't take himself too seriously. He was much better with children than she'd expected. Perhaps even better than he knew.

But she still couldn't help thinking he was all wrong for her. No matter how he made her feel when he touched her—humming and alive, as if everything within her had been wired with electricity. No matter what he said or did.

The circumstance that had brought them back together again—her pregnancy—was famous for being the shakiest, most flawed foundation for marriage. You didn't have to look very far to find couples who had wed for this reason—filled with good intentions and foolish hope—only to wind up in divorce court. It was ridiculous to think she and Mark wouldn't.

And then where would she be? What kind of havoc would that wreak on her family?

He returned to the table, and Jenna straightened with a sigh. This time he sat beside her, facing outward, his elbows propped behind him on the table. He'd bought a draft beer, and by the slight grimace on his face as he took a sip, she could tell it still wasn't the quality he was used to.

After a few swallows he turned his head to look at her.

He was closer than she liked. His nearness made her light-headed.

"My turn to ask questions," he said. "What was your husband like?"

She stared at her clasped hands, trying to think how to respond. She didn't mind the question, not really. Her marriage to Jack Rawlins and their subsequent divorce had long since ceased to be an issue. She drew a deep breath and looked at him. "You want the answer I would have given you when we got married? Or how I would have described him a year ago, after the divorce was final?"

"I want to know what made you think marriage to him was desirable."

She told him. All the little things that had drawn her to Jack. All the ways he'd made her feel special and valued. He'd been a dreamer, impetuous and fun-loving, and he'd encouraged her to fight for independence from her family, something she'd never have accomplished on her own.

When she finished, she gave Mark a rueful look. "Of course, the biggest thing going for Jack Rawlins in *my* book was that my entire family hated him. He was forbidden fruit from that moment on."

He sent her a puzzled frown. "This issue you have with your family. After having met them, I can see that they're very protective of you. But why is that such a bad thing?"

"It's not bad," she said with a shake of her head. "It's just frustrating. You were an only child, so you have no idea what it's like to be the baby of the family. Especially the only girl. Everything you do or say gets second-guessed. No one takes you seriously." She took a calming breath, realizing how easily she could sound irrational about them. "My brothers and father are in North Carolina right now, getting the family cabin ready for winter. I'm getting ready to make an offer on a house of my own, and I'll bet you they're sitting around the dinner table right now debating the best way to talk me out of it."

"You're pregnant. You're unmarried. You have two growing boys on your hands. Now you want to buy a house? Isn't it understandable that your family would worry about the added stress?"

"I can handle it," she claimed. "They need to let go."

"Maybe," he said in a considering tone, "they haven't been willing to let go because you weren't ready to have them let you go."

She pulled away, casting him an annoyed look. "What's that supposed to mean?"

He made a small sound of protest. "I don't want to fight with you, and I can see I've touched a nerve. I'm just saying that your divorce put you through the wringer. You've probably had a lot of doubts. Maybe you haven't been ready to reassert your independence, and your family sensed that. It's possible, now that you're eager to go after it, they'll pull back on their own."

"They haven't so far, and my father and brothers aren't known for picking up subtle hints."

He shrugged. "Maybe they'll surprise you."

"That wouldn't be a surprise. That would be a heart-stopping shock."

"I think you underestimate them. I watched them with you at the picnic. They're crazy about you and your sons. And as annoying as it was to be quizzed like a street criminal about my intentions, it made me kind of envious. When you grow up as an only child, you'd give anything to know there's someone else on your side."

"Sometimes they aren't on your side. Sometimes they're standing in front of you, blocking your way."

He shrugged again. "I guess it's just the different ways we grew up. But I can't help but think that it would be nice to be part of a family like yours. Knowing where you belong. Who loves you. Who could never hurt you."

His comments made her look at him more closely. She realized she didn't know what his family life had been like.

But just as she was about to ask, he said, "You know, if you're really considering buying a house, I can make that happen. Marry me, and I'll give you any house you want."

Jenna sucked in a breath. Money. Was that all he thought she needed? Security? Financial freedom? What about good old-fashioned love between a man and a woman?

With a frustrated shake of her head, she said, "Please don't say things like that. I'm perfectly aware of how easy your money could make my life. But as attractive as that offer is, you can't buy me."

"I'm not trying to. Please don't feel insulted. I'm only reminding you of the fringe benefits I'm offering."

"Can we talk about something else?"

"All right. Let's talk about your divorce. Was it ugly?"

That topic of conversation wasn't much better, but at least it didn't make her uncomfortable.

"It wasn't ugly," she said. "Maybe that's part of what I resent. The fact that he didn't care enough to fight for anything from our marriage. Not even the boys. Don't get me wrong, I'm very grateful he didn't, because I can't imagine not having them in my life. But it hurt to realize he could turn his back on them—on everything—that easily."

It surprised her that by the time she finished speaking, a sizable lump had formed in her throat. She was long past regrets over her failed marriage. Or so she'd thought.

An awkward silence descended. She looked down at her plate, fiddled with the slice of pizza she'd barely eaten. It looked cold and unappetizing.

When he leaned closer to her, she drew a sudden, deeper breath. Their eyes met. He searched her face while she went very still.

"Your ex-husband was a damned fool," he murmured.

A curious fluttering sensation started in the pit of her stomach. Such a silly reaction. He was so close she could see the faint pulse below his jawline. She wanted to press her fingers against it, feel the life thrumming there. What was wrong with her that she could never seem to keep her head around this man?

He grinned. "You've got that suspicious look in your eyes."

"Not suspicious," she denied reflexively. "Cautious." She tried to make her voice crisp. She licked her lips, realizing that she'd failed completely. Finally she looked him directly in the eye and admitted, "I don't want to be hurt again, Mark. You make me feel like I'm sliding downhill very fast—without anything along the way to grab on to."

He brushed his forefinger with whispery gentleness across her upper lip. They might have been marooned here, just the two of them, for all the notice she took of the people around them. "Maybe you shouldn't try to grab on to anything. Maybe I'll be waiting at the bottom, ready to catch you."

She wanted to move back, but not a cell in her body seemed to be at her command. "I don't see you there."

"Maybe you just need to look harder," he said in a light, teasing voice. When she glanced away, he asked, "What's the matter?"

"I wish you wouldn't say things like that."

"Why? I'm being sincere. I've been honest with you from the start about my intentions. There are so many ways I can make you happy, Jenna. And I'm not just talking about the money."

Desperate to get back on more even footing, she indicated their surroundings with spread hands and a disparaging glance. "What? Give up this lifestyle? How could I?"

He grimaced. "I'll admit it *would* be difficult."

"Bad pizza and weak beer are staples in my family. I can't see them becoming part of yours."

He took the final swallow of his beer and made a face

as he pushed the empty bottle across the table. "I'm discovering that when the company is right, the most mundane meal becomes a feast."

She couldn't help laughing at that. "No wonder you were on the Most Eligible list. Were all of you issued some sort of manual? *A Thousand and One Ways to Turn a Girl's Head?*"

"Of course." He leaned close enough that his voice was only a soft rumble against her ear. "Want to find out what I learned in the chapter on kissing?"

He began to stroke her back slowly, seductively. She straightened, feeling the blood leave her cheeks. "I think we've already covered that part."

"You mean last night? That was just practice."

"Mark—"

He nuzzled her neck. "Didn't you say your father was out of town? We could go back to your place, put the kids to bed. Work on our technique."

A warm wave of dizziness washed over her, but it wasn't just Mark now. It was something else. Something unknown and frightening. "Mark—"

"Wait until you see what the manual says about foreplay."

She clutched his arm to keep from swaying. "Mark! Stop!" She closed her eyes tightly for a moment, then opened them again. But the room had started a slow spin, and she couldn't seem to make it go away. "Get the boys, will you? I want to leave."

Her tone must have alerted him that something was wrong. He frowned, giving her a sharp, worried look. "What is it?"

"Something's...not right. I feel sick to my stomach. And a bit faint. I think we should go to the hospital."

THREE HOURS LATER Mark drove them home from the emergency room. The boys were asleep in the back seat, but that wasn't the only reason neither she nor Mark barely spoke as he maneuvered the dark streets of Atlanta.

Jenna's obstetrician had met them at the hospital. The doctor believed her symptoms were caused by nutritional deficiencies, but was concerned about the small amount of bleeding. Jenna had blood work done and was now under orders to spend the next forty-eight hours in bed. She was to rest while they waited for the test results and to see if there was any further bleeding.

Jenna tried not to read too much into the doctor's expression, the slight hesitations. But the truth was, she was riddled with fear, terrified that she was going to miscarry.

The house she'd grown up in looked oddly cold and uninviting as they pulled into the driveway. She'd forgotten to leave on a light.

The boys roused as Mark came around to her side of the car, indicating he intended to carry her inside. Jenna tried to refuse. It might worry Petey and J.D., and her obstetrician had said she didn't need to be treated like an invalid. Mark listened to her protests, then ignored them as he lifted her with ease and carried her up the walkway. The boys trudged along in front of them.

She had to admit it felt good to be in his arms. Protected and safe. The way she'd felt at the hospital when he'd held her hand and stroked her arm gently as they'd waited to hear what her doctor had to say. She should have thanked him for those moments, should have told him she was glad he was there with her, but the thick, heavy fear that had settled around her heart had left her speechless.

He took her upstairs and into her bedroom, setting her down on the bed as if she were made of porcelain. She sat up awkwardly, giving him an embarrassed, wobbly smile.

"Sit still," he instructed. "I'll put the boys to bed and be right back to help you."

It was her guess that he wouldn't be gone long, but she

couldn't bear the idea of him helping her undress. She scooped up her nightgown from the bottom of the bed where she always left it and had just settled it over her hips when he came back into the bedroom.

He frowned to see her sitting on the side of the bed. He sat down beside her, giving her a smile as he tucked a stray wisp of hair behind her ear. "Damn, I see I've missed my opportunity to help you out of your clothes."

She knew he was trying to lighten the mood, but she couldn't quite manage another smile. Did she look anything like she felt—insubstantial and a little lost?

"Are the boys all right?" she asked. In spite of her repeated assurances to the boys that she was fine, the pair had been white with worry at the hospital.

"They were almost asleep before I got them into bed. Do you want anything to drink?" he asked. "Something to eat?"

She shook her head. The elastic cuff of her nightgown was worn and too loose. She fiddled with it, absorbed in making it stay in place at her wrist.

"Talk to me, Jen," Mark said softly, running the back of his hand along her arm.

Her chest felt too tight to allow her to answer.

He reached out and began rolling the sleeve of her nightgown up over her wrists. "It'll be all right," he said. "Everything's going to be fine."

She looked at him then. "You don't know that."

"I've met your family. The McNabs are a hardy bunch."

He finished pleating her sleeve into place. Wordlessly she offered her other arm and watched his movements. The silence between them grew. Not companionable, but melancholy and lifeless. She felt chilled to the bone, but against her flesh, his touch seemed warm and reviving.

"When I found out I was pregnant," she said in a quiet tone, "I wanted the problem to just go away. I don't feel that way now, but I can't deny that I didn't want this baby at first.''

His head was bowed as he focused on his task, but she saw the corners of his mouth lift ruefully. ''So you think you might be punished for having unkind, selfish thoughts? God might take this baby away? I hope that's just your fear talking, because if it's not, I'll be doing a slow roast for the devil.''

''I don't want to lose this baby, Mark.''

His head jerked up. ''You're not going to,'' he said in a calm, steady voice.

So few words. She wanted desperately to believe them. She felt foolishly close to tears. He looked as he always did—self-assured, composed, not a worry in the world. But the skin along the knuckles of his hand were dead white against her royal-blue nightgown.

He finished the second sleeve and gave her hand an indulgent squeeze. Rising, he said, ''Time to get under the covers and go to sleep. We can talk more in the morning.''

She frowned. ''You're coming back?''

''I'm not going anywhere. How comfortable is that couch downstairs?''

''You can't stay here.''

''Sure I can,'' he said, lifting the covers so she could slip between the sheets. ''Your father and brothers are out of town. It's too late to call anyone else. It's settled.'' As though soothing a child, he brushed hair away from her forehead, then planted a quick kiss on her brow. ''If you need anything during the night, don't get up. Just call out. I'm a light sleeper.''

He turned off the bedside lamp, plunging the room in darkness. She watched his silhouette move among the shadows of her room.

''Mark…''

''Hmm?'' he said from the doorway. The hall light was

off, as well, so he was no more than a black ghost against an even blacker void.

"Thank you for staying. I'm sorry you have to sleep downstairs. I mean, the couch is old and awfully uncomfortable, and you're probably used to the best."

She heard him chuckle. "I'm not that spoiled. I'll manage just fine. Go to sleep, Jenna."

CHAPTER TWELVE

FUNNY HOW in the throes of passion every woman was unique.

In his dream Mark was with Jenna, reliving that one marvelous night in New York. There were moments that still stood out in his mind even after all these weeks, even after all that had happened. But it was her breathing he remembered most.

The way it came hot and fast when he touched her. Those soft, frantic little nips of air she'd tried to catch when he ran his fingers slowly down her abdomen and beyond. The shivery, incredulous gasp she gave as he whispered in her ear all the things he intended to do. *Lovely. Perfect.* He remembered every single breath.

And somewhere between sleep and consciousness he could hear them now. The slight whoosh of air in. Out. In. Out. *Ah, Jenna. Wait for me, sweetheart.*

He was smiling when he opened his eyes—and discovered Darth Vader inches from his nose.

Darth Vader with a pint-size body clad in pajamas printed with space ships. J.D.

Mark blinked, tried to focus. He put his hand out, letting it fumble over the mask until he found the knob that turned off the ominous breathing sounds the toy made. "Morning," he said in a voice that sounded rusty and thick. "Any chance you could back off a bit, Darth?"

The kid took a couple of steps away from the couch, then tilted the mask so that it rested on the top of his head. He frowned at Mark. ''Did you know you smile when you sleep? Can we have hot dogs for breakfast?''

Mark levered himself upward. He scrubbed his face with his hands. He was a night person, and from the looks of the sunlight coming in the windows, it was barely sunup. Through the doorway he could see Pete sitting cross-legged in front of the television in the family room. The sound was turned down, but a couple of cartoon mice seemed to be busy beating the crap out of a cartoon cat.

''Does your mother let you have hot dogs for breakfast?'' Mark asked.

''No.''

''Then I'm guessing my answer has to be no, too.''

''Mom's still asleep. We left her alone, like you said last night.''

He patted the kid's shoulder. ''Good boy,'' he said with a yawn.

J.D. moved back to join Pete. Drawing a fortifying breath, Mark went quietly upstairs to check on Jenna, as he had a couple of times during the night.

She was still asleep. He stood beside the bed and watched her for a few moments. Those dark lashes that were longer and thicker than any woman had a right to have lay against cheeks that were pink with life now, no longer white with fear. One hand was folded under her chin. It moved infinitesimally with every breath. She looked relaxed, sweetly at peace, vulnerable. He had the undisciplined thought that he'd like to wake her with a kiss, draw her close just out of a powerful need to touch her. He wouldn't of course. She needed the rest.

Last night still seemed like a nightmare. Those hours in the emergency room had crawled by. It was frustrating to realize that there was so little he could do, no money he could throw at the problem, no team of experts he could browbeat into giving him quick and easy answers. Nothing.

In many ways the baby he and Jenna had created hadn't

really existed for him until last night. Before then, it had remained a nameless, faceless challenge that would have to be dealt with sooner or later. Like a thorny business deal that wouldn't come together until both parties sat down and worked out all the details.

But now suddenly, crazily, everything had changed. A fierce sense of his responsibility had gripped him. The baby had become real. Because Jenna's fear was real.

She sighed heavily, and her lashes fluttered open. She looked up at him with a groggy, faint smile and scooted farther away, an invitation for him to sit down. He did, taking her hand so that he could brush her fingers with a kiss. Last night her flesh had been ice-cold. This morning it felt warm and supple.

"Did I wake you?" he asked.

She shook her head. "My internal clock. Time to get the boys ready for school."

"They're up. I've got it covered. Hot dogs have already been vetoed for breakfast."

"There's cereal in the pantry."

He was glad to hear it. Truthfully, he'd never tried to cook a real breakfast. That was what Mrs. Warren, his housekeeper, was for.

She stretched an arm over her head and gave a contented sigh.

He had to look away from her momentarily, had to pummel his senses into submission, because desire was there in an instant, hot and hard to control. "How do you feel?" he asked.

"Rested. Like last night was just a bad dream." She gave him a satisfied look. "I'll get up in a minute and deal with the boys."

"No, you won't. I'll deal with them. At least for the next forty-eight hours."

"What? No. You can't."

"I'll try not to be insulted by your obvious lack of confidence in my ability," he said on a short laugh.

"Your family's out of town. I'm available. What's the problem?"

"The problem is…" She stopped, looking frustrated.

"You don't want me mucking around in your life when you're trying so hard to get me out of it," he finished for her. "But this is doctor's orders now. It's two days. Not two years."

"I have very good friends who can help me."

"Who?"

"Lauren can come over." She frowned. "Oh, no, she can't. She's leaving today for a photo assignment in Maine. I'll have to ask Vic."

He laughed out loud at that. "Oh, I'd like to see her with your kids. One grubby hand on her best suit, and they'll both get banished to their room."

"It's true she doesn't like kids very much," she admitted.

In the end, he talked her into it, although he had to promise that he wouldn't treat her like a complete invalid, wouldn't hover, wouldn't boss her around and most of all, wouldn't hesitate to consult her if he ran into problems with the boys. He agreed to get Pete and J.D. off to school and then go to work at the Atlanta office, since there were still accounting problems to deal with. In return, she promised to stay in bed.

"What would you like for breakfast?" He posed the question just as he was about to close her bedroom door.

"Dry toast and milk? Maybe some fruit?"

The way she asked made him think she didn't have much hope that he could pull off such a simple request. He scowled at her. "You know, you're going to feel awfully humbled when forty-eight hours are up and I've succeeded beautifully. There's nothing here that I can't handle."

OF COURSE, life came with certain…challenges that could make a person want to cry uncle. Mark met a couple of them that afternoon and evening.

Up until then, he'd done really well. Pete and J.D. had helped him sort through their wardrobe. They looked presentable, if not exactly coordinated. He'd dropped them off at the elementary school with only one missed turn. He'd settled Jenna in for the day with a stack of magazines and books, bottled water and the portable television from the family room. He'd even managed a fruit salad for her lunch. Leaving the telephone number to his Atlanta office and cell phone by her bedside table, he went to the office and slapped everything into his briefcase that he planned to work on the next couple of days at Jenna's dining-room table. He called his department heads together for a quick meeting, letting them know they could reach him by cell phone but it had better be damned important. Then he stopped off at a grocery store with a short list of items designed to please young palates.

He was pretty proud of that particular decision. He'd considered setting up home delivery of gourmet meals with a local catering company, then decided against it. The boys probably wouldn't eat anything that looked remotely good for them, and Jenna was likely to think he'd taken the easy way out—using cold cash to solve problems he should have been able to handle on his own.

Later in the day he picked up Pete and J.D. after school and got them settled playing in the living room. Jenna had been sleeping every time he checked on her. Everything seemed to be on track for dinner. So all in all, he thought, he'd managed things nicely.

Then disaster hit.

Tuesday, it seemed, was laundry day.

Mark had never done a load of laundry in his life. No matter how screwed up his childhood might have been, he'd come from a life of privilege. He hadn't even washed a pair of jeans in college. There were any number of girls willing to take on that chore to impress him.

He followed J.D. into the utility room beside the kitchen. The kid had his arms full of clothes and had made it pretty clear that something needed to be done if he was going to have anything clean for peewee soccer practice.

Mark stood before the washer and dryer, awed. He'd seen a set before, of course, but he'd never seen anything as intimidating as the Dominator Combo 2006.

They sat there like white, bright, hulking SUVs. The 2006 had to refer to the number of dials and gauges there were between the two machines. Surely on a level with the cockpit of a jumbo jet.

Over the top of his dirty clothes, J.D. looked up at him. "Grampa and our uncles got it for Mom last Christmas," he explained.

"Nice," Mark said absently. "Where do you get in?"

J.D. giggled, then sobered immediately. "Are you really gonna get inside?" Then looking at Mark suspiciously, he added, "Do you know how to wash clothes?"

"No. Do you?"

J.D. shook his head and pointed toward a shelf over the combo. Boxes and bottles, like a lineup of soldiers, stood waiting to do wash-day war. Bleaches. Brighteners. Static reducers. Things to get stains out. Things to put softness in. Mark stared at them and made a mental note to give his housekeeper a raise when he got back to Orlando.

He took the clothes from J.D. and tossed them into the washing machine. They looked pitifully small in the cavernous tub.

A basket of waiting laundry sat beside the washer. "Might as well make it a real load," he told J.D., and upended those items into the machine, as well.

The kid gasped, and his eyes went wide. "You're gonna do all of it together?"

Mark frowned. "Not a good idea?"

"Mom always does a bunch of different ones. And she likes to read these." He pulled out the tag from the back of his shirt so that Mark could see the garment-care instructions.

Better think this through a little. He seemed to remember one of his college roommates ending up with a bunch of pink underwear because he'd forgotten to pull out a pair of red socks. He reached into the washer and removed everything he came across that was white. One of the first things he encountered was a bra, all lacy and delicate, dangling at the end of his hand like a fish on a pole.

"Mom wears that," J.D. told him.

"I figured."

He tossed the item back into the basket, trying not to envision Jenna wearing it. And *not* wearing it.

"Go find your brother," he instructed J.D. "Tell him to get his laundry together and bring it downstairs. Quietly, so you don't wake up your mom."

After the boy trooped off, Mark twisted a few of the dials on the machine. The washer growled and jerked, started dispensing water, stopped, then began ticking like a bomb. That didn't seem like a good sign. He shut it down.

He couldn't let this thing get the best of him. Time to call in an expert. He yanked his cell phone out of his back pocket and punched in his housekeeper's number, then remembered that she'd taken vacation time while he was in Atlanta.

Time to use my second lifeline. He dialed the office in Orlando, praying that Deb hadn't gone home yet.

She hadn't, God bless her. She picked up his call on the second ring.

He didn't waste time with greetings. "Deb! Help!"

"What's the matter?"

"What do you know about doing laundry?"

"That I hate it more than vacuuming."

"Ever hear of the Dominator 2006?"

"The Cadillac of washers and dryers."

"I'm trying to use one." He lifted a dusty booklet from

one of the shelves, leafed through it and then tossed it back down. "I just found the instruction manual. I think it takes a degree from M.I.T. to operate this thing. Can you walk me through it?"

Deb was great at not wasting time asking questions, but clearly she couldn't resist revealing her shock. "*You're* trying to do your own laundry? Do you have a camera around? I want a picture of that."

He scowled into the phone. "Just help me out here. When I turn it on, it sounds like it's…digesting something. Or someone. I'm not kidding." J.D. had come back and was now tugging on the tail of Mark's shirt. "Hold on a minute," he told Deb.

He gave the boy his full attention, and J.D. made a face that said bad news was on the way. "Petey says you can't order him to do anything, and he doesn't care if his laundry gets done or not."

That sounded worse than trying to deal with the Dominator. Pete had been subdued this morning and even this afternoon. Mark had chalked it up to the late night or kids and their moods and left him alone, but maybe something was going on in the boy's head that needed to be addressed.

He returned the phone to his ear. "I'll call you back, Deb. Do some research on this thing, will you?" She was still talking when he snapped the phone shut.

He left J.D. carefully sorting clothes into different colors and went upstairs to the bedroom the boys shared. Spiderman vied with spaceships for opposite sides of the room. Pete was seated at the foot of his bed, his knees drawn up around his chin, a pile of dirty clothes covering his sneakers.

Mark hunkered down on the floor facing him, then reached out to tap his knee. "As another guy, I understand liking to hang out in our favorite clothes as long as possible, but I hear Tuesday is laundry day in the Rawlins household. Want to hand those over? Or do I have to send J.D. in to blast you with his space cannon?''

The boy tucked his face into his knees until all Mark could see was a pair of very hostile dark eyes. ''You can't tell me what to do,'' Pete said in a muffled voice. ''You're not my father.''

One thing about kids, Mark thought, they were seldom subtle. In his early years in journalism, he'd gone toe-to-toe with terrorists, the most slippery politicians, even a couple of serial killers. He realized that, right now, he would gladly have faced any of them, rather than one surly seven-year-old boy.

He drew a breath. ''No, I'm not your father. But I'm trying to help your mother. Why don't you try helping her, too?''

Pete's eyes flashed hotly. ''Why? It doesn't matter. She's just gonna die, anyway.''

That took Mark aback. God, where had that come from? ''What? Of course she's not going to die.''

''She could. My friend Shawn Blake told me his mother almost died when she had him, and that lots of moms die when they try to have babies they shouldn't. You don't go to the hospital all suddenlike unless something bad happens to you.''

''Lots of people have to go to the emergency room,'' Mark said in the most logical voice he had in his arsenal. ''For a lot of different reasons. But your mother is not dying, Pete. She had a scare about the baby last night, and the doctor wants her to rest a little. That's not the same as dying.''

''How do you know it won't be like that?''

The boy sounded so full of bleak anguish that Mark reached out to touch him. Pete didn't as much flinch away as shrink into himself. The message was clear, though. He didn't want that kind of comfort.

Mark had to admit he didn't know what to do. If Jenna married him, he could give her a life free from worry and hassles. He could protect her, provide for her. He might even one day manage to conquer the Dominator.

But he had nothing to draw from when it came to handling her children. No manuals. No cheat sheets. Not even past experience in his own family. Everything would have to be off-the-cuff. Gut instinct. Plain dumb luck. And frankly, he wasn't sure he could trust that.

But Pete was waiting for him to say something. Anything. Guarantees seemed too arrogant. Promises seemed too vague. Maybe, like Jenna, the kid had a practical streak in him.

"Well," Mark began, trying to sound as if he'd given the matter a lot of thought, "I guess I think everything will be all right because I know that your mother's a smart woman. She'll do exactly what the doctor tells her. And the doctor's smart, too. If she wasn't, I'd get the best baby doctor in the whole country to come and see your mom."

Pete lifted his head a little. Mark could tell he was listening.

"And we're smart, too," Mark went on. "You and me and J.D. We'll take good care of her and not let anything bad happen. And when she has this baby, we'll all sit around and congratulate ourselves on just how smart we were." He ducked his head, trying to make direct eye contact. "What do you say, Pete?"

The boy took a few moments to consider that. Then he asked, "Are you gonna be here when the baby gets born?"

That was a path Mark didn't want to take. Cautiously he replied, "I *want* to be here."

"J.D. isn't really that smart," Pete said very seriously.

"Then it's a good thing he has you to help him find his way." He plucked a couple of shirts off the boy's toes, feeling as though he'd been trying to maneuver his way through a dark cave and had just come out into the sun. "I could use a little help myself," he said. "What do you know about that monster downstairs that washes your clothes?"

"It's scary."

"Yeah, I know. Let's go see what we can do to tame it. Before it eats your little brother."

THE SECOND CRISIS came later that evening and from an unexpected source. J.D. Just when Mark was beginning to let his guard down.

He knew he'd gotten off easy last night. The boys had been tired, so they'd been asleep on their feet by the time Mark got to their bedroom. But tonight they found a dozen excuses to delay lights-out, after an endless bath time that made wrestling an alligator seem like a walk in the park.

Clearly both J.D. and Pete missed their mom's presence, but Mark was determined that she wouldn't be disturbed for such a small chore. How difficult could it be to scrub two small bodies and trot them off to bed?

Evidently, more difficult than he'd ever imagined.

The boy's bathroom looked like a toy shop, with action figures and miniature submarines lining the side of the tub. Pete and J.D. played more than they washed so that Mark never was completely sure they'd done a thorough job. By the time he'd gotten them out of the tub, clothes littered the floor, along with what seemed like a dozen wet towels. Water was everywhere, including all over him.

His sense of humor had eroded a little. What had appeared to be a fairly simple task had ended up consuming more than an hour, and neither of the boys were taking anything he said seriously.

He pulled the plug on the bathwater, then began collecting towels. Pete and J.D. stood giggling in the altogether, sliding on the wet tiles as they shoved at each other.

"Why don't you two put on your pajamas?" Mark suggested firmly as he pulled them apart.

"Mom always helps us," Pete replied.

"Surely you can manage to put on your own for just one night, can't you?" J.D. was fishing around in the cooling bathwater, searching for a plastic space warrior and getting wet again. "J.D., stop," Mark said in his best imitation of a stern father. "Go get into your pajamas."

The boy blinked up at him. "But Mom—"

"Your mom is asleep. I want her to stay that way. Come on, you guys. We can do this without help from your mom. Now go. *Quietly.*"

They trooped off without another word. Mark gathered dirty clothes and placed them in the hamper. Could the wet towels go in there with them? Hell if he knew. The bathroom was still filled with steamy heat, and a line of sweat trickled down his back. He lifted two pairs of grubby sneakers by the laces, wondering if he was supposed to do anything special with them.

No sounds came from the bedroom the boys shared. Good. Maybe he'd convinced them to settle down. On second thought, maybe he ought to check on them.

The bedroom was dimly lit. A night-light cast deep shadows against the walls. From his bed, Pete smiled at Mark. That seemed like a good sign.

"Okay," Mark said with a sigh. "Are we ready to settle down?"

Pete frowned at him. "Mom always reads to us."

He'd been afraid of that. No easy way out, it seemed. He looked over at the bookcase. "One story. Then lights-out."

Mark was about to pull up the bedside chair and turn on the overhead light when he realized that J.D.'s bed was empty. "Where's your brother?" he asked Pete quickly.

Pete pointed under J.D.'s bed.

Mark bent down. Sure enough, J.D. was under there,

surrounded by a blanket, his trusty space cannon and enough space toys to guard a small galaxy. The kid's wide, dark eyes stared out at him. He'd changed into his pajamas, and it looked as if he had every intention of spending the night under the bed.

Not you, J.D., Mark thought. *I thought I had you on my side.*

Mark smiled at the little boy. "What are you doing, J.D.?"

"That's where he goes when he's upset," Pete offered from the other bed.

Mark glanced at Pete. "What's he upset about?"

Pete shrugged.

Mark bent down on one knee. "J.D., come out from under there."

J.D. shook his head. His eyes were glistening in the pale light.

"What's wrong?" Mark asked, trying to put a little more understanding into his tone. Only problem was, he didn't understand this kind of thing at all.

"I want Mommy."

He wasn't sure he had the patience for this. He wasn't superdad, no matter how well he'd managed today. Guilt. That always worked, didn't it? "You want your mother to get well, don't you?"

"Uh-huh."

"Then she needs her rest. And she needs you to be a brave boy and go to sleep in your own bed. So she doesn't worry."

"Mom lets me sleep under here anytime I want."

Pete made a snorting sound of derision. "No, she doesn't. He's just trying to get his way."

"J.D.—"

"You killed Captain Hollister!" J.D. suddenly accused.

Mark scowled. "Who?"

"Space commander of the whole Alpharegus galaxy," the boy explained. Then in a rush he added, "He was in the tub. Mom always takes out all our stuff before she empties the water, but you didn't, and you wouldn't let me get him. And now Captain Hollister's got sucked into a black hole.''

"He went down the drain," Pete translated.

That was what all this was about? Pure astonishment made Mark speechless for a moment. Then, "I'm sure we can find him," he told J.D. "I'll take the drain apart in the morning if I have to."

The boy's lower lip trembled. Mark could clearly hear sniffling. "He needs help *now*."

"He can cry all night when he gets going," Pete threw in.

"You're not helping, Pete," Mark said over his shoulder. He bent closer to J.D., who had pushed farther back against the wall so that he was nearly out of sight. "Okay, take it easy. I'll see what I can do."

He straightened and headed back to the bathroom. He'd no more than glanced in the bathtub when he found both boys standing at his side. "Go back to bed," he said.

Pete lifted his hand. "I have a flashlight."

Mark took it out of Pete's hand and peered into the drain. He supposed it was possible a small toy could slip down inside, but it didn't seem likely. Was this a stall tactic from J.D.? How would Jenna handle this?

"I don't see a thing," he said to both boys, settling back in front of the tub on his knees.

"Grampa has tools," J.D. suggested.

"J.D., I promise, tomorrow…" The boy looked crestfallen. Might as well concede defeat, Mark thought. "Where are they?"

"In the hall closet."

"Stay here. Do not go into your mother's bedroom. Do not make any noise. Got it?"

They nodded in solemn unison.

Mark rummaged around in the downstairs closet until he found a small tool caddy. He'd never done much in the way of home repair. But he recognized the need for a screwdriver if he was going to play handyman.

Five minutes later, with both J.D. and Pete looking over his shoulder, he got the drain covering off. He flashed the light into the hole, but could see absolutely nothing. Captain Hollister might really be a goner. And Jenna might have a whale of a plumbing problem on her hands if the space commander was stuck farther down.

"Nothing clogging the drain," he said at last. "Are you sure…?"

J.D. was shaking his head vigorously and looked on the verge of tears again. Mark glanced away, wondering if, after all this, he really would have to wake Jenna so she could deal with the loss of the good captain and a wailing six-year-old.

A balled-up washcloth lay in one corner of the bathtub. Something green stuck out from under it. Mark scooped it up and shook it. A tiny plastic hero plinked into the tub.

He held it out to J.D. "Anybody you know?"

J.D. hopped up and down with excitement. He snatched the figure out of Mark's hand. "Captain Hollister! I forgot I put him in the washcloth space capsule so he could be beamed on a mission."

"I see," Mark said. "You couldn't have remembered that *before* I tore up the bathtub drain?" J.D. just looked at him. Rhetorical questions were wasted on this little guy. Mark stood. "Let's go back to bed before he ends up in more danger."

J.D.'s brow furrowed. "He doesn't come to the bedroom. He's a bathroom space commander."

"Fine."

J.D. set him firmly in the toy basket on the back of the toilet. The three of them marched back into the bedroom. Pete went to his bed without a word, but J.D. glanced up at Mark. "Can I still sleep under it?"

"No. Go…to…sleep. Both of you."

"Are you grumpy 'cause you're sleepy?" Pete asked from his bed.

"I'm not grumpy. I'm just not used to trying to get anyone else ready for bed except me. And I can be done in fifteen minutes."

"Mom does it all the time."

"Yeah, well, she's tough, and she's had more practice. Now, no more stalling. Good night."

"G'night," J.D. said, agreeable at last.

Mark turned off the light, listening to the sounds of yawns and settling covers in the meager light.

"Mark?" Pete's voice called out.

"Yes?"

"You said you would read us a story."

Mark sighed heavily and flipped the light back on. He knew when he was beaten.

AT TWO IN THE MORNING, Jenna got up to get a drink of water from the bathroom. Having spent the entire day in bed, she wasn't a bit sleepy, but she knew better than to disobey the doctor's orders and violate her agreement with Mark. One quick swallow of water and then back to bed.

With that mission accomplished, however, she couldn't resist taking a short turn around the house, just to make sure everything was all right. The place was dead quiet now.

Earlier she'd been brought dinner on a tray. Petey and J.D. had spent time with her this evening, but they were clearly uncomfortable to see their mother forced to stay in bed, and probably even bored. She felt isolated, missing the interaction with her children, wanting to do something besides lie in bed and worry. But a promise was a promise, Mark reminded her. So she'd stayed put. Now she couldn't imagine any harm in checking to see what devastation had befallen her tidy little world.

She checked on Petey and J.D. first. Their faces in sleep always undid her. They were sleeping like angels, both of them looking so sweet and innocent an outsider would never have guessed they could be holy terrors. She gave them each a kiss on the forehead.

As she left the room, she was surprised to see clean clothes stacked neatly on top of their dressers. That had to be Mark's doing. Her sons could build entire cities out of two sheets and a towel, but folding their own clothes seemed beyond them.

The rest of the house looked surprisingly well kept. In the moonlight she saw no signs of dirty dishes, no board games with all the pieces scattered everywhere, no shoes to trip over.

In the pearled light coming through the living-room windows, Mark was asleep on the sofa. Still dressed in the casual clothes he'd worn that day, he might have been any husband who'd come home from work and decided to take a nap on the couch.

His features were indistinct in the shadows, but he heaved a sigh that sounded for all the world like relief. He moved restlessly again; the couch was too narrow for broad shoulders like his.

His eyes opened, and he blinked up at her sleepily. "Jenna? You all right?"

"Yes," she whispered. "Just getting a drink and checking on you guys."

He closed his eyes, smiling agreeably. Without even being aware of it really, she reached out to brush a lock of dark hair back from his forehead. Touching him felt good.

"Sorry about the tub," he muttered softly. "I'll fix it in the morning."

"The tub?"

"Captain Hollister. J.D. thought I killed him, but—" he yawned "—I didn't."

"That's good," Jenna said. "Go back to sleep, Mark." He let out another drowsy sigh. "You, too."

She pulled the throw over his shoulder, then lifted the

hem of her nightgown and went up the stairs. Back in bed, she punched her pillow into a better position and turned onto her side. *Stop thinking about him,* she ordered her brain.

But sleep was still a long time coming.

CHAPTER THIRTEEN

"YOU WON'T FORGET to pick us up?" Pete asked as he hopped out of Mark's car and joined his brother on the sidewalk in front of the elementary school.

"I won't forget," Mark promised for the third time. So far he hadn't completely mismanaged this domestic stuff. You'd think by now the kid would have a little faith in him.

"I have batting practice after school, and they get mad if you're late."

"You won't be late."

The boy gave him a hopeful smile and then jogged off to join J.D.

Mark pulled the car back into traffic. Mentally he ran through the list of things he planned to accomplish today. It shouldn't be that difficult. Anyone with a head on his shoulders and a detailed appointment calendar ought to be able to manage it. But for some reason he was having a hard time concentrating.

He suspected part of the problem was lack of sleep. Jenna's couch didn't make a very comfortable bed, and besides tossing and turning half the night, he'd been up and down a dozen times to check on things. Was that Jenna calling out to him? Were the boys up and into mischief or just getting a drink of water? Was that sound in the backyard really the sprinklers kicking on or was someone trying to break into the house?

At home he'd never had to worry about anyone but himself. Up in his tenth-floor condo, he might as well have been living on the moon. And one benefit to that kind of isolation—you slept like a baby.

He didn't want to think about what he'd discovered in the past twenty-four hours—that this parenting thing was a lot tougher than he'd expected. When he'd shown up on Jenna's doorstep, he'd made some pretty big promises about his willingness to commit to her and their child, but he'd never really factored in what two additional children could add to the equation.

Pete and J.D. were good kids, but instant parenthood took a lot out of a person. They were full of a million questions and endless energy. They could develop attitudes at the drop of a hat. And they were constantly testing him to see how much they could get away with.

He hadn't wanted to go to Jenna for advice. But was he saying the right things? Making the right choices? What if he inadvertently hurt one of them? Feeling vastly inadequate for the first time in his life, Mark just didn't know how he was measuring up.

Hell, what was he worried about? They were just two little kids. He could handle them. He'd conquered the Dominator 2006, hadn't he?

Maybe one of the reasons he was so tired and in such a dispirited mood was the situation at work. The Orlando auditors were still yammering about the possibility of embezzlement at the paper.

He'd been avoiding it too long, mainly because the ghouls in accounting kept pointing fingers at his Atlanta controller, Dale Damron. Mark had handpicked Dale six years ago for that job. They'd gone to college together. He trusted the man completely, and he wouldn't believe there was anything out of the ordinary there. Not without proof. Lots of it.

But today was the day he had to finally dig into the records he'd brought to Jenna's house. And if they revealed the worst, that Dale was somehow stealing from the company, from *him,* then he'd have to deal with it.

Quietly he opened the front door. Jenna was probably still asleep.

That proved not to be the case, however, when he heard her call down to him. He took the stairs two at a time and eased open her bedroom door. She sat against the headboard, the sheet tucked tightly around her waist. Damned if she didn't look just as appealing in the harsh light of day as she had last night.

"I want to get up," she said.

He leaned against the doorjamb and crossed his arms over his chest. "Sorry. Until your doctor calls, that's not an option."

"You said you wouldn't boss me around."

"And you said you'd follow doctor's orders."

"I'm going crazy here. I've read everything, written a dozen letters, watched all the television I can stand and reorganized my recipe file. I have to have something to do besides lie here and contemplate my navel for hours on end."

"Omphaloskepsis."

"What?"

"Omphaloskepsis. The act of contemplating your navel to reach a higher meditation. It'll be good for you."

"Well, I'm going to omphaloskepsis my way into breaking out of this house if I don't have something better to do. I'm not going to be responsible for what happens. But I promise you, it won't be pretty."

He came into the room, right up to the bed, where he could scowl down at her in a deliberate effort to intimidate. "Come on, Jenna, be a good girl—"

"I *have* been good," she said. "Now I want to be useful."

"I'll bring you socks to sort."

She refused to be put off. "What are you doing today?"

"Boring stuff. Going over some files from work. My accounting team in Orlando seems to think there are discrepancies that can't be explained."

She brightened and sat up straighter. "Accounting audits! That's right up my alley. Let me help."

"You have to stay in bed."

"Then do your work up here," she countered. She patted the space next to her, giving him a playful look. "I've got a seat saved for you."

He couldn't help where his thoughts took him. "You and me, side by side in bed. Why doesn't that idea sound more like my idea of heaven?"

"Because we'll be *working*," she said in a determined, no-nonsense tone. "No funny business. Go get your stuff and let's get started."

He gave the suggestion serious consideration. Surely they could be friendly but keep the relationship on professional terms. With her present state of health still unknown, it wasn't as though they could do anything. But oh, the temptation.

He motioned toward the bed. "We stay on top of the covers. Not under them."

"Of course."

His eyes landed on the neckline of her nightgown. It was conservative, but not nearly modest enough. "I'm not made of stone," he told her. "Put on a robe. I'll be right back."

They piled pillows against the headboard for back support. Mark pulled off his shoes, then sat beside her with his laptop. Jenna sorted the files he took out of his briefcase, and very soon the rest of the bed was littered with paper, computer disks and various reports. He didn't tell her that the Orlando team suspected Dale. He wanted to see what she came up with on her own, if anything.

Mark found the work tedious; he liked to wheel and deal, not crunch numbers. Jenna, however, seemed invigorated by it. They worked most of the day, stopping only for a brief lunch. Sometimes they went an hour without saying anything, each absorbed in reviewing files, but often they compared notes, dug through the numbers together, tracking items that didn't jibe. The silence between them became companionable.

By early afternoon, they were both frustrated. Every lead went nowhere, but at least they'd found nothing to implicate Dale. The witch-hunt the Orlando accountants were on would have to wait until they came up with something more concrete.

Mark yawned and tried to focus on the line of numbers marching across the page he held. He slid down on his spine, finding a more comfortable position on his side where he could pillow his head on one arm. He looked over at Jenna. From this angle, all he could see was her profile, the slim column of her neck. She was deep in concentration, her lips pursed as she ran down a long list of data from some report.

It was sweet of her to give this problem such close attention. Not exactly fascinating stuff. Not exactly the kind of activity he usually indulged in on a big, soft bed. He reached out to move his hand up and down her backbone in a lingering rhythm. Under his fingers, her robe was satiny smooth, the kind of material that made you think of warm nights and cool sheets.

And yet, he didn't feel the need to go any further, even if they could have. It felt nice to be together like this. He'd never have guessed that he could pull sex out of the equation and still enjoy himself with a woman.

She turned her head toward him. "I know what you're thinking."

"I'll bet you don't."

She removed his hand from her back and placed it firmly on his own hip, giving it a final pat. Her mouth tilted into a smile. She lifted one finger and wagged it back and forth at him—a refusal to play any games.

I'm losing my touch, Mark thought, stifling another sleepy yawn. *In bed with a scantily clad woman, and all she wants to do is read accounting reports...*

He must have fallen asleep, because the next thing he

knew Jenna's voice called him back from the brink of dreams. "Mark, wake up. I want to show you something."

He opened his eyes. Jenna was stretched out beside him, her face so close he see each tiny eyelash. He reached over to run the back of his fingers across her lips. They parted slightly. "Okay, show me whatever you want," he said. "But if I'm dreaming, don't wake me."

She caught his hand and gave the tip of one finger a playful nip. "You're not dreaming. Listen, I want to talk to you about your accounts-payable records."

He sighed heavily and pushed himself farther up on the pile of pillows. "Lord, you do know how to put a damper on things."

Jenna swung upright to scan a computer report that stretched in an accordion fold from one end of the bed to the other. "Do you know if Atlanta's reader circulation is up or down from last year?"

"Of course I know. It's up."

"What percentage?"

"Year-to-date, we're up seventeen percent."

She tapped her steepled fingers together thoughtfully. "That has to be it."

"What has to be it?"

She scooted around to face him. "I think you do have an embezzler. In your accounting office."

Mark's gut sank like a stone. He didn't want to hear this.

"Not possible," he said stubbornly. "We have internal controls, a clear separation of duties, independent audits twice a year."

She waved away that argument with one hand. "You can't stop a clever employee who's determined to steal from you. It happens all the time in the best of companies."

She lifted one of the reports off her lap and dropped it on his. Thick and detailed, it contained purchasing records for the past year. Beside many entries, Jenna had made notations in red ink.

"Check this out," she said, pointing to one of the entries she'd marked. "One of your biggest expenses is paper, and for years you've done business with United Press Works, a supplier well-known in Atlanta. We use them ourselves at the magazine." She brought her finger down to another entry. "But this year, for some unknown reason, you've gone to a second supplier, as well, Fine Print. Comparing last year's total paper consumption with this year, you're up sixty-two percent. And the year's not even over yet. So…if circulation is up only seventeen percent, how can you be going through more paper than the U.S. mint?"

He thought about it for a moment, then met her waiting gaze. "Larger circulation, more ads. The news hole goes up proportionally, so we'll blow through more paper."

"Not this much more."

"You think Fine Print is a dummy account."

She nodded and reached for the Yellow Pages on her bedside table. Flipping to the listings marked Paper, she said, "If it's not, then they need to reconsider their advertising budget. They're not even listed in the phone book."

"Because they don't exist."

"Well, I've never heard of them, and that's what made me curious. Last year I put out bids to every paper company in town to try to get our costs down. And look at this," she said, pulling yet another report across her lap. She was excited, an accounting Sherlock Holmes. Only, the guilty party she fingered as the culprit in all this might still turn out to be his old friend. "According to your warehouse records, none of Fine Print's deliveries ever had a packing slip or shipper's list. Either your warehouse guys were very sloppy about checking in received goods or—"

"They never got them in the first place."

"Right. And in spite of a company policy that states every shipment has to have a packing slip to get paid, all the invoices were approved. Authorized by one person."

He didn't want to ask. But he had to know. "Who?"

"Harvey Dellarubio. The assistant controller."

His heart skipped a beat, then did a relieved somersault. He was so profoundly glad to hear anyone's name but Dale's. Without even thinking, he took Jenna's head in both his hands, pulled her to him and planted an enthusiastic kiss on her slightly parted lips.

She looked stunned. After a few moments of complete speechlessness, she gave him a soft, feminine smile and said with a small laugh, "Gosh, when I talk accounting to Vic, all I ever get is 'Good job, Jenna.'"

If she only knew. Relief washed through him, and with it came another sensation, less definable but more exquisite in its power, one that made his heart reel.

His thumbs caressed the sides of her face, those lean, high cheekbones, then the sweet curve of her jaw. "Jenna," he said softly, "you're an incredible woman. Do you know that?"

Her eyelids dropped as though they had weights on them. She bit her lip, then raised her eyes to look at him again. "You ought to see what I can do with a P & L statement."

She was nervous; he could tell by the quaver in her voice. He turned her loose, aware he could go no further with her, not right now, anyway. He cleared his throat, squinting down at the report in front of him and not seeing a damned thing. "Okay, so let's say it's Harv Dellarubio that's the bad guy here. How do I prove it?"

He watched her swallow convulsively, then turn her attention back to the matter at hand. "You could call purchasing and have them pull the contract with Fine Print. See if he negotiated it. Find out where Fine Print's checks are sent. I'll bet it's a post-office box, and it would be interesting to see who picks them up. I'd have payroll do an audit, too. See if he signed off on any personnel requisitions. A lot of times there will be phantom employees getting paychecks, as well.''

Mark shook his head in disbelief. ''I think this guy's been with us for years.''

''That's usually the way it is. I'll bet he never takes vacations. Probably works long hours. An embezzler can't afford to have the boss going through his desk. It's too dangerous.''

''I'll make a few calls.'' Suddenly remembering that the afternoon was slipping away, Mark glanced at his watch. He scrambled off the bed, yanking on his shoes. ''I have to go. Time to pick up the boys.''

''You've got plenty of time.''

''I can't be late. Pete would never let me live it down. Oh, and don't forget, he's got batting practice today, so we'll be at least a couple of hours.''

She gave him a strange look.

''What's the matter?'' he asked.

She blinked, seeming to come to. ''Nothing really. It's just that you sound so…so daddylike right now. Like you're really part of a family and you know how it's supposed to work.''

''I told you, I'm a quick study. And once I set my mind to something, eventually I get it right, so don't underestimate me.'' He stretched across the bed to give her a quick kiss and flick her nose playfully with his finger. ''Now find me something else I can take to the auditors. I'll be back before you know it.''

She nodded. ''I'll do my best. What culinary delight have you got planned for tonight's dinner, Chef?''

He grimaced as he tucked his shirt into the back of his pants. ''I have to admit, once I've done macaroni-and-cheese and burgers, we're in uncharted territory.''

''Tell you what,'' she said with a grin. ''Tonight the

boys and I will take pity on you. We'll order out. What do you say?''

"You've got yourself a deal.''

THOSE COUPLE OF HOURS flew by.

Right after Mark left, the doctor's office called. Jenna's test results reflected iron-deficiency anemia. Jenna's relief was so great she didn't even mind the doctor's lecture on eating healthier foods. She promised to stop by the office the next day to pick up vitamin supplements.

Some sort of celebration seemed in order. By the time Mark returned home with the boys, she'd whipped up the family's favorite meat loaf and mashed potatoes. She met the three of them at the front door.

Mark frowned when he saw that she'd changed out of her nightgown and into shorts and a T-shirt. "You're not supposed to—''

"The doctor's office called," she interrupted with a broad smile plastered across her face. "Everything's fine.''

She gave him the rest of the news. Petey and J.D. hugged her and so did Mark, although his lasted a little longer and she felt his lips coast along the shell of her ear. She shooed the three of them upstairs to get cleaned up while she poured iced tea and milk into glasses.

Dinner was noisy and fun. The boys and Mark seemed to have developed some secret language all their own. There were inside jokes and looks that passed among them that Jenna had no understanding of. She didn't mind. It was good to see Petey and J.D. so animated.

Occasionally Mark's eyes met hers, and each glance they exchanged felt as revealing as a kiss. The conversation remained light and easy, but sometimes he'd raise an eyebrow at her; or his lips would quirk in amusement—a silent communication to her. It made her feel unsteady, as if all that bedrest had softened her bones.

The truth was, tonight it felt like *family*.

She couldn't help comparing it to the bitter farce her marriage to Jack had become. He had never really connected with his sons, had never seemed to want to. Most of the time he found their behavior irritating, and no amount of pithy lectures and displays of exasperation from Jenna had changed a thing.

She sat at one end of the table, listening to Mark capture the boys' attention with a riddle. If she agreed to marry him, life could not always be like this—a cozy family meal centered around shared laughter and common goals and mutual caring. Could she create a new background with Mark, begin new traditions with someone who claimed not to believe in love?

It might never be the fairy-tale marriage she'd always dreamed of, but how many unions were these days?

Those questions still pestered her mind even after dinner had been cleared away and the boys trooped into the living room to watch television. Jenna had taken the last glass off the table when Mark caught her close, settling his hands on her hips.

"Time to kiss the cook," he said so softly the boys couldn't hear.

He nuzzled the side of her face. She angled her head, so that his mouth connected with hers. He gave her a deep, lazy kiss.

It would be so easy to be with him, she thought. The easiest thing she'd ever done.

When he squeezed her hand, she raised her eyes to his. "I'm glad the baby is all right," he told her.

"Me, too."

"You're not still worried, are you? You were very quiet toward the end of dinner."

"I was watching you and the boys," she said. "Thinking how nice it felt to be sitting there, just the four of us."

A gleam ignited in his eyes. "It can be like that every night, Jenna. All you have to do is say yes."

She shook her head. "It *can't* be like that every night. No one's that lucky. What are you going to do when Petey gets disrespectful or J.D. flunks math? Or you can't get any sleep because of 2:00 a.m. feedings or bouts of colic or teething?''

He grinned at her. "Have you ever considered working for Planned Parenthood? You make parenting sound like an eternity spent in the dentist's chair.''

"Sometimes it feels like that. And forget about the kids for a moment. Think about how your life could change. What are you going to do when you're face-to-face with rampant crabgrass or plumbing that goes haywire? Or air-conditioning that goes on the fritz in the middle of summer?''

His eyes were twinkling now. He tried to look distressed, but his mouth just wouldn't stop smiling. "Where are we going to live? In the Amityville Horror?''

"Be serious," she admonished, punching him lightly on the chest. "Do you see yourself enjoying those kinds of challenges?''

"No. But the phone book is filled with companies that do.''

"Will that be the answer for everything? Gardeners and housekeepers, and maybe even a nanny to keep the kids out of your hair? I want someone who can embrace life in the suburbs, not find a way to keep it at arm's length.''

"So we'll both have to make some compromises to make this work.''

She stroked his shirt, wishing she could get through to him. Beneath her hand she imagined she could feel Mark's heart pounding, strong and sure. "I think I know all the things marriage to you will bring me.'' She looked up. "Some of them are wonderful. But for the sake of your own happiness, don't you think you ought to consider what I'll be able to give you in return?''

"Jenna—''

"Mark! C'mere!'' J.D. called from the living room. "This is our favorite show!''

"I'm being summoned," Mark said with a regretful smile.

Jenna nodded. "I'll collect your things. I'm glad you were here, but now that the test results are back, there's really no reason for you to spend the night again."

He tipped up her chin. The look in his eyes was playful and sexy. "I can think of one. Can't you?"

She pushed out of his arms before her defenses crumbled. "Not one that would make things any easier."

Upstairs she sat on her bed and tried to think. In spite of her worry over the baby's health, the day had been so wonderful. The quiet, easy companionship she and Mark had shared. Intimate and yet comfortable. She'd never experienced that with any other man.

What am I waiting for? Why don't I just give in and thank God?

Awash in emotions she hadn't dealt with in years, Jenna reached across the bed to snag Mark's briefcase. She wouldn't think about it anymore tonight. Dealing with practical matters always seemed to clear her head. She would just concentrate on making all the records they'd torn apart today turn back into a tidy pile of reports and files.

The notes she'd made about the assistant controller's possible embezzlement, the suspicious records she'd encountered, those all needed to go in Mark's briefcase where they could be easily retrieved. But when Jenna flipped the latches open on the case, more files slid out of one of the side pockets.

Tapping them back in order, she was about to return the paperwork to the briefcase when she happened to notice the heading of the top file, and her hand stilled.

Written in heavy black letters, the header read SHELBY.

A more high-minded individual might have refused to even glance at it. Anything having to do with that relationship was clearly none of her business. But she couldn't help it. Shelby was supposed to be firmly in the past. Why would Mark still be carrying around a file on her?

She glanced quickly through the contents, telling herself that a hasty peek was somehow better than a thorough search. Right away she began to feel better and could see there was no real reason to worry. There were only a few documents, and most of them seemed to be the last legal maneuverings of joint ventures they apparently no longer had an interest in maintaining.

And then she came upon the prenuptial agreement he'd wanted them both to sign.

One corner was crumbled, and Jenna was pretty sure it was the very same copy Shelby had tossed in Mark's face in New York. He'd probably stuffed it in the file, thinking that eventually he'd return all these documents to his attorney.

Jenna told herself there was no reason to linger over it. Of all the documents in the file, this would definitely have to be considered off-limits. Still…

In a way, wasn't she justified in satisfying her curiosity about it? Mark had proposed marriage to her, too, and she had been giving it serious consideration all evening. Didn't she have a right to know what kind of stipulations he might ask for?

Jenna couldn't imagine the prenup creating the same reaction in her that it had in Shelby Elaine. Mark's money was the last thing she cared about.

Satisfied that she had reason enough, Jenna scanned the few pages quickly. She cut through the legal mumbo jumbo, and when she read the real core of the agreement, her breath stalled in her lungs. For a moment she actually felt light-headed again.

The prenuptial had nothing to do with money at all. No division of property. No settlement figures. No claims against any estate should the couple divorce.

Instead, it carried the cruelest stipulation any woman in love would ever want to see.

...should either party, during the course of marriage wish to take a lover, this action shall not constitute legal grounds for divorce...

Legal permission to have a wife—and a lover.

CHAPTER FOURTEEN

SHE COULDN'T believe it. But it was right there in front of her. That one stipulation made up the heart of the document.

Heart. That was a strange word to describe an agreement that would allow your husband to keep a lover on the side. An arrangement to which you would be expected to voice no objection.

No wonder Shelby Elaine had called off the marriage.

Jenna supposed she herself had no right to be angry with Mark. He'd never pretended to believe in happily-ever-after. That was just the kind of man he was. A realist. Practical. Logical.

Damn him.

But if it wasn't fair to be angry, she couldn't help feeling a sense of leaden despair. Grief for a dream that could not survive reality, a dream she'd only recently begun to think might be possible. When it came right down to it, he was worse even than Jack. At least her ex-husband had had the decency to realize that he couldn't keep both a wife and a mistress forever.

Jenna didn't know how long she sat staring at those words. Long enough that she began to feel her breath come with effort. Something, a feeling, really, made her look toward the bedroom door.

Mark.

No use pretending she hadn't read the agreement. He stood close enough to see it. She watched his face go through a subtle change as he understood that in the span of ten minutes their budding relationship had shifted and reshaped.

The silence became intolerable. Jenna tossed the prenup on top of Mark's briefcase. "It fell out while I was trying to organize everything. I suppose I should apologize for reading it."

"Don't. Just let me explain."

She stood, prepared to leave. She wasn't sure she could bear to be in the same room with him for any longer. "You don't have to," she said briskly as she started to move past him. "What I think doesn't matter."

He caught her arm. When she tried to pull away, his grip tightened subtly. "It matters to me," he said. He motioned toward the bed. "Sit down." And then in a softer tone added, "Please."

Drawing a deep breath, she sat, her back ramrod straight. She refused to do anything but stare at him. How could she stand to hear what he had to say? What possible justification could he give for such an agreement?

Mark didn't sit on the bed beside her. He took the chair near the window, sitting on the edge of it and resting his elbows on his knees.

He frowned at her in concern. "You're very pale."

"Do you want me to pretend I'm not shocked? I don't think that's possible."

"I would never want you to pretend anything with me, Jenna. That's one of the things I admire about you. Your honesty."

Jenna blinked. She wasn't in the mood to let his particular brand of flattery weave its spell. She lifted her chin. "Very well. How's this for honesty? I think the condition you wanted from Shelby Elaine is insensitive and immoral. What woman in her right mind would want a man under those circumstances? And what arrogant, conceited...*ass* would expect her to sign it?" She shook her head vehemently. "Asking the woman you love—"

"What makes you think I was in love with Shelby?" Mark cut in.

Jenna narrowed her eyes. "You expect me to believe that you weren't?"

The corners of his mouth lifted almost imperceptibly. "I expect you to believe what I told you the first day I met you. Shelby and I approached marriage like a partnership, a business deal that could benefit both of us. It was never hearts-and-flowers between us—at least, it wasn't for me."

She had to admit, he'd been honest about that. Still... "All right. So it wasn't the romance of the century."

"No. And I never gave Shelby reason to think it was or ever would be. Unfortunately the closer we got to the wedding date, the more I began to suspect that she might be falling in love with me."

"How horrible," Jenna said, unable to resist the sarcasm.

Mark stared at her, and she wondered if he had difficulty keeping his features as impassive as they looked. "It is when you've specifically tried to set up a solid, sensible arrangement between two consenting adults. When I realized she was hoping for more, I asked my attorney to create the prenup with the harshest stipulation I could think of. I thought it was better to spell it out in black-and-white *before* the wedding. Before it was too late." He made an impatient movement with one hand. "I couldn't promise her any more than what we'd agreed on, and I wanted to be sure it was going to be enough for her."

Jenna hadn't counted on this explanation, and for a moment she wasn't sure what to say. Finally she murmured, "I think you got your answer on that one."

He rubbed his jaw, as though reliving the instant Shelby's hand had connected with his face. "Yes. I did."

She opened her mouth to say something, then closed it. She glanced away, both baffled and aghast. Wetting her lips, she looked back at him, determined to sort through the whole incredible mess. ''I guess that's something I don't understand, Mark. Why would you want such a bloodless, sterile relationship? That's not what marriage is about. What marriage should be.''

His smile was no more than a faint, grim curve. ''Maybe it would be easier if I tell you what I *don't* want from marriage. And why.''

His voice sounded odd. The look on his face was one of resignation. He rose, moved to the window and stood gazing out for a long moment. There was nothing to see there. Though a moonless night had descended, the streetlights hadn't come on yet. He turned around at last, leaning back on the heels of his palms against the windowsill. ''My father's family came from old Savannah money,'' he said. ''He was an only child. Spoiled rotten, arrogant, very self-absorbed. When he went off to Harvard, he met my mother, who worked in one of the local restaurants. They eloped a week later.''

''A love match.''

''Yes. A grand passion,'' he said flatly. ''And when my father's family found out, they threatened to disown him. She was everything they hated—middle-class, a Yankee, pretty, but too…vulgar for their genteel family tree.''

Mark fingered the drapes absently, staring into space as though lost in thought. The harsh set of his mouth made him look distant and entirely different from the man she'd come to know these past few days.

''My father was forced to drop out of school to find a job that could keep them from starving,'' he said. ''The break with his family really threw him. Maybe the marriage would have cooled quickly, anyway, but whatever passion had drawn them to each other died almost before the ink was dry on the marriage certificate.''

He gave Jenna a wry glance. ''Unfortunately my mother was already pregnant with me. There went any chance for annulment.''

He tilted his head back as though the rest of the story were written on the ceiling. Jenna waited quietly, seeing the pulse beating hard and fast at the base of his throat.

"Dad's family eventually forgave him. They were prepared to accept my mother, but by then both my parents were miserable. My mother was a passionate woman. She believed all my father's early promises, and she couldn't understand why he didn't seem to love her anymore. She cried and begged and screamed at him constantly, but the more she fought to regain his love, the more emotionally removed he became. Over the years he went openly from one affair to another, never trying to hide his disgust for her clinging desperation."

Mark moved suddenly, propelling himself away from the window. She watched him prowl back and forth at the end of the bed. Some of her earlier anger had begun to be replaced by sadness.

"It must have been awful for you," she said.

A strange expression crossed his face, that she couldn't interpret. "You can't imagine the kind of numb fortitude it took to simply endure every day in our house. All I knew was that marriage was a battlefield where everyone got bloody. Including me."

"Why didn't they just divorce and be done with it?"

"My mother wouldn't let him go. And I think there was a petty part of my father that enjoyed creating a thousand little horrors for her."

She could only imagine what life had been like for the little boy he'd been. What misery he must have known. Every breath Jenna drew felt like a jerky effort to push past the wedge in her throat. "I'm so sorry, Mark," she said. "Really sorry."

He turned and came to sit beside her on the bed. "I'm not telling you this to gain your sympathy. I accepted my parents' flaws years ago. My father was a coldhearted bastard. Mother was an emotional minefield. But I learned a few things from them. I learned that giving someone unrealistic expectations, making promises you can't or won't keep, is the worst kind of cruelty. And that marriages based on grand passion are destined to turn ugly, because nothing that explosive can last forever.''

Jenna shook her head, staring at him in miserable disbelief because everything was starting to make sense. Terrible sense. ''Your parents' marriage failed because of who they were. That doesn't mean you can't…''

The words died as he took her by the shoulders. He held her still, looking down into her eyes. His own were intense and hard. ''You don't understand. I couldn't endure one month, one *day,* of a marriage that bore any resemblance to my parents'. And I'd certainly never put a child through that kind of hell.''

''You would never do that.''

''I don't intend to take that chance.''

''So then…what?'' she asked a little desperately. ''You plan to go through life without ever falling in love? Real love?''

His hands fell to his lap. ''I didn't say that. I'm saying that marriage for me can't be based on wild, romantic notions that some greeting-card company has brainwashed us into believing. What's wrong with a relationship built on trust and friendship, common goals…''

''Don't forget occasional great sex,'' she couldn't resist adding bitterly. ''Just to keep things from getting boring.''

He frowned deeply. ''I take it you don't agree.''

She looked down at her hands, trying to think. When she spoke, her words were measured. ''I guess I'm just trying to envision the kind of future we could have. Living a polite, calm, sensible existence. Like two roommates.''

''It wouldn't be like that.''

''Why wouldn't it? That's what you wanted from Shelby Elaine.''

''*Our* situation is completely different. Shelby has great ambitions for her career. We wouldn't have had children.

You and I are connected in a way that Shelby and I never could have been.''

Her head jerked up and she gave him an incredulous look. ''Because of the baby? Children aren't a miracle cure. They didn't save my marriage. And from the sounds of it, your birth didn't save your parents', either.''

''I don't expect it to be easy,'' he said with a slight note of impatience. ''With all the thought I've given this, do you think I want a marriage to start out this way? But it's too late for that now. All I'm saying is that there's no reason why we can't work toward that kind of goal together.''

Something very raw and painful moved in her breast. ''I can't promise you that, Mark.''

His hand plowed violently through his hair, and he rose. ''Why not?'' he asked. ''Dammit, what's wrong with it? If you think about it sensibly…''

His words stalled as she stood up from the bed, too. She felt as if she were going to break into a million crazy pieces. ''Trust and friendship and all those other things—of course I want them out of a marriage. But why do the two have to be mutually exclusive? I can't help it, Mark. I *am* a hearts-and-flowers kind of woman. I want that heart-fluttering feeling you get when you see your husband walk into the room. For God's sake, Vic and Lauren and I founded an entire magazine dedicated to that sort of relationship. I want the fairy tale. And if you don't, then maybe you really *are* wasting your time.''

''Didn't your marriage teach you anything?''

He spoke carelessly, probably without thinking, but the knife went deep just the same. She felt the sting of tears and she looked away, trying to clear the logjam in her throat.

He placed his hands around her arms, stroking gently. ''Jenna, I'm sorry,'' he said. ''That wasn't fair.''

''No, it wasn't,'' she agreed, then swung her head back to meet his eyes again. She wanted to sound detached, distant, but with Mark she never seemed to quite pull it off. "Marriage to Jack taught me that a lot of frogs can masquerade as princes. I have to be careful. But the right person will still be able to sweep me off my feet." Her lips curved in an ironic twist. "I fell into bed with you easily enough."

Mark's head tilted and he looked at her closely. "Are you saying I'm the right person?"

"I was beginning…"

She broke off, frustrated. How could she bear to tell him that all night she'd been thinking that very thing? That in spite of all her protests, she suspected she'd fallen in love with him. How could she tell him that when he'd just made it clear he'd never risk his heart for her?

She drew a deep, fortifying breath. "Ultimately it may not matter what I want. I still have to consider what's good for Petey and J.D., as well as this new baby. It's their future, too."

"So what do we do now?"

"I don't know, I don't know," she said with a sharp shake of her head. "I just need time to think all this through."

"All right. I've got this situation with work to deal with over the next few days. I'll leave you alone. Maybe a little distance will make it easier for you."

"Or convince me once and for all that it just won't work between us."

He made a sound like a chuckle, but there was no mirth in it. "Poor princess," he said with a tender sweep of his hand across her cold cheek. "I'm sorry I can't be what you want."

She was sorry, too, though she'd never have said so. It didn't seem fair that he could throw this curve her way just when she was beginning to hope.

Could she eventually settle for the kind of relationship he had in mind? No shooting stars. No fireworks. Just commitment and friendship and a solid, secure life for her children. There must be hundreds—*thousands*—of women who would be happy to say yes to that. But could she?

Right now she only knew that she agreed with him about one thing. Love could be a very messy problem indeed.

"J.D.!" PETE WHISPERED across the darkened bedroom.

He knew the little doofus wasn't asleep. "Lights out!" Mom had said, but for the past ten minutes Pete had watched the covers jump and jerk on J.D.'s bed, so he knew he was playing with his Captain Treadway action figures under the blanket. "J.D.! Come out from under there."

The covers snapped back as J.D.'s head poked out. By the glow of the night-light, Pete could tell he wasn't happy. "What?" he whined. "I'm not bothering you."

"I want to talk to you."

"You're supposed to be asleep."

"Well, so are you."

"What do you want?"

"Mark hasn't come to see us in two days."

"So?"

"You think he still likes us?"

"I think he likes *me*," J.D. said, and Pete could see his brother's teeth gleam in the darkness.

He didn't know why he bothered to ask his brother anything. He was such a little kid. "What do you think of him?"

"Did you know he's actually seen the space shuttle?" J.D. said in an excited voice. "In person!"

Pete wanted to choke him. Sometimes, like Grampa said, J.D.'s brains were all in his backside. "No, you flea-fart. I mean, could you see him being our dad?"

"I guess," J.D. replied, screwing up his face in thought. "If he ever comes back. Mom should be nicer to him." He turned on his side, facing his brother. "Don't you like him?"

Pete felt all tight inside, like a clock that got wound too much. "I miss Daddy," he admitted.

J.D. sat up on one elbow and just looked at him hard for a minute. It was the longest Pete had ever known him to be quiet. Finally he said in a soft voice, "Everyone says you're smarter than me, but sometimes I think you're dumber than a brain-sucked Cyberlon."

"Oh, yeah?" Pete replied, feeling more like himself again. In a million years he wouldn't want J.D. to feel sorry for him. "Like you know so much."

"I know you talk when you should be listening," he said. "Mom says Daddy's not coming back, and even if he did, she doesn't want him to live with us anymore. Mom doesn't lie. So why keep wanting something you're not gonna get?"

Pete thought that was a pretty mean thing to say, and a bad way to talk about their father, too. But he had to admit, as scared as he'd been about Mom getting sick, it had been nice to have Mark Bishop in the house. Looking after things. Acting like he wanted to be around them.

"Yes. I think Mom and Mark should get together," J.D. said, as though he'd finally come to a decision.

"Maybe Mark will come to see me play ball." As soon as the words were out, Pete wished he could put them back in his mouth. He didn't like to sound as if it mattered one way or the other to him.

"Maybe," J.D. said. "You been practicing. He'll probably come." He flipped over on his side, facing Pete. "I know! We can call him. Ask him to come. Then he can see Mom, too. Do you still got the card he gave us with his phone number?"

Pete threw back the covers and padded quietly over to his book bag. From a zippered compartment, he took out the card Mark had given them in case they needed to call him. He went over to J.D.'s bed and plopped down on it. "What if he won't come?"

"We'll tell him you won't be able to hit anything if he's not there. That you need him for good luck."

Pete made a face. "I'm not gonna say that."

"Why not?"

"'Cause it makes me sound like a baby. Like I'll get all spooked if he's not there to see me hit something. And then I'll look stupid when I do."

"When you do what?"

"Hit something."

"You're not gonna do that," J.D. said, but Pete didn't think he meant to be mean—the whole family knew he stunk. "Let's call him, Petey. And we need to get Mom to wear her blue dress. Something pretty, not old jeans and a sweatshirt."

"Why would she do that?"

"Tell her it's your lucky dress. Tell her you always do good when she wears it."

"But I never do good," Pete said with another frown. "No matter what she's wearing."

J.D. punched him on the arm. "Say it, anyway."

"Okay," Petey said after thinking it over for a long moment. "Let's call him."

They slipped down the hallway. No one was upstairs but them. Downstairs the television was on. They could hear Grampa laughing at some show he liked. The only phone upstairs was in their mother's room. J.D. closed the door gently while Pete dialed the number on the card. The phone rang, but after a few seconds, Mark's answering machine came on.

Pete left a message saying he hoped Mark would come to the ball field tomorrow—he tried not to sound too goofy. When he hung up, he felt disappointed even though J.D. looked pleased. Suppose Mark didn't listen to his messages that much? Or suppose he really didn't want to come? This had been a stupid idea.

They went back to their bedroom. J.D. looked happy. Like he'd found out he was gonna be in the next Captain

Treadway movie. He glanced over at Pete. "So tomorrow, when he gets there—"

"He's not gonna come," Pete said.

J.D. looked really surprised. "Why not? You asked him to."

"He's probably busy. He won't come."

"Mom's right. You're a pestmiss. He'll come. Mom should take a bath before the game so she smells real nice, too. How can we get her to do that?"

Pete refused to talk for a minute. J.D. thought all you had to do was ask someone to do something and they did it. But Pete knew better. Sometimes grown-ups let little kids down. Even for really important things.

"This was a dumb idea," he said at last.

That made J.D. mad. "It's gooder than yours," he said in a hot whisper.

"I didn't have an idea."

"That's what I mean!"

"Go to sleep," Pete ordered his brother.

J.D. settled back down. A few minutes later Pete heard him snoring softly. It was a long time before Pete started to feel sleepy. Maybe J.D. had been wrong about Mark coming to the game, but he was right about one thing: Mom needed to be nicer to Mark, and tomorrow he might get up the nerve to tell her so.

"SON OF A B—"

Mark slid the computer mouse away in disgust. He'd just finished creating a carefully worded, multipage report to the company attorney regarding Harvey Dellarubio's embezzlement. And with one careless, absentminded key-stroke, he'd sent it off into computer oblivion. Four hours of work. Gone.

He snapped the computer off and kicked back in his chair to glower out the window. He didn't like his Atlanta office. The lighting wasn't right. The view, of another concrete-and-glass monstrosity, depressed him. If he ever decided to spend more time with this crew, he'd make changes.

Of course, if Jenna had anything to say about it, there was a very good possibility he wouldn't be here all that often.

He rubbed his eyes, wondering why he was so tired. He thought he'd caught up on his sleep. The problem with Harvey Dellarubio's "creative accounting" certainly hadn't brought the worry and sleeplessness Mark had expected.

After formulating a plan with Dale Damron, they'd called Harvey into the office and steeled themselves for his denial, only to have the guy break down in tears with the first accusation. He'd claimed that living with fear and guilt so long had made him a nervous wreck, and he was actually glad to have everything out in the open.

Over the next two days, Harvey had confessed to one misdeed after another, to the tune of half-a-million dollars taken from the company. The guy seemed repentant and scared. Now all that remained was to figure out how he could, and should, make restitution if they decided not to prosecute.

When Harvey had confessed, Mark had actually considered calling Jenna. After all, she was the one who'd discovered the dummy accounting. He missed her. Had there been any more cause for concern about the baby? How was Pete doing with his batting? He was even curious to see how J.D. had done at soccer.

It didn't really surprise him that he missed the interaction with the boys. Jenna had wondered why he seemed so natural with them, and at first, he'd wondered that himself. Good instincts? A businesslike approach? Calm, consistent treatment? Maybe some of that came into play.

But mostly the answer was rooted in a much deeper truth.

He realized that over the years, in his mind, he'd already lived that kind of fantasy father/son relationship a thousand times. He knew what to say. What to do. Well, *most* of the time, anyway. The moments he'd shared with Jenna's kids were the sort he'd wanted so badly to share with his own father and never had. What a shock to discover that, in spite of all his arrogant protests about the need to live a life grounded in reality, he could fantasize with the best of them.

He wondered what Jenna and her sons were doing right now. He could call, but he'd promised to give her time to think. He'd pushed her enough already. He'd never exposed so much of his past and how he felt about it to anyone before. But he knew now it hadn't helped much. She needed distance and perspective.

Hell, Mark thought, he wouldn't mind getting a fresh perspective himself.

It wasn't that what he wanted out of marriage had suddenly changed. It hadn't. It was just that he had a heck of a time reconciling that kind of comfortable, complacent existence with Jenna as his wife.

Always, *always,* when he'd pictured spending the rest of his life with Shelby, he'd known he could keep his wits about him. His life would stay on the neat, tidy track he'd planned, and so would hers. No emotions mangled and twisted into weapons. Never a danger of losing control.

But with Jenna?

Forget tame. Forget calm. All the skills he'd acquired over years of dating women went right out the window when he touched her. Everything she did made him want more. Anytime she was near he felt his command over every thought, every movement, trickling away like rainwater down a window.

Damn, he was pathetic.

So he, too, needed this time away from her. To think. To recoup. He needed to get away from maverick dreams that made no sense and only brought heartache.

Oh, Jenna, Jenna. If you'd witnessed half the hell there

*was in my parents' house, you'd know why the kind of
love you want is so dangerous.*

She would never know, thank God. His parents were
dead now, both killed in a car accident eight years ago,
on one of the few occasions they'd been willing to ride
together. And since their deaths, he'd stopped raising the
phantoms of those hellish years. The other day with Jenna,
he'd explained as much as he comfortably could.

She'd understand. Eventually she'd see his side of it.

She had to.

He pushed back from his desk, deciding it was time to
go back to his hotel room. He wasn't accomplishing anything here.

Opening up his briefcase, he stuffed a few files inside
and noticed that the message light on his cell phone was
blinking. He caught his breath for an instant. It might be
Jenna. The haste with which he retrieved the message
made him feel like a lovesick teenager.

The caller wasn't Jenna, but it wasn't a complete disappointment. It was Pete, sounding hesitant, but hopeful.
Inviting him to tomorrow's game. He could hear J.D. in
the background, egging him on.

Mark cut the phone off with a smile. For the first time
that day, he dared to hope that everything *wasn't* well and
truly lost.

Jenna might not want to see him anytime soon.

But her kids did.

CHAPTER FIFTEEN

"PETEY, COME ON!" Jenna shouted up the stairwell. "Get a move on."

It was Saturday—Little League game day—and if they didn't get started soon, they were all going to be late. Again.

Jenna dragged a hand through her hair. She didn't really want to go and she wasn't the only one. No one in the family seemed to be in the mood for it. Her father's arthritis was acting up. Christopher had come straight from a fight with Amanda. Trent—who could usually be counted on to entertain them in the stands—had a cold and had turned into a 220-pound baby. Even J.D. was grouchy.

With the threat of rain in the forecast and up against an opposing team that hadn't lost once, today's game promised to be long, boring and painful.

Of course, the past four days hadn't been that great, either.

Four days since Mark had snuffed out the final, foolish dream she'd had about what married life could be like between them. And four days since she'd come face-to-face with the humiliating fact that she might be falling in love with him all the same.

You win. Let's do it. Let's get married. She could see herself saying those words, and only one thing stopped her from calling him up to say so.

Regardless of how the two of them might manage, the boys needed someone permanent in their lives. Someone who would stick it out when times got rough. And Jenna still wasn't certain that Mark could be counted on to do that.

She sucked in a deep breath. A little more time, that was what she needed. Time to see if Mark and her sons could build a relationship. Time to…to be sure.

She walked into the living room, where her father and brothers were waiting. Since they'd returned from working on the family cabin, their attitudes had been doing a gradual thaw. They seemed to be accepting, albeit grudgingly, that Jenna planned to buy the Victorian fixer-upper and regain some independence. Maybe Mark had been right about that. Maybe they just needed to see she was serious and they'd back off.

Jenna scooped up paperwork she intended to work on in the stands. As if things couldn't get worse this week, the latest edition of *Fairy Tale Weddings* had hit a few snags and was in danger of not going out on time. Since Petey was dead last in the lineup, and flowers could bloom in the outfield before he ever came up to bat, she figured it wouldn't hurt to kill two birds with one stone. The deadline for getting the magazine out was so tight she'd probably have to work tomorrow, instead of taking the boys to Six Flags as she'd promised.

J.D. trudged sullenly into the room, dragging his space cannon, along with his feet.

"Look alive, buddy!" Jenna's father said. "You look as grumpy as a beaver with a toothache."

"Nobody listens to nothin' I say," J.D. replied inexplicably. He jabbed one sneaker-clad toe over and over again into the carpet.

"Stop doing that," Jenna said, then counted to ten. J.D. had been impossible today, fighting with Petey and making a general nuisance of himself the whole time she'd been getting dressed. "Are you still sulking about the blue dress? I told you, I'm not wearing one of my best outfits in a grandstand."

"Even if it's Petey's lucky dress?"

"A lucky glove. A lucky rabbit's foot," her father said. "But nobody in softball has a lucky dress, J.D."

Her brothers laughed. They definitely weren't helping matters. She threw them a dirty look. Just then Petey walked into the living room. He wasn't in uniform. By the shape of his mouth, Jenna could see trouble ahead.

Great. I need this on top of everything else.

"Why aren't you dressed?" she asked.

"I'm not going. I quit."

That didn't surprise her. Petey quit at least twice a week, though this was the furthest he'd ever gone in actual rebellion. "You can't quit. Now go get ready. And hurry up."

"I'm not going," he repeated. "Coach says I can quit if I want."

Behind her, she was aware of long sighs and impatient movements from the men in her family. J.D. looked suddenly panicked, his eyes darting back and forth between them.

"You don't wanna quit," he told Petey. "'Member how today you feel so lucky? 'Member how today is gonna be different?"

"Today's no different," Petey said. "It doesn't matter what you think. It's all gonna be the same 'cause nothin's changed. I don't feel lucky. I just wanna quit."

"Petey...." J.D. muttered in a drawn-out whine.

"Shut up, squirt."

Some sort of coded conversation seemed to be going on between the two boys, but Jenna had no patience today for sorting it out. She could tell Petey didn't want to budge, but quitting was definitely not an option.

"Don't talk to your brother like that, Petey." She squatted in front of him, catching each of his thin arms in her hands. "You must have misunderstood Coach Williams. I talked to him this week. He says you need more practice, but that you're getting better all the time."

Petey shook his head. "He just says that 'cause you're my mom. He knows parents like to hear that stuff. What he says to us is different. He tells us all the time that we're a bunch of losers. That we ought to give our uniforms to kids that really wanna play." He caught his lip between his teeth. "He said a girl could hit better than me, and I ought to go play on their team."

Her father made a gruff, dismissing sound. "He's just trying to toughen you up, Petey-boy."

"Dad, please," Jenna said with a look back over her shoulder. "When did he say this, Petey?"

"Last practice. I tried to tell him I been working on a new way to bat so I'll do better, but he didn't listen. He said I don't get paid to think. He said—" Petey's brow furrowed as he tried to remember the conversation "—he said I should consider myself lucky to even be on the team, and if I didn't, I should quit. So I am."

"No, you're not. You're going to finish up the fall schedule. If you want to stop playing ball after that, we can discuss it, but you're not quitting now. As for Coach Williams, I'll speak to him today about the way he talks to you and the others."

Petey jerked in her hold, and his eyes went wide with alarm. "Mom, you can't!"

"Of course I can." Inside, she could feel her maternal instincts behaving like rottweilers. If the conversation had really gone as Petey claimed, Coach Williams needed a talking-to. The man had no right to belittle her son that way.

"The kids will make fun of me!" Petey cried, looking horrified now.

She was aware of movement behind her—Christopher moving forward. "That's not a good idea, Jenna."

"I didn't ask you, Christopher."

Her father came into her line of vision. "Honey, Little League coaches have to be hard on their boys sometimes. They have to get them fired up, make them realize they're part of a team that depends on each player. Otherwise they'd be out in the field goofing around, instead of paying attention.''

''Jen, don't act like such a girl,'' Trent threw in, around blowing his nose.

She felt ganged up on. Petey squirmed in her grasp. She let him go and rose, giving the men in her family a stern look. ''Don't try to turn this into some sort of male-bonding thing. There's a difference between being hard on kids and berating them.''

Christopher pulled off his ball cap and ran his fingers through his hair. She could tell he thought he was dealing with an unreasonable woman. ''You run interference for Petey, and every kid on the team will never let him forget it. His life will be hell.''

''Petey, go upstairs and get changed. Now. J.D., will you run up to my bedroom and bring my black coat out of the closet? I think it's going to be cool today.''

J.D. brightened. ''You could wear—''

''My black coat, J.D.'' Jenna shot a sharp look at her youngest son. J.D. wisely accepted defeat and ran out of the room. The adults remained silent until Jenna was sure both her sons were out of earshot. Then she turned to her father and her brothers, her expression hard.

''Uh-oh,'' her father said with a grimace at his sons. ''I feel a lecture crawling up my backside.''

''No lecture,'' Jenna said calmly. ''I just want to remind you all that Petey and J.D. are my responsibilities. Mine. Not yours. And I'll do what I think is best. I don't need any of you second-guessing me, especially in front of them.''

''We're just trying to help, sis.'' Christopher said.

Jenna crossed her arms. ''Well, it's not working. So butt out, all of you.''

THE GAME, and the day, was just as dismal as it started out.

The air had a real fall snap to it, but off and on it misted lightly, so that rain gear came out and umbrellas popped open in the stands like colorful mushrooms. Since her blue dress was silk, it was a very good thing she *hadn't* given in to J.D.'s bizarre request.

The opposing team was full of pint-size all-stars. In no time the score was embarrassingly lopsided. It wouldn't have surprised Jenna a bit to hear that every one of those little Tiger phenoms had Major League aspirations. Poor Petey and the rest of his Cardinal teammates, even their best hitter, looked as miserable as the gray skies overhead.

When she wasn't watching Petey standing glumly in the outfield or sitting in the dugout, Jenna watched Coach Williams. She never heard him say anything inappropriate. In fact, he seemed more in control than some of the fathers who sat in the stands. But she still felt dismayed that he could encourage Petey to quit.

Right at the end of the fourth inning, the rain picked up for a few minutes and everyone took a break. Seeing this as her chance, Jenna snatched up one of the umbrellas and over the sour looks of her father and brothers, went down the bleacher steps.

Just past the high chain-link fence, Coach Williams and the Cardinal team were huddled in discussion. She waited until they finished, then called the coach over. Petey reached her first, pressing against the fence as if he could push his way through it. He looked at her wildly.

"Mom…don't," he said in strained undertones.

"Petey, it's all right," Jenna said. "Go sit down."

He didn't obey, but by that time Coach Williams had reached the fence. He looked a little surprised to see her, and she nodded pleasantly at him.

"Hi, Mrs. Rawlins," he said. He grimaced over at the scoreboard. "Not too good, huh? But if the rain holds off, we might wipe the smiles off those Tiger faces yet. What can I do for you?"

She was about to speak when she noticed that the

number-one player on the team had crossed to the fence to stand beside Petey. He was one of the kids in the Bear Hollow neighborhood that Jenna disliked—a snotty little carrot top with lashes so pale they reminded her of wood lice. He thought he was better than everyone else, which would have been a lot less annoying if it hadn't been the truth.

"What'sa matter, Petey-poop?" he taunted her son. "Did your Momma come over here to find out why you ain't come up to bat yet?"

Petey ignored him, although he looked pale and worried.

The other boy made crying-baby sounds, obviously determined to get a rise out of Petey.

Jenna wanted to shake the little brat until his teeth rattled. She settled on giving him the sternest "mom" look she had. The kid gave her a nervous glance and then galloped back to the other boys.

In that moment Jenna realized that her father and brothers might be right. There were better ways to handle this than charging in like a lioness defending her cub. And maybe Coach Williams did have to get tougher with the boys than any mother would have liked. This was a *guy's* arena, a sacred world that only males understood and appreciated.

"Coach Williams," Jenna began, sensing Petey's tension even through the fence, "I was wondering if you'd like to come for dinner next week."

"Dinner?"

It occurred to her suddenly that the coach was a divorced man. He might think she was making a play for him. "With my father and the boys," she amended quickly. "We could talk about the last of the fall fundraisers." She looked down at her son and gave him a smile meant to reassure. "And Petey isn't certain he should continue with ball next spring. Maybe you could give us your feedback."

"Sure," the coach replied. "Thanks for the invite."

"I'll give you a call."

He walked back to the dugout, yelling at the boys to quit fooling around and get their equipment back on. The rain was letting up again and they needed to hit the field. She put a finger through the fence and flicked Petey on the nose. He looked so relieved that she hadn't challenged Coach Williams's methods that it was almost comical. "I thought about our conversation this morning. When it comes to you guys and sports, I guess moms don't always know the best way to handle things."

Petey nodded. "Grampa said you didn't understand 'cause you're a woman, and women get sports about as much as monkeys get table manners."

Jenna frowned. "I may have to have a talk with your grandfather about some of the words of wisdom he's teaching you boys."

Petey glanced back over his shoulder. "I gotta go."

"Okay. Go get 'em, tiger."

"Mo-om," Petey complained with rolled eyes. "Don't use that word." He pointed at the other team, where the boys were slapping one another's rear ends and giving high fives. "That's *them.*"

"Oh, sorry. Well, go out there and…beat 'em to a pulp."

"Yeah. Like that's gonna happen." He brightened suddenly. "But I got a new stance, and I'm gonna use it, even if Coach doesn't want me to. Can't hurt, huh?"

"Not a bit," she agreed.

She went back to the stands. Her father and J.D. were huddled under their rain gear playing cards on the seat between them. Christopher and Trent were talking about last week's football game. They all gave her questioning glances.

She scowled at them. "Don't look at me that way. I didn't do it."

Her father poked his head out of his slicker like a turtle coming up for air. "You didn't give him what-for?"

"No, I didn't," she said, enunciating every word. "The timing wasn't right, and you...you guys may have a point. As a woman, I may not understand all the nuances."

"You mean, you think we're right?" Trent asked, sounding incredulous.

"I suppose it can happen once in a while."

They all laughed, even Jenna, and the day got a little better after that. Petey had had one disastrous turn at bat, but maybe he'd improve the next time he was up. She watched J.D. and Trent build a temple out of peanut shells. Her father and Christopher discussed the team's capabilities as if comparing Major League stats. The conversation rolled over and around her, and gradually a lump formed in her throat.

Mark had been right that night at Pepino's. A family that loved you was better than almost anything. They were here for the boys. They were trying to ease up on running her life. Now she needed to ease up a little on them.

Down at the bottom of the stairs, a guy was selling hot dogs. J.D. and Trent were always up for that, and her brother sent J.D. down the stairs with a handful of dollar bills.

Jenna saw her opportunity and took it.

She turned on the bench, looking toward her brothers and father. "Fellows...," she began, not knowing what exactly she wanted to say, but determined to get it out. "I just want to tell you that I know you mean well. I know you want what's best for me, and I love you for it. Between this new baby and a new house, I'm going to need all the family support I can get, and I'm sorry if I've been bitchy. My body's changing, my whole *life* is changing, and frankly, as much as I'm looking forward to it, I'm scared to death."

There was a moment or two of silence. They looked stunned. Then male protests of understanding tumbled

from their mouths, though they probably didn't understand a thing. Christopher looked embarrassed. Her father
took her hand. Trent scratched his head and asked what
they had done.

Her father gave her a narrowed glance. "You gonna
marry that newspaper fellow?"

It was her turn to be at a loss for words. At last she
said honestly, "I don't know. What would you all think
if I did?"

"I don't like things changing," her father said, "but I
guess he'd do. Especially if he made you happy. You've
been as contrary as a handful of coat hangers lately."

"Is he more than just the guy Petey and J.D. called out
of the blue?" Christopher asked her in low tones.

He knew. From the looks on their faces, they all did.
"Yes," she admitted. "How did you know he's the fa-
ther? And please don't tell me you did some new kind of
DNA testing to find out. I'll murder you."

Christopher laughed and shook his head. "I admit we
aren't the sharpest tools in the shed when it comes to
reading you. But we talked about it up at the cabin, and
all three of us said we'd never seen you look at anyone
the way you look at him. You're in love. You ought to
see yourself, sis."

She cringed and covered her face with one hand.
"Don't say that. I don't know. I don't know anything
right now. It's very confusing."

"Doesn't seem confusing," Trent said.

"It doesn't to me, either," her father agreed. "If you
love each other, you ought to be making plans. You don't
have forever, you know. He ought to be making an honest
woman out of you. In my day—"

"Stop," she admonished them all. "Here comes J.D."

She was glad to see J.D. return with an armload of hot
dogs. She couldn't have discussed this topic with them if
her life had depended on it. Especially when she didn't
have any concrete answers.

Ten minutes later it was Petey's turn at bat. Jenna could feel the entire family tense, even J.D.

Sure enough, Petey swung wildly at the first ball. Jenna's heart sank.

Strike one.

He repositioned himself over the plate, ignoring the cat-calls from the other team. There was a man on first, but Petey wasn't likely to bring him home, much less himself. He swung again, but he wasn't even close.

Strike two.

Jenna's heart took a deeper dive. It was heartbreaking to witness this. And heartbreaking to realize there was absolutely nothing she could do.

He never looked up into the stands, but she watched his shoulders pull back. In spite of his earlier attitude of defeat, he was going to tough it out. He really was a brave little soldier, Jenna thought, her heart breaking for him. He leaned over the plate, his feet shifting as he planted himself in a different position, letting one of his elbows drop slightly.

Beside her, her father said under his breath, "Oh, no, Petey-boy. Don't try anything new. Stick with what you know."

In another moment, her son would be called out. Jenna tried to get her game face ready. *Pretend it doesn't matter.*

The pitcher threw the ball. Petey leaned in and, by some miraculous twist of fate, some bizarre accident, his bat actually connected with the ball. It wasn't a powerful hit. Not enough to send anyone zooming across home plate, but it rolled decently into right field. The Tiger fielder hadn't been paying attention. It bounced past him, and it was a good five seconds before anyone got on the ball. By that time, Petey had made first base.

The entire family stared, mouths open. Then they went wild.

Trent whooped like a crazy man.

"Gosh, he really hit it!" J.D. said.

"Where did he learn that?" Christopher asked Jenna.

"Who cares?" her father answered for her. "He hit the damned thing!"

Jenna shook her head in disbelief. It hadn't been a homer. It hadn't been anywhere close to that. But her son, the absolute-worst player on the team, had finally hit something.

"I don't know," she said quickly. She waved excitedly at Petey, who was jumping up and down at first base. "He said he's been practicing a new stance."

"Petey got it from *him*," J.D. told them. He pointed. "They practiced."

They all followed the direction of J.D.'s finger. A man stood on the sidelines. One hand curled into the chain-link fence, and the other waved at Petey. Jenna couldn't see his face, but she would have recognized those jean-clad hips anywhere.

"Mark?" she whispered.

For the second time in less than a minute Jenna was stunned into silence. She stared at the figure until her eyes watered. She watched him make an okay sign with thumb and forefinger, and when she glanced back at Petey, she saw him nod in excitement.

"When did he teach Petey that?" Jenna asked J.D without looking at him.

"When you were in bed 'cause of what the doctor said." Her son looked at her solemnly. "But he's no good in soccer. He said so. And he can't kick nothin' even though we tried and tried. But he came today. I knew he would."

The game progressed. There was no way the Cardinals could win of course, but Petey made it home when a team-mate whacked the ball right out of the park. As delighted as she was for her son, Jenna barely noticed what went on. She couldn't take her eyes off Mark, who never once looked into the stands or moved away from the fence.

It ended shortly after Petey's unexpected triumph. Fifteen to three. The Tigers were disgustingly smug about the win. Coach Williams huddled the boys together afterward for a pep talk, while everyone in the stands gathered raincoats and headed down the stairs.

Jenna stood up, discovering that her knees were slightly wobbly. Not because of all that time sitting, but because of Mark.

Mark, who had come here to see Petey. Who had helped her son with an achievement he'd never have accomplished on his own.

She didn't believe Mark had done it deliberately to impress her, to win her over. It came from a deep well of kindness in him, a compassionate decency that was as much a part of him as that wonderful bone structure and dark eyes. Whatever childhood memories still plagued him, whatever his parents had or hadn't been for him, they hadn't been able to crush that. They just hadn't.

A lot of things became clear to her in that moment, as though a moving blur had suddenly been caught in a clean, sharp snapshot.

She really did love him.

All the words, cries, arguments beating their wings within her suddenly went still. No matter what the future held, no matter what stood in the way of happiness, she wanted Mark in her life.

Maybe there would never be a declaration of undying love. Maybe bringing two growing boys and a new baby into his life would stretch his capabilities to the limit. But she didn't doubt him anymore. She knew he could do it. And she would help him. She'd show him the way.

Because Mark Bishop was a man worth fighting for.

CHAPTER SIXTEEN

ALONE AT THE FENCE, Mark watched Pete Rawlins charge toward him. Most of the boys looked dejected about the loss, but Pete's face glowed with excitement. His hair stuck up every which way, spiky with sweat.

"Did you see me?" he crowed. "I did it just like you said. And it worked!"

"I didn't miss a thing," Mark said, grinning broadly. For years he'd almost always felt uncomfortable around children, but this kid and his brother were different somehow. "You nailed it, Pete. I'm really proud of you."

The boy was jumping in place. He swung around, spotted his family in the crowd and ran toward them, nearly losing his balance on the rain-slick grass. "Uncle Christopher, did you see me? What did you think, Grampa?"

Mark watched the family close around Pete, full of congratulations and praise. Ordinarily that kind of folksy scene set his teeth on edge, but he found himself smiling again as the McNabs eventually came toward him. They were smiling, too, even Christopher, the cop, who Mark suspected would prefer to see him locked up for daring to date Jenna.

He realized suddenly that he didn't give a damn whether they welcomed his presence in their world. It was Jenna he wanted to see, Jenna he'd been waiting to catch a glimpse of in the crowd. And when she shifted and stepped slightly away from that overprotective clutch of males, he finally found her.

She moved through a slant of afternoon sunlight, and

in a rush it all came back, how it felt to hold her, how her lips tasted. His pulse ran with fire. God, less than a week, and he'd missed her so much!

Staying away had been difficult. A time of dreary responsibilities and manufactured duties. One day after the other, night into day, until they'd all become the same to him, all without meaning. Even if Pete and J.D. hadn't called, he knew he'd have come here today. Just to see how Pete did. Just to make sure the boy remembered what they'd practiced. But his motives, so clear at first, had become muddled somewhere along the line.

The truth was, he felt as though all the good parts of his life had been ripped away. The old complaisance wasn't a comfort any longer, because life had turned ugly on him. He would never have guessed it could be that way, but everything before Jenna felt mean and bleak and not worth remembering.

The McNabs reached his side. Jenna smiled at him, her sensuous mouth hinting at any number of possibilities. Her face was alive with joy and intelligence, and he could see gratitude shining in her eyes. The misty rain had planted tiny diamonds in her hair, and he thought again how pretty it was. Just looking at her, he found that an amazing array of fantasies were playing in his mind, some of them shocking in their boldness. He was beginning to wonder if he was addicted to her.

The men exchanged handshakes, unfailingly polite, and yet he couldn't lose the feeling that they were looking at him differently. They were not necessarily hostile, but sizing him up all over again.

Christopher McNab had corralled Petey against him with one arm around his chest—a possessive gesture Mark couldn't miss. "So you've been coaching Petey?"

No antagonism in the question, but Mark knew he had to tread lightly. He gave the man a level look. "I figured it couldn't hurt to try something different."

"I've been working a long time to get his game up."

"He told me how much you've helped him."

Something subtle changed in Christopher's face. Abruptly he grinned. "A fresh set of eyes is probably just what he needed."

The awkwardness of the moment ended as William McNab enthusiastically entered the conversation. "I say we all celebrate with ice cream. What do you say, boys?"

Not surprisingly, that idea was met with a chorus of agreement.

Jenna, however, frowned and shook her head. "I promised my real-estate agent I'd return the keys to that house to her before she leaves the office." She glanced at her watch. "We only have thirty minutes to get across town."

The boys made sounds of disappointment, and Mark found himself saying, "I could take you by her office, then drop you at your house. No sense cheating the kids out of ice cream."

"Or Trent," Jenna's father said with a teasing glance at his younger son.

"I wouldn't want to take you out of your way," Jenna said hesitantly.

"It's not out of my way at all."

"Go ahead, Jen," Christopher said. "We'll look after the boys."

A few minutes later Mark had Jenna settled into the front seat of his car. She gave him the directions to her agent's office, and he pulled into the late-afternoon Atlanta traffic.

Neither spoke for a while. The silence wasn't awkward, but it wasn't as companionable as Mark might have wished, either. Jenna seemed friendly, glad to see and be with him, and yet he sensed some sort of barrier. Nothing he could put his finger on, but it felt as though they'd lost the intimacy they'd gained during the two days he'd spent in her home.

Just as the silence was becoming uncomfortable, Jenna stopped watching the traffic and turned her head toward him. "I want to thank you for helping Petey," she said. "You can't imagine what good that one hit did for him."

"I think I can. He's a good kid. So's J.D."

From the corner of his eye he saw her duck her head and knew that his words had pleased her. "How are you? No more problems with the baby, I hope."

"The doctor says everything looks good. I'm on a new iron-rich diet and taking supplements, so I shouldn't have any more episodes."

"Glad to hear it."

"How did it go with your embezzler?"

"Harv shocked us all and confessed."

He gave her the details of the past few days. Chancing a glance from the road, he caught her nodding in interest, though he sensed something illusory about it.

More silence after that too-polite exchange. Mark wondered if he'd mistaken her welcoming smile at the ball park. What was wrong? She seemed tense and uncharacteristically reserved. He wanted to ask her if she'd begun to see marriage in the same way he had, but feared that one argument about that subject was quite enough to disrupt a peace as fragile as theirs.

To make matters worse, they encountered an accident that had traffic snarled for miles. It soon became apparent they couldn't possibly make the real-estate agent's office in time.

Mark pulled his cell phone out of its holder and extended it to Jenna. "Would you like to call and tell her we can't make it? We can stop by her house if she really needs to have the key back."

She nodded and took the phone. Instead of inconveniencing them, the agent was perfectly agreeable to letting Jenna drop off the key in the morning.

"The owners won't mind that you have a key?" Mark asked.

"They live out of state. I think they're going to accept

the offer I made. They didn't mind me going in to take a few measurements.''

"So you're really going to do it.''

"It looks that way.'' She turned her head toward him suddenly. "Would you like to see the place? I could give you a quick tour.''

"I'd like that.''

That odd tension seemed to lessen a little.

She gave him new directions, toward the outskirts of town. Eventually they reached a neighborhood of narrow, brick-lined streets, where ancient oaks shaped like candlelabras dripped moss and atmosphere to make shady canopies across the road. The houses here weren't particularly fancy, but they looked inviting and well cared for.

They pulled up to a corner lot, where a decent-size Victorian house sat, decked out in peach and beige and lots of white gingerbread trim. As they got out of the car, he saw that it could stand a coat of paint.

Jenna glanced his way. "Now, remember,'' she cautioned, sounding strangely defensive, "it needs a little work.''

A little work was an understatement. He wasn't a professional, but as they approached the place, he could tell right away that the house had been neglected. Mother Nature had taken back the yard. As pretty as the oaks were, their roots, like elderly fingers, had turned the brick walkway into a danger zone. The railing on the front porch wobbled in his hand. The front door and side panels had beautiful beveled-glass inserts, but the door itself was warped.

He tried not to look skeptical as Jenna dragged him through the downstairs rooms, pointing out all the possibilities and little modifications she could make.

The living-room fireplace was deep and impressive, but when Mark ran his hand along the mantel, two bricks fell and almost whacked off one of his toes.

"A little mortar, and you'll never know they were loose," Jenna said quickly when he frowned at her.

There was a room up front that Jenna said would make a perfect office. A nice feature at the back of the house— a small solarium with multipaned windows—brought a wide smile to her face.

"All my plants could be here," Jenna said, looking around the space wistfully. "There's good light..."

"And water." He pointed upward, where several of the glass panes were missing and had been boarded over.

"Cosmetic problems," she said, scowling at him. "Replaceable."

Before going upstairs, she pulled him back onto the wide front porch. She used her hands to block out space against one corner. "And a big wooden porch swing right here," she said. Her eyes were shiny with enthusiasm. "I know it's corny and overdone, but I like the idea of sitting out here on a nice evening, watching the stars come out." She inhaled deeply. "Do you smell that? It's so wonderful."

The afternoon was tinged with the smoky scent that heralded autumn, but he barely noticed it. He couldn't take his eyes off Jenna. She looked so pretty right now. He tried to ignore the tremor of pleasure that went through him, but nothing seemed to exist for him except the need to touch her. Just touch her.

Trying to overcome that urge, he glanced up at the wooden overhang, then cocked a dubious brow her way. "I see some rotted wood up there."

"Don't be a spoilsport," she said with a dismissive wave of her hand. "The report is due back any day now, but the Realtor said nothing the inspector saw indicated that the structure wasn't sound. Can't you see its potential?"

"There's a considerable amount of work to be done."

"It'll be worth it in the end."

She started to move past him, but he caught her and

pulled her close. To hell with trying to resist temptation. He wanted her in his arms.

"Jenna," he said softly, "I don't know where we stand right now, but I meant what I said a while back. If we got married, I'd buy you any place you want, *anywhere* you want. You could build this house brand-new, from the ground up, if it pleases you."

He thought she looked a little disappointed, maybe even hurt. "You don't get it, do you?"

"I'm just—"

"Being practical. Yes, I know. But what you don't understand, Mark, is that, when I first saw this house, I had as many reservations as you do. But almost from the minute I walked in, I knew it could be a home for me and the boys. I felt it."

"Jenna—"

She refused to hear what he had to say. Instead, she slipped out of his grasp. "Come on. Let me show you the upstairs."

She led him up the staircase. He had to admit it was splendid, wide and solid rosewood, with a whimsical newel post shaped like a bird that almost defied description. Nearly every step creaked as they climbed, and when he hit a particularly noisy one, she looked back at him to gauge his reaction.

He smiled, but shook his head.

"Fixable," was all she said.

He grinned back, deciding that, for her sake, he'd try to be enthusiastic about this monstrosity of a house that she seemed determined to make her own.

The funny thing was, he didn't have to try very hard. Jenna's excitement was infectious.

She'd done her homework. When she wasn't giving him a running monologue about all the possible ways she could turn it into a real home, she filled him in on the history of the place—nothing notorious or noteworthy really, but interesting enough that he began to see a certain character in every nook and cranny. By the time they'd reached the last small bedroom at the back of the house, Mark found himself making suggestions, trying to visualize every change she had in mind and even coming up with solutions to problems she hadn't solved yet.

The little bedroom had a bay window that boasted a view of a large backyard. The massive oaks that from the back porch had looked like roof killers to him suddenly seemed ideal for J.D.'s tire swing or Petey's tree house.

"Guess what I envision for this room?" Jenna asked, and before he could answer, she said, "The nursery."

He nodded thoughtfully. "I can see it."

She pointed toward one of the corners. "I could put a rocking chair there."

"No. Over by the window. So you can watch the boys play while you feed the baby."

"Yes, you're right," she replied after a thoughtful pause. "All the carpet upstairs is new, so I wouldn't have to replace it. I can't settle on a color for the walls, though."

"What's wrong with blue if it's a boy, pink if it's a girl?"

"Very logical," she said with a teasing tone. "I'd expect that from you."

He watched her survey the room with pursed lips and a brow crisscrossed with wrinkles. He'd never been more fascinated by the sight of her, standing in the fading light, making plans for the nursery, the place where their child would find love and tender care. When she envisioned herself here, was there hope at all that she saw him by her side?

She brought her hand to her chin. "I was thinking lavender might be nice."

"Lavender!" he said with a laugh. "You mean like 'old lady and doilies' lavender?" He shook his head. "You wouldn't do that to a boy, would you?"

"Maybe you're right," she said. "Once children get to

the toddler stage, they usually like a stronger color. But I do hate to paint, so it would be nice to keep it the same color.''

''Painting is not that big a deal.''

''Fine. Then *you* can do it when the time comes.''

Their eyes met in a moment of curious intimacy. She looked a little startled. Vivid color stained her cheeks. She was fully aware, Mark realized, that she'd committed the hideous faux pas of assuming that he would be here in the future.

In an obvious effort to ease her embarrassment, she moved toward one side of the room. ''I was thinking the crib should be here.''

Mark crossed the room slowly. He took her in his arms, and it pleased him enormously that she didn't resist. ''Jenna…''

She smiled weakly. ''Well, that's the grand tour. We can leave now. Everyone's probably wondering where we are.''

His thumb smoothed the tiny laugh lines that bracketed her mouth as he gazed at her with frank sexual interest. ''You're an amazing woman, Jenna Rawlins. But you are absolutely no good at pretending, are you?''

''No,'' she admitted, ''I'm not.''

''So what do you want? Right this minute.''

''I want you—'' her tongue came out to lick her lips ''—to touch me.''

He pulled her closer, settling her against his chest. Bending his head, he brushed his lips against the side of her jaw and with one finger tucked wisps of fine hair behind her ear. ''We don't kiss enough,'' he murmured. He pressed his mouth to the base of her throat, where the skin was like sweet, yielding velvet. ''I've missed this. This little spot right here.''

He heard her draw a sketchy breath. ''That feels nice.''

''Does it? How about this?''

"Lovely," she said faintly as he planted a line of kisses along her throat.

"Do you want me to stop?"

"No."

"I didn't think so. Do you understand what I want to do with you right now?"

"We can't," she said on a soft note of alarm. "This isn't officially my house yet. There's no furniture."

He flicked a glance down at the carpet, then gave her a slow smile. "We can improvise."

"Mark!"

"Yes?"

"We mustn't. It's completely inappropriate."

"Very."

She appeared to think about it for a heartbeat. Then she grinned at him. "Should we lock the front door?"

Pointless to pretend any longer. They both wanted it. He kissed her.

A long kiss. A pressure that started lightly and experimentally as he traced the line of her mouth, then deepened into something more demanding and passionate, something that eventually brought a sigh of pleasure from Jenna.

Mark's hands came up to grasp the lapels of her coat. "This," he said as he nibbled gently at her lips. "Take this off."

He pushed the coat from her shoulders and she let it slide down her arms to pool at her feet. Together they worked buttons loose—her blouse, his shirt—with languid care and smiles for each bit of skin revealed.

When at last they were naked, he laced his fingers with hers, feeling the warmth running from palm to palm as they sank and knelt face-to-face, only inches apart.

She was as beautiful as he remembered. He reached out to touch her nipples. He liked the way they looked, peeking out from between his fingers like a couple of tiny, perfect rosebuds. She closed her eyes and moaned as he stroked them, learning again the shape of her breasts, their unique contours. He watched a host of fascinating expressions flicker across her face, as though she'd fallen into some slow, secret dream.

His hand moved lower. She drew in her breath sharply, making her abdominal muscles taut and quivering. Her stomach was flat. He thought of how she would look in a few months, rounded with the weight of his child.

The thought of the baby made him glance at her in sudden concern. "Jenna," he said softly, "can we do this?"

"If we don't, I'll go mad," she said, and her voice held only tender amusement.

"I meant, what about the baby?"

He'd started to take his hand away, and she kept that from happening by laying his fingers back against her skin. "It's fine. Really. Don't stop. Please don't stop."

"You're so beautiful."

She laughed lightly and gave him a rueful smile. "Wait until the baby gets bigger. I assure you, you'll find me quite unattractive."

He shook his head. Threading his fingers through her hair, he tugged until she met his eyes. "Nothing about you will ever be unattractive to me. Not the body that carries my child." He bent his head to touch his lips to her breasts. "Not the heart that already loves it."

She wrapped her arms around him, held him close. Unexpectedly her hand closed around him. Her grip, gentle and electric, made him gasp with pleasure.

His pulse thrumming, he brought his hands around her slim back and lowered her to the carpet. He wanted to go slowly, make it special, make it different from the first time. He thought fleetingly of holding back and knew he couldn't. He was fast losing his capacity for control, so great was the sweet, throbbing heat between his thighs.

He slid into her, gently, slowly, waiting, waiting—letting her adjust. The moments seemed to stretch into forever. Then he felt her tighten and squeeze on him, her legs drawing up, sliding against his. Soon he wasn't sure which one of them was trembling.

They were knitted together now so tightly that when she arched upward, asking for more, he groaned as a feeling like an electrical current jolted him. Beneath him her flesh was slick with perspiration. He nuzzled the side of her face, saying things, foolishly loving things, into her ear he would not have thought could pass from his lips. She clutched him, breathing faster. And then she began to shudder.

"Mark," she gasped, curling her fingers into his hair. She bit her lip, trying to stifle the sounds of pleasure that hung in her throat.

"Shh," he whispered hoarsely. "It's all right. I'm here. I've got you."

And then he wasn't sure he had her at all because something changed. The slow, rolling motion of her hips against his created a blunt pressure within him that built and built...till it was excruciating, overwhelming. His pulse surged. His breath came out in a harsh exhalation, and a moment later his body convulsed in orgasm.

They collapsed against each other and lay there quietly for long moments, neither speaking.

Mark pulled Jenna against his body, cradled her in his arms, and all he could do as he listened to his heart settle back into its normal rhythm was stare at the ceiling, as if the startling truth were written there.

He thought he could finally understand what his parents' marriage must have been like in those very early days, before bitterness and resentment gnawed it to bloody pieces. That wild hunger between them had led to *this*—a desperate need to hold on and not let go, to feel your mind lunging for something faraway. To the lovely discovery that another person could heal you and bring you a peace that curled through a thousand empty places in your spirit.

Making love to Jenna gave him all those feelings of belonging he'd craved his whole life, and for the first time ever, he could see a distinction between lovemaking and sex.

He wasn't sure the knowledge pleased him. What was he to do with everything he'd believed in for so long? Before she'd robbed him of any satisfaction he'd had with his old life? He wanted to tell her how he felt. He wanted to know if it was the same for her. But how to shape the words?

I'm such a hypocrite. I can't do without this in my life, Jenna. I want all the same things you want. All that crazy, uncontrollable passion. But it's so frightening. Tell me how we can work this out.

That joyful, searing truth was on the tip of his tongue, but in the moment when he would have spoken, Jenna roused, rubbing her cheek against his jaw.

"Mark," she said against his mouth, tickling the corner of it with her tongue. "Do you think we'll ever have just normal sex?"

He laughed. "I thought we just did."

"You know what I mean. In a bed. Without ripping each other's clothes off."

"Give me a few minutes," he said, raising her fingers to his lips. "I'm willing to try again."

She grinned and lowered her head to his bare chest, licking and kissing one of his nipples, teasing it to life, then moving on toward his shoulder. She had the softest mouth. He could feel her breath, warm on his flesh. He closed his eyes, letting the heat of her lips send his blood traveling to new routes.

And then she stopped.

He opened his eyes to find her looking up at him again, and this time a tiny frown marred her forehead.

"Where did you get this?" she asked, running a finger lightly down the length of a jagged scar that cut him from his shoulder to the underside of his ribs.

"Souvenir from a messy childhood," he said, trying to keep his tone light as a cold sensation sharpened in his chest.

He could tell she wasn't satisfied with that answer. The light in the room was poor, a sulky amber color that promised the last of the fading sunset. She twisted slightly in his arms, trying to see more of that old damage. He wondered what he could say to explain it away without ruining the mood.

He didn't have to explain anything. Modern technology intervened. His cell phone, buried in the pool of their clothing, rang.

Sitting up, he found it and flipped it open. Dale Damron was on the other end. The conversation lasted less than a minute, then Mark immediately began sorting through their clothes.

"We have to go," he told her as he pulled on his shirt.

"What's the matter?"

"Harv Dellarubio's been taken to the hospital. He tried to kill himself."

MARK DROPPED HER off at her house. Neither of them spoke much. The interior of the car marooned them in darkness, hiding so much, but he had a feeling there were plenty of things she wanted to say. Now just didn't seem the right time.

When she started to exit the car, he stopped her with a hand on her arm. "We need to talk," he told her.

She nodded. "I know."

"I don't know how long I'll be at the hospital. Let me take you out to breakfast tomorrow."

"I can't. I told Vic I'd come into the office first thing. As it is, I'm going to have to break my promise to the boys to take them to Six Flags."

"It seems a shame to disappoint them."

"It can't be helped."

"Don't cancel it. Let me take them instead."

"I don't know… The boys love Six Flags, and they can be a handful when they're excited."

"I've noticed."

"And they don't really know you that well," she said. "They tend to like the usual family outings to stay…just family."

"All the more reason for the three of us to go together. It will give us a chance to get more comfortable with each other. Then we could have dinner tomorrow night. Just the two of us."

"All right," she agreed with a smile. "Pick them up at nine."

He reached over, cupped the back of her neck and pulled her close for a quick kiss. "Tomorrow night. Wear something festive."

CHAPTER SEVENTEEN

WITH HALLOWEEN less than two weeks away, Six Flags over Georgia was crowded and dripping with decorations. Wispy ghosts hung from trees, skeletons popped out of unearthed coffins. Witches, headless monks and mummys trailing gauze wandered the park in search of victims to terrify.

Personally Mark thought it was all too intense for younger children, but what did he really know? Pete and J.D. sure seemed to love it.

So far the day had gone well. He hadn't been to a place like this since high school, and when the boys found out he was a novice, they took over. Instead of following the plan he'd carefully laid out from the park map, they charged off toward their personal favorites, rides that bogged down quickly with long lines. Their haphazard route made no sense to Mark's logical mind, but their zeal made complaining impossible.

Leading him from ride to ride, Pete and J.D. made sure he had the best seat, pointed out every special effect they thought he might miss, warned him when the scariest moments were coming in the haunted house. All Mark had to do was look thrilled, which, he discovered, was easy and fun.

They ate hamburgers and French fries for lunch, but by early afternoon they were ready for another break. They ordered ice cream from an outdoor vendor and sat on a picnic bench next to a hillside covered in fake tombstones that stood like giant chessmen.

Mark was halfway through a hot-fudge sundae when his cell phone rang. Occasionally during the day he'd had to take quick calls, and with a regretful look at the boys, he answered it.

It was Dale, and Mark prayed it wasn't bad news. Harv Dellarubio's stomach had been pumped clean of the sleeping pills he'd taken. When Mark had left the hospital late last night, everything had seemed fine.

He got right to the point. "How is he?"

"He's all right," Dale said.

Something in his voice made Mark frown into the receiver. "Then what's the matter?"

There was a short silence. "Mark, I think I should resign."

"What? What the hell are you talking about?"

Pete and J.D. had polished off their cones. Mark watched them wriggle impatiently on their seats as he waited for Dale to elaborate.

"This whole thing with Harv," Dale began, "it's really my fault."

"I don't see how. You didn't make him swallow a bottle of pills."

"No, but if I'd been more on top of what he was doing in the office, it might never have come to this."

"Dale, come on. You heard what the cops said. It's not that unusual. Look at the papers. With what's been happening lately—so many execs playing fast and loose with company funds—we're lucky this is all we have to deal with. Even Weatherwax Corp. went through this sort of thing last year. Hold on a minute."

Evidently tired of waiting for Mark to complete the call, Pete was making motions that he and J.D. wanted to wander up on the hillside to inspect some of the tombstones. Mark nodded.

"Stay where I can see you," he said.

They raced off toward the break in the stone wall. While Mark absently watched them investigate the fake graveyard, he listened to Dale explain how he'd done a lot of soul-searching during the night. How he felt he'd let Mark down. How he couldn't shake the feeling that in some way he'd been less than vigilant in office procedures and so Harv had found it easy to embezzle.

Dale was fully wound up. He went on and on, and when he finally paused for breath, Mark took the opportunity to say, "That's a load of crap."

"I'm serious. You heard Harv tell us that making those department cuts last year helped him keep what he was doing under wraps. *I* made those cuts, Mark. *I'm* responsible."

"And who told you to make those cuts? Me. Does that mean I should resign, too? You're internalizing this too much."

The boys were back now. J.D. frowned at him, and Pete looked blatantly hostile at finding Mark still on the phone. The kid opened his mouth to say something. Mark lifted his hand to stop him, then held up one finger, indicating he'd be done in just a minute. Pete's features became even surlier, but it couldn't be helped.

Mark turned his back on them, hunching over the table so that no one could overhear his conversation. "For God's sake, Dale. Dellarubio stole half a million dollars from the company. The investigator said whatever embezzlers admit to taking, the real figure is probably twenty-five percent more. The guy needs help. I'm sorry he didn't see any other way out than taking an overdose, but *we* didn't bring him to that point. He did it to himself. Hell, we haven't even said we're going to prosecute yet."

"I still think I should resign."

"Well, I won't accept it, dammit. Get some sleep. We can talk tomorrow, and I'll give you a dozen reasons why I need you to stay. All right?"

Dale agreed reluctantly. Mark snapped the phone closed before the man had a chance to change his mind. He'd have to apologize to the boys for taking so long. Surely, without giving them any of the nasty details, he could make them see he'd had no choice.

He swung back around. Neither Pete or J.D. were anywhere in sight.

HE WAS JUST LIKE Daddy, Pete thought as he pushed through the wave of human traffic coming toward him.

He'd been thinking that Mark Bishop was different, but he wasn't. Daddy had always been more interested in doing anything other than spending time with him and J.D. The family had never gone anywhere without his father getting bored with them and talking on his cell phone or cutting short the outing.

And in spite of the way the day had started out, it looked like Mark thought that way, too. He might not be daddy material, after all. Maybe Mom had tricked him into taking them to the park today. He probably couldn't wait to dump them back home.

"Pete! Stop!" J.D. hollered behind him.

Petey swung around on his brother so suddenly that J.D. plowed into his back. "Stop dragging your feet, runt. The line for Raging Rapids is gonna be a mile long by the time we get there."

"We shouldn't have left Mark," J.D. said with a worried look toward the ice-cream stand. With all the people crowding the walkway, they couldn't see much.

"Why? He doesn't want to be with us. We're just a lot of bother. He's got business to take care of, or didn't you see?"

"You're acting stupid. And Mark's not gonna like that we ran off and left him."

"Then go back if you want."

Pete took off down the walkway again, knowing J.D. would follow. J.D. always did what Pete said, even when he didn't really want to.

Sure enough, he heard J.D. call after him. "Petey, wait!"

They reached a narrow bridge that crossed a small stream, the turnoff to the Raging Rapids ride. Everyone moved like turtles, and in front of him some stupid girl blocked the way, crying because she'd dropped her box of popcorn.

Impatiently Pete cut away from the crowd and ducked under the railing. A grassy slope led a few feet down to the stream, with another slope leading back up on the other side. Nobody was supposed to take that shortcut— his mom had told him he'd better never try a stunt like that—but he'd been to this park often enough to see that plenty of people did it when they got tired of waiting for slowpokes.

The dirt under the grass was looser than he expected, making his feet slide a little out from under him. He reached the bottom and was about to holler over his shoulder for J.D. to be careful when he heard his brother's cry.

He turned just in time to watch J.D. tumble headfirst down the slope like a toy. He landed a few feet away, facedown in the water.

Petey scrambled around fake boulders to reach his brother. "J.D.! J.D.!" he screamed. "Somebody help!"

He splashed into the stream and yanked J.D. onto the bank. J.D.'s eyes were closed. There was watery blood all over his face. Petey thought he might be sick right there and then.

He'd killed his brother.

MARK SPENT a few minutes checking out the area around the ice-cream stand to no avail. He was more annoyed than frightened. This morning they'd all agreed to stick together. If the boys had wandered off and gotten lost, it surely wouldn't take long to find them. The park probably dealt with this kind of problem all the time.

Maybe Pete and J.D. were headed toward the Raging Rapids ride—it was where they'd wanted to go to next. He'd give them hell for running off this way. He went quickly in that direction, scanning the crowd as he pushed through them.

By the time he reached the bridge over the stream, he became aware that the crowd seemed to have come to a dead halt. Something was going on, maybe street performers. The boys could be waiting for him here.

But as he glanced around, he heard snatches of conversation.

"...some kid fell down the hill. They never listen..."

"I heard he was underwater for a long time..."

"Why weren't his parents watching him?"

"...poor little guy..."

Mark's heart began galloping in his throat. He felt ice-cold suddenly and shoved his way toward the top of the slope. His breath stalled as he saw Petey at the bottom, surrounded by a small knot of bystanders.

And J.D. lying on the bank beside him, not moving.

Mark plunged down the incline. He pushed strangers out of the way and didn't stop until he was finally able to kneel at J.D.'s side.

The boy was pale and unconscious. But breathing, thank God.

Mark swiped wet hair from J.D.'s forehead, careful not to touch a nasty-looking bruise that had already begun to bloom. "J.D.? Wake up, buddy."

"I don't think you should touch him," someone said. "Paramedics are on the way. Is he your kid?"

"My son," Mark said without looking up.

"He's not your son! He's my brother!" Pete shouted at him. Closer now, Mark could see that Pete's face was streaked with tears, pale with the same fear that had a stranglehold on Mark. "He's dead!" Pete cried hysterically. "He trusted you, and it's all your fault!"

In the face of Pete's angry hysteria, Mark was speechless, but he couldn't deal with that now. He struggled to recall everything he'd learned about what was the most appropriate action to take.

Help me, God. Tell me what I should do.

Luckily the park's emergency crew arrived just then and immediately took over. Mark backed off so they could do their job, his legs feeling as though they'd turned to oatmeal.

Pete started to move forward, and Mark hauled him back, pulling him out of the way. The boy struggled against him for a moment, then subsided.

Eventually they got J.D. back up the slope. The paramedics questioned Pete about how long his little brother had been facedown in the water. Mark knew they must be worried about the possibility of brain damage if he'd been without oxygen too long. Mark's gut was clenched so tightly he couldn't breathe.

"They'll take him to Atlanta General," one of the paramedics told Mark. "The park will drive you there so you can meet up with the ambulance. Is there someone you should call?"

Unable to take his eyes off J.D.'s still form, Mark nodded.

Jenna. He had to call Jenna.

But dear God, how was he going to find the words to tell her?

THE WAIT WAS agonizing, like some grotesque enemy.

The emergency room of Atlanta General was full of patients. Everywhere Mark looked were ominous signs of just how desperate the situation could be. Blood-spattered, empty stretchers. Nurses hurrying back and forth between examining rooms. Someone crying uncontrollably, the sobs climbing to a new plateau every few minutes.

With Jenna's health scare, Harv Dellarubio's suicide attempt yesterday and now this, Mark felt he'd had more than his share of hospitals lately.

In a chair beside him in the waiting room, Pete sat stone-silent, apparently in shock. Mark could understand that. When they'd first arrived, he'd felt a strange, stifling sensation seizing him by the throat. But after a while, he didn't feel anything but numb.

Jenna should be here soon. He'd called her house, told her father briefly what had happened and asked him to see to it she got to the hospital as quickly as possible. Driving herself here alone, with all kinds of horrible scenarios probably circling her brain, seemed too much for one person to bear, and Mark's guilt increased tenfold.

He didn't know what to say to her. How could a couple of minutes of inattention produce such potential for disaster? What excuse could he offer?

The truth stared him in the face. There was none.

Your fault, you bastard. Couldn't you see this coming? What did you expect?

In crazy, unguarded moments lately he had let himself imagine something else for his life. Wonderful years with Jenna as his wife, her sons coming to think of him as their father, a baby to bring them even closer. Maybe another one a few years later. Last night—*it seemed so long ago now!*—he'd even envisioned himself seated beside her on the porch swing, enjoying the evening breeze. He'd never anticipated miracles, but that kind of simple, domestic bliss wasn't so preposterous, was it?

He should have known better. And right now, with J.D.'s life hanging in the balance, he had to rip open the scarred-over hurts that had been sleeping for years and simply face facts.

He *was* his father's son.

The outer E.R. doors opened with a whoosh, and Jenna, her brother Christopher and her father rushed in. Mark stood. Petey sprang out of the chair and ran to his mother, slamming against her and clinging.

She cupped his cheek and kissed him, then made a beeline for Mark. Her dark eyes, full of fear, met his. "Tell me," she said.

"The doctor is still with him. There's no word yet."

Her lips went white, and he thought she was struggling

against the urge to burst into tears. Both her father and brother looked at him silently. If they were casting any blame on him, Mark couldn't see it.

Christopher squeezed his sister's shoulder. "I'll check in at the nurses' desk. Let them know we're here."

Jenna nodded absently. Tucked against her side, her older son was beginning to cry softly. She bent to catch his face in her hands. "Petey, stop crying," she said with gentle command. "Your brother is going to be fine."

Petey glared at Mark. "I hate you," he said explosively. "It's all your fault."

Jenna lifted candid, troubled eyes to Mark. He felt as though his blood was corroding.

"Jenna..." he began quietly, and could go no further. He wanted to hold her, to explain, but didn't dare.

"No, it's all right," she said, and Mark wondered if he imagined the tiniest hesitation in her voice. She seemed a little bewildered, as though trying to put the pieces together. "He's just frightened."

She led Pete back over to the line of chairs, and they sat down together. Wrapping her arms around him, she leaned against the wall behind her, looking scared. Pete ducked his head into her stomach and refused to budge. Her father sat next to her, hunched over and suddenly looking every one of his advanced years. Pretty soon Christopher joined them.

Security from the park showed up to fill out an incident report. Mark pulled the man into a quiet corner and answered his questions as best he could. Every so often he glanced in the direction of Jenna and her family, but he no longer felt as though he was one of them. They'd become like people in a play.

Just when he thought that he couldn't stand waiting a moment longer, that he would get up and raise holy hell if someone didn't come out right now and tell them what was happening, the doctor pushed through the double doors. Everyone rose, expectant and fearful. As Mark approached, the man was just giving them the news.

Except for a small cut on his forehead and a couple of bumps and bruises, J.D. was fine.

Mark felt euphoric.

"Thank God," Jenna whispered.

She glanced at Mark. The relief in her eyes made him miss a couple of heartbeats. He wanted desperately to pull her into his arms, but he couldn't help feeling as though he'd lost the right.

"Can we see him?" she asked the doctor anxiously.

"For a few minutes," the man replied.

Jenna gave Mark a small, hopeful smile. Then she turned and followed the rest of her family through the double doors.

CHAPTER EIGHTEEN

ATLANTA'S GREENBRIAR HOTEL wasn't the bland, functional kind of place Jenna was used to staying in when she traveled, but it didn't have the Old World charm of the Belasco in New York City. The Greenbriar was bright and sleek, with lots of glass, mirrors and lush greenery. She suspected Mark had chosen it because his newspaper office was two doors away.

She got on the elevator and punched the button for the penthouse. It seemed ironic to be in this situation again, heading up to the top floor of a hotel to see Mark.

This was hardly the same, though. For one thing, she didn't have on her best suit. Glancing into the mirrored wall of the elevator, Jenna realized that she couldn't have looked less put together. Her hair was a dark, tangled mess. No makeup. She wore her oldest pair of jeans and the wrinkled blouse Petey had cried all over.

The other difference was her mental state. Meeting face-to-face with Mark Bishop in New York to do that interview, she'd felt fearful and not up to the job. Inadequate.

Today, however, her nerves fluttered with a certain uneasiness. Because for a couple of hours now the same thought had been running circles in her mind.

Something in her relationship with Mark had gone very, very wrong.

She had come here straight from the hospital. J.D. had already been sitting up in bed, hardy little creature that he was, annoyed because he'd have to wait until he got home tomorrow before he'd be reunited with his space cannon. She'd finally left him sleeping, with Dad sitting by his bedside and Christopher taking Petey home.

J.D.'s accident had given her some terrified moments, but Petey's state of mind had been almost as worrisome. At J.D.'s bedside he'd suddenly turned into a weeping, guilt-ridden mess. Around hiccuping sobs, he'd given a rambling account of what had happened at the park, particularly his part in it, and ended up begging J.D. not to hate him. J.D., never one to miss an opportunity, had graciously forgiven his brother, but Jenna had a feeling he planned to get a lot of mileage out of Petey's remorse.

The only problem to be dealt with now was Mark.

She knew the incident had stunned and frightened him. One look in his eyes at the hospital had told her that. What she didn't understand was why he'd left without a word.

She glanced back in the mirror, realizing that one hand was unconsciously rubbing small circles on her abdomen. *Come on, baby. Let's find out what nonsense your father's thinking.*

Jenna had to knock twice on the door to Mark's suite; it took him that long to answer. When he pulled the door open, his expression was cold, detached. She studied his features, trying to see beyond the facade, wanting to see into his heart.

He didn't bother with greetings. "How's he doing?" he asked. "The doctor said—"

"He's fine," she reassured him quickly. "They're going to keep him overnight for observation."

"Thank God."

She looked at him expectantly. "May I come in?"

When he didn't answer right away, her heart lurched. For one horrible moment, she thought he might actually refuse. He seemed so stiff and unapproachable.

Finally he stepped aside so she could enter. The penthouse was all modern elegance—black and cream and burgundy. She hardly noticed, because she immediately became aware of two suitcases and a briefcase sitting beside the couch, obviously ready to be taken downstairs.

She'd expected trouble, but nothing like this. She turned toward him, fighting to get the words out past the lump in her throat. "You're leaving?"

His gray eyes had gone so dark they looked black. The hurt there made her want to hold him, even as it made her want to slap him.

"I've booked a flight back to Orlando," he said. From the nearby desk, he lifted a cream-colored piece of stationery, then set it back down. "I was just writing you a note to explain."

"That would have to be one heck of an explanation," she replied a touch acidly. She tilted her head, noticing that the stationery was still blank. "Doesn't look like you got very far."

"I think it's for the best."

"Best for whom?"

"Best for all of us."

"I see. May I ask why?"

He shifted, crossing his arms across his chest. "You were right. I can't stick it out through the tough times. I don't want the kind of responsibility that goes with having a wife and family."

The best thing in her existence besides her children, and he was deserting her. The thought fired her anger. It wasn't going to end this way. Not if she could help it.

She gave him a tight, narrowed look. "So you're breaking your promise."

"Yes. I'm sorry. I shouldn't have—"

"What about the baby?"

"I'll make sure you have everything you need."

"Except a father."

He blinked at that. "I can't. I'm not daddy material. I'd be no good at it."

"What about us?"

"Us?" He repeated the word as though he derived

some private satisfaction from disliking it. "We had fun. Some great sex." He drew a deep breath, and Jenna knew he'd decided to take a tougher stance. "But I'm just exactly what you've accused me of being. I'm one of your frogs masquerading as a prince. A coldhearted bastard that you don't need in your life. You had it right all along, Jenna."

They looked at one another for a long, silent moment. Then Mark snatched up a few toiletries that lay on the couch and began stuffing them into one of the side pockets of his suitcase.

She swallowed hard. She wanted to cry, but then something took hold of her inside. This wasn't Mark. This wasn't the man she'd come to love. And she wasn't going to let him get away with it.

Quietly she said, "You told me yesterday that I wasn't very good at pretending. I think *you're* not very good at lying."

He jerked upright. "Don't be foolish—"

"I love you, Mark."

His lips parted in a hiss of exhalation. "Jenna, don't—"

"I love you just the way I told you I would. With all my heart. With every cell in my body. With everything in me that I have to give. You make me feel—"

"Stop," he ordered. "Dammit, just stop."

She shortened the distance between them until they were only inches apart. "Why? I'm not ashamed of it." She gave him a small smile. "The funny thing is, I think you love me, too. Just the same way."

"I don't," he said with a sharp shake of his head. "And if you'd grow up and stop wanting some fairy tale—"

"Believe me, I see you completely as you are. I don't see you as my white knight. You make mistakes. You're trying to make one now. I could list a half-dozen ways you drive me crazy. But you're also the kind, decent, caring man I fell in love with."

As though something inside him suddenly snapped, Mark swung away. He paced over to the windows, turning after a moment to look at her. "I'm also the guy who nearly got one of your kids killed."

She could feel herself paling. "Is that what this is about? What happened to J.D.? Yes, it was frightening. Yes, we were lucky. But it was an accident, Mark."

"I was supposed to be watching them."

"So you'll know better next time. Do you think I never screw up? It happens."

"Not to me, it doesn't. I won't let it."

Her chest hurt. She couldn't seem to breathe properly. The silence grew again. She began to hate this sleek, cold place. Finally she said in a quiet voice, "You're a lot of things, Mark Bishop. But I never thought you were a coward. What are you so afraid of?"

He walked back to her slowly. The look in his eyes was terrible, blank and without life. When he was directly in front of her, he gathered the hem of his polo shirt and in one smooth movement pulled it over his head so that he stood, bare-chested before her.

"I'm afraid of this," he said softly, pointing to the scar she'd noticed yesterday. In the bright light of day, it seemed larger, more jagged. "This is what my father did. Not through any intentional abuse. Just careless disregard for anything but his own interests. I was four."

She couldn't take her eyes off the scar. "What happened?"

"He was supposed to be watching me. But he'd had a fight with my mother, and she'd stormed out of the house. He needed a drink to calm down, and since I was playing in my room, he didn't see any problem with leaving me there alone while he went down to the store. Only problem was, I didn't stay in my room. I was running around and fell into the glass coffee table."

"Oh, God, Mark—"

"It shattered into a million pieces. One of them pierced

a lung. I nearly bled to death before Dad came home and found me.''

She was speechless, filled with nausea. She reached out, gently running her fingers along the scar. Mark didn't move, but his muscles twitched spasmodically under her hand. So much hurt here, she thought. And so much more than just physical…

''I don't want to be like him,'' Mark continued. ''I don't want to hurt a child just because I haven't got what it takes to be a good father. I tried to fool myself for a little while because I wanted it so much. But it just won't work, Jenna.''

Her gaze lifted to his. ''You could never be like that. I've seen you. Your instincts are terrific. Your father might have been a self-absorbed son of a bitch, but that isn't who you are.''

''You don't think so? Ask Pete. You heard him. He hates me.''

''Petey tells me he hates me almost every time we have a disagreement. That's what kids do. They say cruel things when they're angry or scared. They want to hurt you before you hurt them.''

''If you'd seen his face—''

''I'm telling you he didn't really mean it. He told me that what happened was his fault, that he'd deliberately run off with J.D. just because he was mad at you.''

''You can't brush it off that easily.''

''I know my boys, Mark. They're crazy about you. They need you.'' She reached into her purse, suddenly remembering the note she'd stuffed in there this morning. Filled with the fierce, desperate need to make Mark understand, she unfolded the piece of school-notebook paper and pushed it toward him. ''After you dropped me off at the house last night, I found this on my pillow. I was going to share it with you tonight, but I think you should read it now.''

He took it from her, frowning at the childish scrawl.

Petey had written the note the day of his success on the ball field, so he'd probably been feeling close to Mark. But J.D. had signed it, as well. Jenna knew it by heart already, and as she watched Mark read it, she remembered every word of it again.

Dear Mom—
We like Mark and think he would make a good daddy for us and the baby and a good husband for you, too. We worked hard to get him to come here. Now you have to be nice so he will stay.

Love,
Your Sons,
Peter Rawlins
James David Rawlins

Mark looked up from the note. He seemed surprised, like a man coming suddenly awake in a strange place.

"I think my father helped with the words last night," Jenna said. "I realize that Petey wrote this *before* what happened today, when they were both excited from the game. Probably while we were…at the new house. But it doesn't change things. He wants you in his life, Mark. Does that sound like a boy who hates you?"

He scanned the note again. Instinct told her that she'd gained some ground, but was it enough to sway him? The agony of knowing that it could still go horribly wrong had begun to terrify her.

"Well?" she prodded, trying for a lighter tone. "Just how 'nice' do I have to be to get you to stay?"

He lifted his face. "I don't want to hurt you, Jenna."

"You won't. Unless you go away now. Unless you do something you'll regret for the rest of your life."

"I want to believe you." He shook his head. "God, Jenna, you don't know how much—"

"Mark," she said, starting to feel panicky. Her voice

broke with emotion as hot tears formed behind her eyes. "If it was just me, I think I could eventually accept the fact that you don't love me enough to stay. I could be strong, raise this baby by myself. But please don't hurt Petey and J.D. Please don't do that."

She ducked her head, staring down at her clasped hands. Her throat hurt with the force of her frustration. A tear struck her wrist, large enough to be embarrassing, but she didn't care. Nothing mattered if she couldn't make Mark understand.

He was suddenly in front of her, lifting her chin so that their eyes met. "You think I don't love you?" he asked in a voice that was thick and warm. "Right now all I want to do is show you how many ways I need you. When I think about you, I want everything—the magic, the music, all those romantic things that you treasure and I've been running away from my whole life." He cupped her head in his hands, using his thumbs to brush away tears. "Do you know when I fell in love with you?"

Unable to speak, she shook her head.

"When you asked me if I wore boxers or briefs."

Her lips parted in surprise. "But that was right after we met."

He smiled at her. "You were the first woman who had ever made me question what I wanted out of life. I think that's why I was such a bastard on the phone the next day. Anything to keep you from getting any closer."

She touched his face, trailing her fingertips along his chin as though trying to memorize every angle and curve. "Don't go, Mark. Please. I love you so much."

He put his arms around her. "Jenna," he said softly against her hair. "I love you. What can I do? I want to be everything you want. I want to change."

She pulled back, eyeing him seriously. "No, you mustn't. I've been giving it a lot of thought. Who you are is the man I fell in love with. Please don't change."

He grinned, rubbing his fingers against her chin. "We can make this work, can't we."

It was a statement, not a question, but Jenna nodded agreement, anyway. "I've never been more certain of anything. It will be difficult sometimes. There will be moments when we'll wish we could run away. But we won't. Because we love each other. Because this is what we've both wanted all our lives."

He kissed her then, tilting her head back to make a sweet, unbearably gentle connection with her lips. Between kisses he said her name over and over, his embrace sure and loving. She took what he gave her and gave him everything she had in return.

A long time later she opened her eyes and smiled up at him, full of dreamy contentment. "So it's settled."

"It seems that way," he said absently, still nibbling the skin along her jawline.

"I do have one request," she said. "Actually I think it's more of a demand."

"Anything you want."

"I want a prenuptial agreement drawn up."

He looked quizzically at her. "What do you want in it?"

"No lovers outside of the marriage. Ever."

"Of course," he replied solemnly.

"And your name, it has to come off that Ten Most Eligible list. You're not on the market anymore."

"Princess," he said with a laugh, "don't you know? I took my name off that list the first day I met you."

EPILOGUE

"HOLD STILL, sweetheart," Mark coaxed. "Only one more button."

"No, Daddy, no," his daughter complained, making a face and pulling at the high collar of her red sweater. "Too hot."

Mark pushed Evie's hands away gently and resettled her sweater in place. He probably shouldn't bother to tell the child about the cold snap that had arrived the night before, throwing Atlanta into a chilly pre-Halloween turmoil after months of unseasonably warm weather. At two, Evie's main concern these days seemed to be wearing as few clothes as possible.

"It will be cold in the park today," he explained. "You have to bundle up."

"Don't want to," the little girl replied.

Refusing to cooperate was another one of Evie's favorite things to do now that she'd hit what the parenting books called the "terrible twos." Jenna swore their daughter had inherited his stubborn streak.

"Sorry, sweetie pie. Daddy says you have to."

The child frowned darkly, but a moment later she toddled off happily to play with her toys, which were collected in one corner of the room.

Mark watched her fondly. Evie was an achingly beautiful little girl. Sweet-natured most of the time, an infectious laugh, and smart, much smarter than most kids her age. The child he and Jenna had created that night in New York was everything any parent could want and more.

With Evie finally dressed, Mark turned toward the window that looked out onto the backyard. When he and Jenna had bought the Victorian, he'd been sure he'd hate this backyard. Just like the house, it had needed a lot of attention, the kind of work he didn't enjoy. The kind that called for an expertise he didn't have. But he was a hopelessly easy mark when it came to making Jenna happy, so he'd gone ahead and signed the papers, then set about learning how to turn a crumbling eyesore into a real home.

He knew every inch of it now. Especially this backyard. From the tiny garden he'd helped Jenna plant in the back corner to the small fish pond they'd put in to the fort he'd built for the boys in the cradle of the oak's gigantic arms.

Not all of its rebirth had been a rousing success. They'd had to call in his father-in-law to save the barbecue pit Mark tried to build. Before he'd figured out how to keep them out, owls and raccoons had carried off three of the Koi he and Jenna had brought home for the pond. And a month ago he'd begun a territorial war with some moles that seemed determined to chew up his new grass. It was a war the moles appeared to be winning.

But the backyard bore his imprint. And he'd discovered he liked it that way.

Through the glass he watched J.D. and Pete playing on the swings. They were dressed and ready to go to Aunt Penelope's birthday reunion in the park. Even from here he could see that their cheeks were as bright as new apples from the cool fall air.

Mark tapped on the glass, drawing their attention. They smiled and waved at him, and he mimed a look at his watch, then gestured for them to come inside. Always ready to take the lead, Pete nodded and jumped off his seat, nudging J.D. ahead of him.

Jenna's boys were his now, too. He'd officially adopted them, and he couldn't have loved them more if they'd been his own blood. And he was pretty sure they felt the same way about him.

J.D. had had little problem taking to Mark. He was an easygoing kid who saw life as an adventure and met every challenge with curious delight. It probably didn't hurt that his new stepfather shared his interest in the space program and never minded long discussions on the possibility of life on other planets.

Pete had been another story. He was a handful, strong-willed and obstinate at times. But he had also been desperately eager to have a father figure in his life again, and over time he and Mark had found their way with each other, developing a closeness that seemed rock-solid.

He thought about all the worrying he'd done early in the marriage and how foolish it all seemed in retrospect. There were still times when his gut clenched at the thought of making some crucial family decision, when he wondered if he was saying or doing the right thing for all of them. But whatever fears he'd had were always chased away quickly. Because Jenna was there with him, helping him every step of the way, and whenever he looked at her, somehow every crisis seemed manageable.

That adjustment for him, the realization that he could be a good father and husband, that he could share both trouble and triumph with another human being, hadn't been easy, either. Sometimes Mark felt as though the last three years of his life had been spent trying to find a path through an alternative universe.

Frightening.

Exhilarating.

Unbelievably rewarding.

It wasn't that he'd changed really. It was more a case of redefining priorities. He still cared about the business. He still kept a close eye on the bottom line and oversaw every acquisition, every shift in market share. The newspapers were doing well, even the Orlando market, now that he'd promoted Deb to a top-management level.

It was just that, from the day he'd married Jenna three years ago in her father's living room, he'd stopped feeling the need to fill every minute of every day with business. He still went in to work, but now he couldn't wait to get back here.

Home.

He'd discovered that making a living wasn't nearly as crucial and satisfying as making a life.

And that, he was getting pretty good at.

"Daddy, hug." Evie's voice drew Mark out of his thoughts. Her small body attached itself to his knees, almost knocking him off balance.

He smiled down at her indulgently—and discovered that, except for a pair of frilly panties, she was completely naked.

Evidently he wasn't as in command of the situation as he'd thought. Twenty minutes of struggling to make sense of a little girl's jumper and tights had all been for nothing.

"Evie," Mark groaned. He began scooping up articles of clothing, while his daughter still clung to his leg like a barnacle, giggling the entire time. "We're going to be late, and your mother is going to blame me."

"No, I won't," Jenna said from the doorway of Evie's room. "Even *I* can't get her to stay in her clothes these days."

Mark looked up and smiled as his wife came toward him. This was one of the unexpected delights—he never got tired of looking at Jenna. He'd thought that eventually he'd get used to it. That there would be times when he'd be too tired, too distracted, that sooner or later she would become a steady, pleasant presence in his life.

But it never happened that way. He never lost that little leap of his heart when she entered the room, that slightly breathless feeling he had when he saw her for the first time after an absence of only minutes. It was such a foolishly romantic reaction. It was embarrassing to realize that he was still so besotted with Jenna that he couldn't control his own body.

"Help!" he appealed to her as he shook the leg Evie had attached herself to. "I've grown a wart."

Evie giggled and clung harder.

Just then the boys burst into the room, full of enthusiasm and energy, loud and excited about spending a day with all their cousins. Evie adored J.D. and Pete, and they adored her, even though they'd been disappointed to discover there was a whole new world to learn about having a sister. Squealing, she detached herself from Mark's leg and ran toward them.

"Look, Evie," Pete said, holding out his hand to his sister. "Look at the cool rock I found. See the sparkly flecks in it? I'll bet that's gold. Do you know what gold is?"

"It's not gold," J.D. refuted with a frown. "It fell from some planet. It's not just a dumb Earth rock."

The three of them hunched over the pebble in Pete's hand, their faces displaying identical interest. Mark and Jenna watched them with pleased grins. The boys were so gentle with Evie, especially Pete.

Jenna crossed to Mark and turned, offering her back to him. "Now do *my* buttons. Unlike Evie, I promise I'll keep my clothes on."

"In that case," he said with a low laugh, "I'm not sure I want to."

He handed her Evie's jumper, sweater and tights, then set about closing the tiny buttons along the back of Jenna's blouse. She could probably have managed on her own just fine—there were only three, after all—but he loved this ritual between them, this little game. He'd always been crazy about her back and neck, and now he let his hands travel slowly, lightly, up her spine, playing gently against the silky flesh. Jenna drew a deeper breath every time his fingers touched her, but she didn't move. He knew her well enough now. Everything in her was focused on the soft, sure feel of his hands on her flesh.

Eventually the task was done. The bare back of Jenna's

neck was like a work of art to him, and also one of her most sensitive spots. He dipped his head and placed his lips against the small, delicate vertebra that disappeared beneath the edge of her blouse.

"All finished," he said softly, savoring her warm, sweetly scented skin.

She looked back over her shoulder. The smile she gave him sent his nerves zigzagging. "I wish there were more."

He turned her around, pulling her against him so that he could kiss her properly. The thought skittered through his addled brain that nobody kissed the way Jenna did. "Remind me to take you shopping tomorrow," he said, nuzzling the fine hairs against one of her ears. "All new clothes. With a million buttons in the back."

"Gross!" he heard Pete exclaim. "No kissing this early."

Jenna and Mark smiled at being caught. Without looking at their son, Jenna said, "Boys, take Evie downstairs and get your jackets on. We'll be down in a minute."

Both boys giggled. "Mo-om," J.D. said. "We can't take Evie to the park like this."

"Oh." Jenna pulled out of Mark's embrace, realizing that she still had Evie's clothes clutched in her hand. "Not a good idea," she said with a grin. "Come here, Evie."

Their daughter obeyed. Jenna knelt, and in an amount of time that made Mark feel depressingly inept, Jenna had the little girl ready to go. She gave her a kiss on the nose, then sent her gently toward the boys, who had discovered that their sister's toys weren't completely uninteresting.

"The three of you go downstairs," Jenna said again. "We'll be right down. I want to talk to your father a minute."

"Don't take long," Pete said, scrunching up one side of his nose and mouth. "I don't want to be late. Uncle

Trent promised to sit in the dunking booth no matter how cold it gets today."

"Can we get a pony?" J.D. asked, galloping one of Evie's stuffed unicorns along the back of her play table.

"No," Jenna replied.

"I was asking Daddy."

"No," Mark said.

"I didn't think so," J.D. conceded.

The boys marched out of the room, Evie hot on their heels. They made so much noise going down the stairs that the neighbors probably heard them.

When it was quiet once more, Mark pulled Jenna back into his arms. He grinned down at her. "You're not going to try to persuade me that we need a pony, are you? The backyard just isn't big enough."

"No. But we might want to consider adding on to the house. The doctor's office called. We're pregnant."

The grin faded from his mouth. He knew he must look dumbfounded. "What? How can that be?"

"Well…" Jenna cleared her throat, and he witnessed color rise in her cheeks. Even after all this time, she still blushed easily. "I think we know *how*. The question is, what do you think about it?"

He glanced down at her stomach, touching it lightly, trying to imagine how small their child must be right now. Then he looked up at her. Her eyes were shining, full of love and fragile elation, and he let the pleasure of that moment flow through him.

"I love you, sweetheart," he told her around a trio of soft, whispery kisses. "I love you for wanting my babies. I love you for not giving up on me and making me the happiest man who ever lived."

She laughed and when she pulled back at last, she cocked her head at him. "You know, I think you're turning into an incurable romantic."

"When it comes to loving you, I'm completely hopeless."

He hugged her close again. Over the top of her head, he said almost in awe, "Another baby. A sister for Eve."

"Or maybe another boy," Jenna speculated. "Goodness knows, I need another male in my life."

"Let's tell the kids. Right now. And call Lauren and Vic. Hell, why don't we let all the McNabs know today?"

"Slow down," Jenna said with another laugh. "We don't have to tell everyone right this minute. We have time."

"Right," he said. He took her fingers, touching his lips to the back of her hand. "But let's at least tell the boys, if not the whole family."

She nodded agreement, and he led her out of the room.

Family, he thought as they went down the stairs. He still couldn't get over how good that word felt. How big a void family could fill. Why had he been running from it so long when it offered such a sense of purpose? Such a feeling of belonging?

Maybe you needed the right woman. The right kids. The right reasons to try.

He had all that now. The certainty of that rang true in his heart. And he wasn't doing such a bad job. No doubt about it.

He was getting the hang of it.

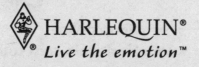

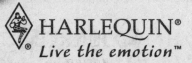

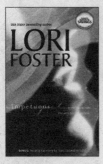

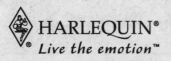

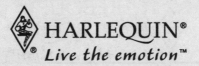

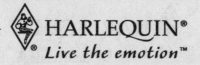